Carbisdale

Margaret Alty

Published 2016 by arima publishing

www.arimapublishing.com

ISBN 978 1 84549 691 3
© Margaret Alty 2016

Printed and bound in the United Kingdom

Typeset in Garamond

Swirl is an imprint of arima publishing.

arima publishing
ASK House, Northgate Avenue
Bury St Edmunds, Suffolk IP32 6BB
t: (+44) 01284 700321

www.arimapublishing.com

To my brother Bill

a nostalgic reminder of when we
were young and invisible

Chapter One

HILARY

I walked with Kirstie as far as the escalator, savouring these last few moments of being with her and already anticipating the sad emptiness I would feel the moment she had reached the top and had disappeared from view. My beautiful and self-sufficient daughter, no longer a schoolgirl flying back to England at the beginning of a new term, but it made no difference to my emotions as I watched her as I had done so many times before as the escalator bore her up to Departures and, as she had done the very first time she had gone off to boarding school, turning round at the top to blow me a kiss.

Feeling sorry for myself and wishing Pete could have been with me, I walked slowly back towards the car park, stopping at the W H Smith kiosk to buy a newspaper. I had reached the cash desk when a copy of "Art Review" caught my attention, not that I had any more than an average interest in art, but because of the portrait painting on the front cover. I had never seen the painting before, but that wasn't necessary; I had only been fourteen when my mother sat for Charles Grayson and as I stared in awe at the way he had brought out her rather ethereal beauty; the high cheekbones, the slightly downwards slanting of the vivid blue eyes, the scarlet-painted Clara Bow lips and the unruly auburn hair, all brought back to me just how lovely she had been. Not that I realised this at the time; she was my mother, a person I had taken for granted all my life. It wasn't until years later I realised what she really looked like, and I'm sure if she had lived longer she would have still retained that something extra which separates an attractive woman from a beautiful one.

'Do you want to buy the magazine or not?' the tired looking woman behind the desk asked and becoming aware of the long line of customers behind me, realised I must have been standing there for several minutes.

'Sorry,' I apologised, giving her a note to cover both the newspaper and the magazine, 'but I got carried away.'

With an exasperated raising of eyebrows, making it abundantly clear exactly what she thought of people who 'got carried away', she took the note, slapping the change on to the glass counter which was obviously crack-proof, and looked over my shoulder at her next customer. What happened to thank you, I wondered, also what happened to Scottish hospitality, recalling the road sign as I'd crossed the border earlier in the week: "Welcome to Scotland" it had proclaimed. Really?

Turnhouse Airport is only eight miles from the centre of Edinburgh and, in spite of it being a Friday evening when the exodus to and from the city was at its peak, the journey only took me twenty minutes to reach the first set of traffic lights at Haymarket and, as invariably the case, they were against me for the remainder of the way to my hotel, but I wasn't in any hurry; the whole evening stretched out ahead of me, glancing at the clock on the dashboard. Six-thirty; Kirstie would be airborne now, imagining her settled in her window seat, flicking through the in-flight magazine, excited and optimistic about the new life she had chosen for herself in a part of the world where she had grown up. Hong Kong, where even after the 1997 handover to the Chinese there continued to be opportunities for westerners, provided they were prepared to accept the energetic competitiveness which contributed to the success of the old colony. There was a time, not so many years ago, when I couldn't have ever envisaged leaving; after my divorce it hadn't been easy to stay on, but the company I worked for paid well, including the added perk of a serviced apartment in Causeway Bay overlooking Victoria Harbour. All of this changed though when I met Pete. I had been on holiday in England for three weeks, mainly to see Kirstie during half-term and visiting those friends I had kept in touch with over the years. One of them, Mandy, whom I had known since our college days, introduced me to a colleague of hers, Pete Fisher. The attraction was mutual and for the remainder of my stay we were inseparable, trying to cram as much as possible into the last days before I had to return to Hong Kong. Less than a year later, we were married in Oxford where Pete had lived all his life. Knowing Kirstie would soon be back in Hong Kong, re-visiting all those places she and I used to go to, wasn't making me feel nostalgic; far from it. It had taken me a long time to find equilibrium to my life and with Pete I had achieved it. Too cautious, and a little too superstitious, I knew I would never become complacent.

"Channings", the hotel where Pete and I had stayed when we had come up to Edinburgh to see Kirstie, and where she and I had spent the two nights after the graduation ceremony at Edinburgh University, was in the Stockbridge area of the city; a beautiful Edwardian town house looking out on to private gardens, remembering Pete's pleasure when he had learned that the arctic explorer, Sir Ernest Shackelton had once lived there. Window boxes, suspended from the black-painted railings on either side of the short flight of steps up to the front door, were filled to over-flowing with geraniums and honeysuckle.

I was in my room freshening up, having decided to eat in "Channing's" brasserie, when my mobile rang and, guessing it might be Pete, hurried to answer it.

'Hello, sweetheart,' he said, 'everything alright?'

'Yes, fine, I've just got back from the airport; your timing is perfect.'

'How was Kirstie; sad to be leaving?'

'You know Kirstie,' I laughed, 'all she could think about was her adventure as she described it this morning.'

'She's young.' reading the sympathy in his voice; how well he knew me. 'I know.'

'Good news, Hilary,' he said, 'I'll be back home on Wednesday.'

'That's wonderful, a whole week earlier than you had expected.'

'Yes, thanks to the efficiency of my team; they've worked solidly these last couple of weeks and now only the final tidying up has to be done, labelling, cataloguing and completing the paperwork.'

Pete's position as senior archaeologist attached to Oxford University meant he often had to spend time away. I had become accustomed to these periods of absences; my work as an illustrator, now freelance and working from home, couldn't be more diverse, although quite frequently with deadlines to meet, meant my hours could be erratic.

'What do you plan to do this evening?'

'Have a meal in the brasserie.'

'You're making me envious; our diet here leaves a great deal to be desired, not what you would call *haute cuisine*.'

'Too much pasta?'

'Too much pasta, but the Italians love it!'

'I'd better not suggest we go to "Santinis" when you get back, then.'

'Not for a couple of weeks; give me time to recover.'

'I had a really weird experience today, Pete, which transported me back twenty-six years.' going on to tell him about seeing my mother's portrait.

'My goodness; how did you feel when you saw it?'

'Amazed I suppose. I'd never seen the actual painting, but I remember her sitting for Charles Grayson. I haven't even looked at the magazine yet; I expect there will be a profile on him, but I'll be bringing it home anyway, so you'll be able to see for yourself.'

I ordered a gin and tonic from the bar, and taking it with me to one of the tables, opened the magazine. As I had thought, and hoped, there was an article on Charles Grayson, alongside what must have been a fairly recent photograph of him. He had aged considerably since the time I had last seen him. He would have been in his early thirties then, I hadn't known his exact age, only that he looked younger than my own parents and those of my friends, which would make him now about sixty, but he had the appearance of a much older man. His hair was now white and not as thick as it used to be, but the premature sign of aging was more than that; he looked tired, worn out, as if those intervening years had taken their toll. Reading through the article, it appeared he had been more than moderately successful, receiving several acclaims for his work in Britain and overseas, with a number of his paintings currently being exhibited in the Scottish National Portrait Gallery in Edinburgh. I looked again at the front cover and was reminded of Sir James Gunn's style, probably his most famous painting being "Pauline in the Yellow Dress" which I'd seen recently in the National Portrait gallery. In both paintings there was an iridescence about their subjects, the dark, although detailed background, strengthening this effect. There was no mention made of Charles Grayson's personal life; it was merely a documentary of his career as a portrait and landscape painter from when he left school after winning a scholarship to Edinburgh School of Art and up to the present where, having remained living in the family home in Calder Bay, continued painting. It was interesting to learn he used part of his house as his studio and gallery, the opening times, including the telephone number of the gallery being included at the end of the article.

Calder Bay, equidistant between Arbroath and Montrose on the east coast of Scotland, once a fishing village but for many years a popular seaside resort and where I had spent six years of my life. Although my parents were Scottish, I had been born and brought up in England. We used to spend holidays with my grandparents, but as they lived on the west coast there was no occasion to travel any further, therefore Calder Bay and that part of Scotland was virtually unknown to me, so much so, when I first arrived I often felt I was in a totally different country. Charles Grayson and his sister Beth lived across the road from us in Green Lane although somewhat misnamed as people used to always refer to it as a road, probably because it ran the full length from the centre of the town up to St. Paul's church at the top and, as with many of the houses in Calder Bay, the Graysons' was stone-built, but had been much neglected; the stone blackened by years of grime, the whole edifice made even gloomier by thick clinging ivy, which on the upper floors had been allowed to grow unchecked, attaching itself to the window frames and completing obscuring the windows.

Rob, my first husband, had come from Aberdeen, but during our marriage neither of us returned to Scotland, making the excuse to anyone who asked that the journey from Hong Kong was too long, especially with a young child. A poor excuse and not entirely true; I never knew the reason for Rob's reluctance, but I had other reasons for not wanting to go back. I had been fourteen when, after being in Calder Bay for about two years, we moved from our first house to Green Lane. Shortly afterwards,

I began to overhear snippets of conversation and to witness things which would have been best if I had remained in ignorance. I had never told anyone about this; not even my mother. She had always been my confidante, but she was the last person I could talk to and even if I had found someone else I had the sense to realise I wouldn't be believed. I had, therefore, over the years been able to keep these memories well and truly buried. It's possible that in hindsight and maturity I may have been over-reacting. I don't know. But, seeing my mother's portrait and reading about the man who had painted it, had acted as an opener, permitting me to take a further look into the past. I was being far too fanciful I knew, putting the magazine away in my bag, the phrase, "out of sight, out of mind" taunting me.

I had a delicious meal, choosing the smoked salmon platter; a mouth-watering concoction of perfectly cooked salmon with capers, lemon oil and *crème fraiche*, goat's cheese, beetroot and a walnut salad, rounding it off with a lemon *crème brulée*. By the time I had finished and was appreciating the remainder of a half bottle of Pierre *André*, a wine from the Bourgogne area and recommended by the head waiter, my thoughts were back on an even keel, looking forward to getting home the next day and catching up on all those odd jobs I'd been promising to tackle for far too long.

So much for good intentions. I left "Channings" shortly after nine the following morning, had reached my car, placing my overnight bag on the back seat and pulled out the route map which I always kept in the glove compartment, at the same time switching on the radio which was still tuned into Kirstie's favourite station, Capital Scotland, and had to fiddle around with the tuner before I found Radio Two. Pulling away from the kerb, the presenter, whose name I missed, was introducing his Friday morning guest. Charles Grayson's voice hadn't changed; I would have remembered and recognised it anywhere, although hearing it now on the radio was not only out of context, but was weird. If I was a superstitious person, I thought, I would be taking this as an omen, of what kind I had no idea, but as I joined the traffic in the main road, I found myself compulsively drawn to take the A8 out of the city instead of the A7 south. This road was unfamiliar to me and I had no time to question what I was doing, needing all my concentration to make sure I didn't miss the A90 for the Forth Road Bridge.

It was eleven when I took the exit from the motorway on the outskirts of Dundee, pulling into the service station. I needed a respite, time to think and try to understand what I was doing. By now, I should have been a good part of the way to Oxford, but instead, here I was, only twenty-odd miles from Calder Bay. There was a paved terrace outside the cafeteria from where I see my first glimpse of the sea, sparkling in the brilliant sunshine of the July morning, and I took my coffee out there.

I sat, sipping the sweet milky coffee, feeling the warmth of the sun on my face, idly wondering now why I had been so rash; I very seldom made decisions without first thinking them through. It wasn't too late to change my mind, but not sure whether I wanted to or not. Was this hesitation a sign of shying away from confronting, although metaphorically, what had happened twenty-six years earlier? On the other hand, it might not be such a bad idea to face those mental demons and perhaps discover they weren't demons after all. I might even enjoy seeing Calder Bay again, which would undoubtedly have changed a lot since I was last there.

I left the motorway at the first junction and followed the coastal road, passing Broughty Ferry, Carnoustie and Arbroath before sweeping round the bay, arriving in Calder Bay as the clock above the town hall was striking one. It had been an easy drive and I wasn't tired, but needed a walk to stretch my legs, but first I needed to book into a hotel. The ones I remember in the High Street were still there: "The Kinloch", "The Royal" and "The Shipwreck", and I decided on the "The Royal" as it was the only one I had been in before. Parking was no problem as there was plenty of space at the back of the hotel and in the hope they would have a vacancy, I took my bag in with me.

The reception area was exactly as I remembered, even the carpeting, Blackwatch tartan. Everything looked spotless; gleaming brass stair rails, enormous gilt-framed mirrors on either side of the staircase and tubs of orange and yellow chrysanthemums by the counter. I was given a room on the second floor which gave me a magnificent view of the bay; the tide was coming in, the water a brilliant blue as it slowly covered the sand. The window was open and I could smell the sea, taking a deep breath and inhaling the sheer purity of the air. I had forgotten that, I thought, moving away to unpack the few things I'd brought with me; cream linen trousers, cotton tops, only two dresses; a sleeveless powder-blue sheath and my standby, 'the little black dress'; two pairs of shoes; flat strappy sandals and black courts. My toiletries were the bare essentials and I set these out on the glass shelf above the hand basin in the bathroom. Before going downstairs, I unzipped my ipad case, relieved to see there was an email from Kirstie, eagerly devouring every word she had written: "Hi, Mum. Arrived safe and sound, HK's new airport is something else! Quite a reception waiting for me! They all send their love. Will keep in touch, lots of love and kisses, Kirstie." My day was now complete, wondering what she would say if she knew where I was. I would give Pete a ring later. He would be surprised, but no doubt intrigued for I had told him about that other time in Calder Bay. Pete had been the only one I had eventually confided in, but by then, it wasn't much more than a fading memory.

I walked up Green Lane slowly, wanting to savour these moments, passing familiar buildings which triggered off various memories: the Italian ice cream parlour where I had spent many hours, graduating as I grew older from strawberry milkshakes to cappuccinos with generous sprinklings of brown sugar; the house next door belonging to Miss Hayward, the piano teacher, and someone who used to frighten me to death trying in vain to teach me how to play, much to the disappointment of my father who was a brilliant pianist; further along, where the three sisters used to live; I never knew whether they were triplets but to me they looked identical, incredibly old-fashioned; gray crimped hair, tweed skirts and brogues, and as to age, naturally I couldn't even guess, but they always went out together and never appeared to talk to anyone; and now I was coming up to Charles Grayson's house which looked exactly as it had done; if anything, the ivy had reached an impenetrable stage; it was impossible to see any of the top windows, hardly an enticing place for anyone wanting to view his work, but perhaps the rear of the property was an improvement. I was now at the opening to "Carbisdale" where the Henderson family lived and for all I knew some of them may very well still be there. Not with any intention of making myself known, I walked along their side pathway to where I knew I would be able to see the house and from that distance it was unlikely I would be noticed, and then, reaching the end I came to a complete standstill. There was no house. "Carbisdale" no longer existed; no roof or walls remained, only the ground floor was visible, with a few of the interior walls still in place. The workmen must be having their lunch break because there was nobody around. Demolition equipment was parked on the churned up front lawn, alongside a massive truck fully loaded with rubble of what used to be the Henderson's magnificent property. I found the whole scene so unbelievably sad, and wanting to be away before the workmen returned, I turned round and walked back along the path towards Green Lane.

The main entrance to "Carbisdale" was in Carlogie Road at the top of the lane and was on my right-hand side. I was about to walk across the road to the church when I saw a notice had been pinned to the gatepost. There it was, in black and white. Planning permission had been granted by the Calder Bay Council for the construction of six two-bedroom luxury apartments, work to commence on the 7th of July and scheduled for completion on the 12th of January next year. Morrison Estate Agents, twenty-seven High Street, Calder Bay, had the sole selling rights on the properties. Bitterly disappointed there hadn't been a preservation order on the building, I turned away. I didn't go inside St. Pauls, but instead, walked round to the cemetery. Although so close to the main road it was a peaceful spot; most of the graves I noticed had been well tended, even the very old ones. I wandered along the narrow gravel pathways, all the time trying to puzzle out what must have happened for such a drastic decision to be made. I always understood that "Carbisdale" had been in the Henderson family for two or three generations. And, more importantly, where were they all now? After I left Calder Bay, Janice had been the only one I had kept in touch with, but regrettably, the letters between us became fewer and fewer, until eventually they stopped altogether. I had hardly known their father; he'd been widowed when Dougie was born and spent more time working than he did at home. Miraculously, none of them seemed to mind, not even Dougie; Mrs Baird, their housekeeper, looked after their daily needs: fully stocked food cupboards, an abundance of fresh fruit and vegetables and regular supplies of clean clothes. Looking back, I wondered how she had coped with only the help of a daily cleaner who must have spent most of her time clearing up after them all. Janice was the same age as I was when I first knew them not long after we had moved into the house across the road; Aileen, the eldest, had been eighteen and had that summer left boarding school; I think it was in Cheltenham; then there was John and to me the best looking of them all. He was three years older than me and I was madly in love with him, but of course he had no idea. Bobby was eleven and I suppose he was a bit wild; my father used to call him a rascal, but he was a likeable rascal and always managed to extricate himself from any scrapes. Dougie, 'the baby' of the family was only nine; he was a quiet boy, never had much to say for himself, just tagged along with the rest of us.

Memories, I sighed, and too many of them, but that was how I was feeling that afternoon and for the second time that day wishing Pete was with me; I needed his down-to-earth common sense to bring me back to the present. I continued along the path, glancing at the inscriptions on the gravestones, but there were no names I recognised, not that I expected them to be. During the six years I'd lived in Calder Bay, although I had made friends in secondary school, I could scarcely remember their names now, but close to the church wall I saw two I recognised; they hadn't been there long; the squares of grass at the side of the grave waiting to be put back into place, although the inscriptions on both of the gravestones had been done: "Sarah (Sadie) Northcot, beloved mother of Carla, died peacefully on the 17th June, 2003, aged sixty-six" and the other one, "Elizabeth Grayson, beloved sister of Charles, passed away on the 20th

June, 2003, aged sixty-two."

Charles' sister. I could just about remember what she had looked like: tall, like her brother, with thin features, her only redeeming feature being her hair, a thick mane of dark hair falling below her shoulders, which I had thought incongruous compared to the rest of her; no make-up, at least I never saw her wearing any, and even during the summer always wore trousers, the only concession to the warmer months being what looked like the same black linen ones.

Sadie Northcot, on the other hand, had been an entirely different kind of woman. Eccentric, flamboyant, so much so, I had convinced myself she must have been an actress at some time in her life. She had seldom ventured out, living two houses along from us and once, when Janice and I were collecting for the church jumble sale, she had greeted us dramatically, dragging us inside. She gave us a full carrier bag to take back with us saying "these clothes, my dear girls, will never be worn by me again", but before we could escape, she had insisted on showing us dozens of old photographs, all black and white; she was in all of them, exaggerated posing for the camera, which further convinced me she had been on the stage at one time. We hadn't known she had a daughter, she had never said. So, I thought, looking again at the inscription, she hadn't been all that old then, only thirty-eight. When do you start thinking like that; in your teens anyone even nudging twenty, as Aileen Henderson was, we considered to be old and ten years later, having passed that milestone, people, especially females, in their thirties and forties were ancient. Janice and I had both agreed when we'd finally managed to escape and were walking back to "Carbisdale" that Sadie Northcot, whether she had been famous or not, was just an old has-been. How cruel young people can be.

There were two graves next to each other at the far end of the cemetery, in deep shadow from the overhanging branches of an oak tree; it was quieter here; the thumping and clattering of machinery from the direction of "Carbisdale" which had started up as soon as I came into the cemetery, was barely audible. Two vases of yellow and red roses had recently been placed on the grass in front of the graves. Father and son, my breath catching at the back of my throat: "Jack Henderson, beloved husband of Myra who passed away on the 2nd April 1966, and loving father to Aileen, John, Janice, Roderick and Douglas, passed away on the 4th July 1993, aged seventy-six" and as I read the inscription on the second gravestone, the tears were running unchecked down my cheeks. "Robert (Bobby) Henderson, died tragically on the 4th July 1993, aged twenty-nine." Poor Bobby. Even at the age of eleven he had lived life to the full, squeezing everything he could out of it, almost as if he knew he had to, intuitively perhaps, that his life would only be a short one. And to have died on the same day as his father; what could this mean? Was it one of life's cruel coincidences? Also, a further coincidence, they had died exactly ten years ago today. The roses looked fresh; perhaps someone from the family had been along earlier, if they had that could mean whoever it was lived locally. I didn't think it would have been Janice; she lived too far away in Kendal. It may have been Aileen; I knew she still lived in Calder Bay, although I didn't know about the other two.

I took the long way back to the High Street and continuing down to the bay and trying to fathom out what could have happened ten years ago, but it was hopeless; I might never learn and even if I did, what good would it do. Bobby had gone, and although Janice had never said as much, I had always thought he had been her favourite brother. How devastated she must have been when he died. Tragically, the inscription had said. Did this mean he'd had an accident? There was only one person I could think of who might be able to tell me, but as I walked back along the High Street, I wasn't sure whether I wanted to ask him. Charles Grayson would know. He'd been friendly with Jack Henderson and often on a Sunday they would spend afternoons playing chess, but somehow I didn't think he would be all that approachable. I'd hardly ever spoken to him, but then what would we have had to say to each other. I was still a schoolgirl, my knowledge of painting negligible and what I had learned would be of no interest to him; a man in his thirties already making a name for himself in the art world. Even if I did decide to approach him, now would probably not be the right time. He had only recently lost his sister. I suppose he must have been fond of her and it would appear she had never married; she had been a strange woman, some years older than him and I couldn't imagine them having a great deal in common. I had no idea how she filled her days. She may have had a job, but I don't think she did. In fact, I realised after all this time, she must have led a fairly lonely existence in that drab mausoleum of a place, surprised she and Charles hadn't made an effort to make the house more welcoming to anyone wanting to have a look round his gallery. To have had the gallery specifically mentioned in a prestigious magazine such as "Art Review", with presumably a wide circulation, must imply he wanted visitors.

It was almost six when I got back to "The Royal" and, deciding to have a shower before going down to the bar for a drink before my meal, I switched on the television before going into the bathroom. Emerging five or six minutes later, feeling considerably refreshed with one of the hotel's large white fluffy towels wrapped round me, I caught the newsreader mid-sentence: "..... the remains of what is believed to be that of a woman were discovered this afternoon by demolition workers in Calder Bay. My colleague, Sandra, visited the scene in the grounds of the once locally-owned property and was able to have a few words with the foreman."; the studio immediately being superimposed by the frontage of "Carbisdale", blue and white striped tape cordoning off the whole area, and focusing on the woman, a clone of her studio counterpart. Facing the barrage of press cameras, she turned to the man standing beside her, her microphone positioned as close to his face as she could manage: "I understand you were the first to see the body?" she asked him somewhat unnecessarily I thought; poor man he looked so shaken anyone could see he'd had a shock, but she appeared to be oblivious.

"Aye," his voice shaking, "that's right."

"Where was it exactly?"

"In the old wash-house over there." pointing behind him.

"Wash-house?" allowing a frown to mar her perfectly smooth forehead.

"Aye, it's where the servants of the big house would have done the washing; they would have heated up the water in the boiler, no washing machines in those days;" he added, presumably for her benefit. Probably fed up with her, I thought, feeling sorry for him. He'd already tried to move back from the microphone, only to have her quickly extend her arm, until she had the microphone exactly where she wanted it.

"I see, and whereabouts in the wash-room was the body?"

"Inside the boiler, someone had crammed it in there, but I didn't notice it then, it was too dark in there; it wasn't until the JCB had hauled the boiler out into the open."

"Do you think the body had been in there a long time?"

"I've no idea; by the state of it, I would say so, but that will be up to the experts. I'm in the demolition business, lassie."

That's put her in her place, I thought; she should have known better than to ask such a stupid question. The television cameras zoomed in briefly over to where tarpaulin had been erected shielding the policed activity, before returning to the studio. Not wanting to hear or see anything else, I switched off the set. I was finding it all so difficult to take in. The sheer horror of what I had heard was so shocking, so unbelievable. A woman's body, the newsreader had said. And possibly it had been there for a long time. How long? And why there? A multitude of questions were emerging and I was making an effort to ward them off, to keep my mind clear. The fact that none of this had anything to do with me was immaterial; the knowledge that a woman had been murdered and an attempt had been made to conceal the body in the grounds of "Carbisdale", was bordering on the bizarre.

I had yet to phone Pete, hesitating over whether I should tell him about any of this. Up to now, taking the mobile from my bag, I had refused to consciously consider the possible consequences of what I had just heard, but if I did, realising in advance what his reactions would be, I would have no choice but to bring those long-buried suspicions to the surface and face facts, however painful.

Chapter Two

CHARLES

It was an illusion, but for a fraction of a second as I saw her leaning forward to read the inscription on Bobby's gravestone, I thought Natasha had returned. The resemblance was remarkable; the way she was standing, with one foot slightly in front of the other and her head tilted to one side, was exactly how I remembered her. I had never noticed the likeness before, but then Hilary had only been a kid then, about fourteen probably. I'd seen her often when she'd been round at the Henderson's, and I remember Marion commenting that her daughter was becoming as wild as the rest of the Henderson children.

She hadn't seen me and that suited me; I was in no mood to talk about the past, retracing my steps back to the church gate; I could return later to place the small pot of petunias, Sadie's favourite flowers, by her graveside. Sadie had been a good friend these last few years since Jack had died and I was going to miss our talks. She'd had a wicked sense of humour which had appealed to me; also she had been a good listener and an avid art lover. If it hadn't been for her friendship, Beth having, as far as I was concerned, long ago reached saturation point in respect to any conversational skills, I would no doubt have left Calder Bay; moved closer to Edinburgh, but I'd left it too late. While I hoped to have a good few more active years left, I knew I was far too set in my ways to adjust to any new environment. I should have gone years ago, but then there had always been Beth; cloyingly possessive, demanding more and more of my attention, something I had been no longer prepared to give. Dying, as she had, suddenly, and ironically only three days after Sadie, had provided me with something I had not experienced before, which was freedom to think independently, and equally as important, the freedom of movement. Bitter thoughts, but that was how I was feeling. The irony of their graves being next to each other hadn't escaped me either. The two women had been neighbours for years, although it was unlikely they had known each other, especially as in the latter years, Beth seldom left the house. Naturally enough, she hadn't approved of my friendship with Sadie, but I had by then learned to ignore her sarcastic remarks with the unpleasant sexual innuendos. Beth's jealousy had been dangerously close to the surface, but as she was losing any interest she may have had in life, her influence over me had also lost its strength.

When I reached the gate, I turned round; Hilary was still there, her hand resting on the dark grey marble of the gravestone, as if reluctant to move away. Why should she have come here after all this time? It must have been about thirty years since she left Calder Bay; surely there couldn't be anyone she would have come especially to see? Maybe she was on a nostalgic visit. It was possible.

She must be in her forties now, although looked younger; she had Natasha's olive skin tones and the deep blue, almost violet eyes, and as I walked back to the house I thought about her; she had been Marion's daughter and although they were close, I always thought she preferred Natasha; mesmerised, I suppose, by the glamour Natasha exuded and it would have been just like her to intentionally woo her away from her mother, if only to upset Marion. Was Hilary married; if so, where was the husband? There was an air of serenity about her which she must have inherited from her mother. Natasha could never have been described as serene. Far from it; she'd been fiery, unpredictable and hell-bent in making trouble if she didn't get what she wanted. She had been in her late twenties when she came to Calder Bay that first summer after Marion and her family moved into the house across the road from me, and hadn't wasted any time in making herself known; there were no subtleties with Natasha, she always came straight to the point, as she had done within the first couple of days. "I want you to paint me, Charles," she had pouted, leaning against the window frame in my studio, the top buttons undone, revealing more than a glimpse of frothy white lace, "in the nude. Only in the nude. You like my body, don't you?" she'd asked when I didn't answer immediately.

Of course I had given in, with only the slightest of misgivings. She had been right; she had a lovely body; slim, but rounded, her skin flawless, seeming to glow in the late afternoon sun streaming through the window and on to my canvas. I had painted nudes before, many times, but the women had been unknown to me; artists' models trained in maintaining the same position without fidgeting as Natasha had done. The end result though had been good and I wasn't displeased with the work and years later received a number of acclaims and for a while it was exhibited in the National Portrait Gallery in Edinburgh. I had almost completed the painting and was adding the final touches, when I made a mistake; I made love to her, not for any overwhelming desire to do so, but because of her provocative persistence and being Natasha, once was not enough. She took to calling in at odd moments during the day, not discouraged when she could see I was working and although I had been quick to tell her so, this made no difference; the unwanted visits continued until one afternoon she issued her ultimatum; either I married her or she would report me for sexual harassment.

It didn't matter that she'd been lying; my reputation would have been tainted, a stigma which no doubt would have remained. I will never know whether she would have carried out her threat, but I couldn't afford to take the risk. I had to think quickly, and the only solution I could think of was to pretend to go along with her, suggesting before we should make such a commitment, we go away for a few days. I had recently purchased a villa in Cap d'Ail, a tiny village on the outskirts of Monaco and had been promising myself a break. I hadn't told Beth about the villa; this was something I intended to keep away from her.

Natasha, true to form, had been quick to agree. I think the idea of spending some time alone with me in what she probably thought of as the exotic surroundings of the South of France was the real attraction. It had been she who had suggested, insisted even, that we keep our relationship a secret, not that I could have described it as such, my view being I was being coerced into doing what she wanted.

"What about Beth?" she had asked.

"What about her?"

"Well," an unfathomable expression on her face, "she won't let you go, especially with me."

"Natasha," annoyed by the implication, "I'm thirty years of age, financially and emotionally independent, "Beth's reaction is of no interest to me."

"Why do you continue to live with her then?"

"We share the same house, Natasha, in which we both grew up."

"She doesn't like me."

"And does that bother you?"

"Err – "for once sounding hesitant, " – *normally*," emphasising the word, "it wouldn't but, quite frankly, Charles, she gives me the creeps."

"In what way?" intrigued in spite of the situation in which she had placed me. I had never discussed Beth with anyone before and could only guess how other people viewed her.

"Oh," making an attempt now to make light of what she had said, "it doesn't matter."

"But I'm interested; go on, tell me what you meant."

"Well, it's the way she looks at you, as if she couldn't bear to let you out of her sight; even when you're in here working, I can hear her hovering around, It's not natural, Charles, that's what I meant by creepy."

This is what becomes, I sighed, unlocking my front door, of permitting the past to insinuate itself into the present. I scarcely ever thought of Natasha, hadn't done for years, and certainly didn't want to now, but seeing Hilary Robertson again had been similar to looking into a three-sided mirror; by slanting the glass, the three images multiplied, growing smaller each time, but it wasn't only Hilary he was seeing, Marion was there, Beth naturally, Sadie, even his old friend Jack and his dead son, Bobby.

I'm becoming maudlin, I decided, walking through to the studio and opening the French windows on to the stone terrace; too much had been happening recently: Sadie dying so suddenly only a week ago, then Beth, which reminded me I had yet to sort out her things, a task I was not looking forward to, but there was no one else, but at some time, it had to be done. At least Sadie's daughter would be taking care of everything.

Sadie hadn't told me about Carla until after Jack had died. I should have been surprised, but I hadn't been. Sadie had been a good-looking woman, clever, intelligent and it was true many years younger than him, but Jack had confided in me shortly before Dougie was born that he wasn't happy with his marriage; he hadn't elaborated, I believe he may have done, but it could have meant he would have had to tell me about the affair with Sadie. I'll never know. He may have anticipated my disapproval, especially the way he treated her after Carla was born. He hadn't been prepared to accept his daughter, although he had provided for her education. To salve his conscience? It was more than likely. I had asked Sadie why she hadn't moved away from Calder Bay, but her reply had been ambiguous: "Charles," she had said, looking at me in that direct way of hers, "one cannot continue running away from oneself." I hadn't pursued it, respecting her privacy. I met Carla for the first time at Sadie's funeral, but didn't have the chance to talk to her, but I had wanted to; she did tell me she would be in Calder Bay for a couple of weeks, arranging the sale of the house, once she had taken care of the contents which I knew to be considerable. She gave me her mobile number and said she was staying at "The Royal".

I spent the rest of the afternoon catching up on tedious but necessary paperwork: acknowledging the handful of condolence letters which had arrived after I had put Beth's obituary in the local newspaper; signing the formal acceptance for talks I would be giving during the Edinburgh Festival next month; completing forms for a solo portrait exhibition in the autumn and, finally, sifting through estimates from Calder Bay and Montrose builders which had come in over the past week and up to now I hadn't had time to look at properly.

For a number of years I had had countless arguments with Beth concerning the deterioration of the house, but she had been adamant; she stubbornly refused, never explaining why; it could have been her paranoid dislike of spending money, but I don't think so; she knew I would have been willing to contribute towards the cost. I really had no say in the matter. The property had been bequeathed to her when my father died giving her full control on whether anything would be done to prevent the encroaching decay in the stonework and the crumbling window frames; the rapid growth of ivy was more than partially responsible for the overall depressing appearance, but now, as she had left it to me in her will, I was determined there would be changes. It wasn't only the exterior of the building which required extensive remedial work; the interior left a great deal to be desired, but that could wait until the builders had finished. I looked again at the estimate from William Lowe & Sons which appeared to be the most favourable, not only in price but in the estimated time they reckoned it would take to complete: two days to strip the ivy away, three to steam-clean the stonework; new window frames, including the supplying and fitting of a new front door, all in all, four weeks. Deciding on this one, I dated and signed the form. It was going to be an upheaval, but couldn't be helped. Very little needed to be done at the rear of the house as about ten or twelve years ago, I had insisted on a conservatory being added to accommodate both my studio and small gallery, the latter only recently opened to the public. There would be no need for anyone sufficiently interested in viewing my work to use the front entrance as they could walk along the path at the side of the building to reach the gallery. Beth hadn't protested as much as I had expected her to when I first broached the subject; one reason I expect because I would be paying for the renovation and the other, which was more than probable, I think she realised if she hadn't agreed, I would use this as an excuse to move out.

With the idea of spending the following day working, hopefully without any interruptions, I decided to walk down to the High Street and post my mail; it would be too late for today's collection, but that didn't matter; there was nothing of such great importance that one day's delay would make any difference. The post office was next door to the "The Shipwreck Hotel" and I called in for a drink before going back home. It was just after six and already there were a number of people in the bar, most of them I recognised, but others, who looked like visitors, easily recognisable by their clothes; the men in shorts, open-necked shirts and deck shoes which, apparently, were currently in vogue amongst holidaymakers this summer. The women, more adventurous in what they obviously considered to be holiday attire for a seaside town, sleeveless, long cotton dresses in various shades of red, blue and yellow, reminding me of tropical birds. In here, unlike "The Royal" further along the High Street, the decor was not traditional Scottish; there was no tartan in sight, or any ancient paintings of Highland cattle or game; instead, fishing nets festooned with coloured weights, imitation brass-rimmed portholes and, at the far end of the bar where there had once been a fireplace, a fairly good replica of an ancient rusted anchor was the focal point. The name of the hotel, "The Shipwreck" may be something of a misnomer; as far as I was aware there had been no shipwreck in close vicinity to Calder Bay. To some, the contrived effect to create a nautical atmosphere probably had no appeal, but I quite liked it; each time I came in I was reminded of many of the old pubs down in the West Country. However, the solid dark oak bar was authentic and so were the lines of optics and beer pumps carrying a good selection of ales.

'Hello, Charles, a Heineken?' Ken Morris asked me as soon as I reached the bar; Ken had been head barman for years from as far back to when I first started coming into "The Shipwreck"; he had to be past retirement age, although he gave no sign of slowing down, appearing just as agile as ever.

'Please, Ken; you look as though you're going to be busy this evening.'

'It's always the same at weekends especially with the holiday season in full swing, but I'm not complaining.' placing the Heineken on the bar in front of me, 'You'll have heard the news, then?'

'No, I missed the six o'clock; what's happened?'

'You live in Green Lane, don't you, Charles?'

'Yes, that's right, about half-way along.'

'Well, you'll know where the old Grange is?'

'"Carbisdale", yes, my house is next door.'

'Well, they found the remains of a woman's body there this afternoon.'

'What! Who did?'

'Workmen, apparently they're demolishing the old place and the body had been in one of the outhouses.'

'My God! I've been at home most of the afternoon, Ted and I never heard a thing, apart from the demolition workers' equipment of course, but as they've been there for the last week, I've grown used to it.'

'Terrible business;' Ken said, shaking his head, 'Bruce McPherson, he's the foreman, was the one who made the discovery; they interviewed him and he looked badly shaken.'

'No wonder; poor man.'

'Yes, the interviewer, an insensitive young miss, was asking him some daft questions, like how long did he think the body had been there. As if he would know!'

'You mentioned remains, Ken, so that would, I suppose, indicate it had been there for some time.'

'That's what he told her; reminded her he was in the demolition business.'

Distracted at that moment by a new surge of customers, Ken moved along the bar to serve them.

I continued to stand there, forgetting to drink my beer, trying to make some sort of sense of what I'd just heard; the remains of the body of a woman, hidden for probably years, in the grounds of "Carbisdale" and only discovered now. It sounded so utterly incredible. I didn't know what to think; the Hendersons had always lived there from as far back as I could remember, right up until fairly recently when the company Jack had owned went bankrupt and John Henderson had been forced to sell-up. I had no idea where John and his wife had gone, only that they no longer lived in Calder Bay. No doubt Janice was still living in the Lake District with her husband and family; only Aileen and Dougie were still in Calder Bay; they would presumably be the first to hear, wondering how they were re-acting to such shocking news. It was inevitable they would be questioned by the police and then, of course, there was the media. Where on earth is all this going to end, I thought, picking up my glass and taking a deep sip.

There was a message on my answering machine when I eventually got home; I'd eaten in the restaurant and had a final drink in the bar chatting to a couple of old friends I hadn't seen for a while, therefore it was quite late by then.

It took me a few seconds to recognise her voice: "Hello, Charles," she said, "sorry to be calling so late in the evening," and adding, although by then I realised it was Sadie's daughter, "it's Carla here, I've just been watching the nine o'clock news and heard about – about what's been discovered in the grounds of what used to be my father's house – quite shocking – I don't really know why I'm phoning you, but I suppose I wanted to talk to someone who knew him – I don't know – sorry," she repeated, "I'm not usually as garbled as this," an attempt being made to laugh, "but I'm finding the news, well, I guess bizarre is the only way to describe it ..... Bye, talk to you soon I hope."

I didn't hesitate and taking out the card she'd given me I dialled her number; she answered immediately.

'I've just got in, Carla,' I said, as soon as she answered, 'and got your message.'

'I just couldn't believe what I was hearing, Charles.'

'I only heard earlier this evening, not from the television news, but the barman at "The Shipwreck Hotel" told me; it must have been on the six o'clock, but I missed it. As you say, it is shocking and yes, unbelievable.'

'And the body has only been discovered now. Why did it take so long, I wonder; they said on the news it had been there for a number of years.'

'Presumably the police will find out who the woman was.'

'How?'

'I'm only guessing, so I'm rather vague; DNA, dental records, and when they've established when she was murdered, they'll check the missing persons' lists over that particular period. Look Carla,' I suggested, 'it's too late tonight, but why don't we meet sometime tomorrow; that's if you'll be able to spare the time?'

'I'd like to see you, Charles, and as tomorrow is Sunday, that will be no problem.'

Before ringing off, we arranged to meet in the lounge bar of "The Royal" around eleven the following morning. "The best made schemes of mice and men gang aft a-gley", I thought, switching off the lights and making sure all the doors were locked, Rabbie Burns had a lot to answer for, but I did want to see her again; the programme I had set for myself could easily be rearranged. I had no sittings until next Wednesday which would enable me to complete two canvases I had been working on before Beth died, this reminding me once more about the chore of sorting out her things. I felt instinctively, and perhaps unkindly, once that had been accomplished I would be in a position to embark on this new phase in my life.

Chapter Three

AILEEN

I didn't hear about the discovery of the body until Sunday morning, having spent the previous day with friends who were in Calder Bay on holiday and it had been late when I returned home and not having an answering machine, I had no way of knowing whether Dougie had been trying to call me.

'Dougie, honestly,' I complained as soon as I heard his voice, 'it is only ten o'clock; what can be so important for you to phone me so early?'

'Sorry, but I thought you should know.'

'What's wrong?'

'I don't know whether anything is wrong, actually, anything which concerns us I mean, but yesterday afternoon, demolition workers found a body in the old wash-house at "Carbisdale" – '

' – what the hell!' increasing my grip on the receiver as the full horror of what he had said hit me.

'It had been there for a long time apparently,' he went on as if he hadn't noticed the interruption.

'And,' prompting him; he always had been slow in coming to the point. If I hadn't known my brother so well, I would have believed he was doing this on purpose, 'what else?'

'I think that's enough, don't you, Aileen?'

'Oh, you know what I mean; was it a man or a woman's body and whereabouts in the wash-house; surely there was more to the news report?'

'Not really, except it was a woman's body and had been crammed inside the boiler, that's about it.'

'I wonder who she was.'

'No doubt the police will eventually suss that out; they usually do, even after a long period of time.'

'I suppose so.'

'Apart from wanting to let you know about this, I thought you should be prepared for a visit from the police.'

'What the hell for? I didn't kill the woman!'

'Of course you didn't. A lot will depend on when this happened and, if it was when we were all still living in "Carbisdale", it stands to reason they are bound to want to question us.'

'So, we, the only two members of the family unfortunate enough to still be living in Calder Bay, will be on the top of their list. Is that what you're saying?'

'I'm sure, if they contact us, they'll also get in touch with John and Janice.'

'Don't forget Karen,' I put in maliciously never having liked the female, unreasonably annoyed that we should be the only people to be singled out for questioning, 'and Mrs Baird.' I added.

'You might as well include Jimmy.'

'Jimmy McIntosh;' remembering our old gardener who had been working for us even before my mother died, 'that might be difficult.'

'Why?'

'Because he died, that's why, Dougie. Old people do, you know.'

'I don't understand why you're taking this attitude, but it's a pity he's gone, not only because he is no longer with us, but if he had been he might have known whether anyone had been inside the wash-house, someone who shouldn't have been, I mean.'

'I doubt it; he had enough to contend with looking after the garden, not to mention the orchard.'

'He had help though.'

'A couple of boys from Calder Bay, yes, but Jimmy was a shrewd old boy; he always kept his eye on them; they would never had had the opportunity to wander off and break into the wash-house just for the fun of it.'

'True. Anyway, it's not good news. You can imagine all too well what people will be saying.'

'Oh, let them, Dougie. Give the old biddies something to talk about.'

I hadn't really meant it when I tried to make light of how too many of the people in Calder Bay would literally have a field day, also there would be more than a few who would even enjoy anything which might, although even remotely, further tarnish the Henderson name. In the wake of John taking the company into bankruptcy, both Dougie and I took the full brunt of what had felt like a social stigma. It had been alright for John and Karen; they couldn't get out of Calder Bay quick enough and the unpleasant fact that John had over the years since my father died, somehow managed to siphon off sufficient money from undisclosed, or more accurately *fudged* income to purchase a two million pound property south of the border, only added to my growing concern about this latest development in the turbulent history of "Carbisdale". We had all been born there, even my father and grandfather; my grandmother used to tell me stories of past family scandals; I never knew whether they were true or not, but at the age of nine or ten I believed everything she said.

I was meeting up with the Blakes again at midday; they would be leaving Calder Bay the following day and had asked me to join them for lunch at "The Royal"; fortunately I had already dressed before Dougie rang and I only had to put the finishing touches to my make-up. Usually, I would have walked from where I lived at the other side of the bay into town, but as I was short of time decided to take the car. I drove past several family groups carrying collapsible sun beds, picnic baskets and cool boxes; the children, with an assortment of beach toys, already in their swimwear. The summer season in Calder Bay was truly in full swing, I thought, turning into the High Street, which was teeming with visitors; the three hotels all had tables and chairs outside on the pavement; different coloured parasols had been strategically placed to shield the customers from what promised to be another hot and sunny day. I parked in "The Crown's" car park and walked into the hotel by the side entrance which led directly into the bar. There was no sign of the Blakes and I ordered a glass of wine from Terry, one of the barmen, remaining at the bar from where I would see them as soon as they came in.

'Aileen?'

I couldn't believe it; after all these years. Only Hilary had ever pronounced my name that way, with the emphasis on the second syllable.

'Hilary!' turning to face her, 'how extraordinary; I never expected to see you again.'

'Hello, Aileen,' she smiled, the same shy smile, 'you look just the same.'

'Older!' I laughed.

'Aren't we all!'

'What are you doing here in Calder Bay? Sorry, that sounded rude, but seeing you again is so – well, so surprising.'

'I suppose it must be; actually,' she went on, 'it's rather surprising to me, it was a spur of the moment decision. I had been in Edinburgh attending Kirstie's graduation ceremony and had started to drive back down south, but changed my mind and came up here instead.'

'To Calder Bay.'

'To Calder Bay.'

'There has been so much water passed under the bridge since you left; for us and, I'm sure for you, Hilary. Are you still living in Hong Kong?'

'No, I left there six years ago; that's when I re-married. Pete and I have been living in Oxford since then.'

'And Rod?'

'We divorced when Kirstie was eleven.'

'And how is she?'

'She's fine; in fact she's in Hong Kong now; she flew out there on Friday. She wants to try and make a go of things over there.'

'That's brilliant -' breaking off, having seen the Blakes in the open doorway, ' – sorry, Hilary, but I've arranged to meet some friends of mine for lunch, so I'll have to go. Will you still be here tomorrow?'

'Yes, I'm driving back down south on Tuesday.'

'Shall we meet for a drink tomorrow then and catch up on things. In here, around six, will that be alright?'

'I'd love to, Aileen.'

How odd I thought, that she should be in Calder Bay at this particular time, wondering whether she knew about the gruesome discovery. She and Janice had been very close friends and Hilary had spent more time over in "Carbisdale" than in her own home, especially during the school holidays. She wouldn't know about Bobby, I would have to tell her tomorrow; in fact, if I chose to, there was a lot I could tell her about these intervening years, mentally calculating when any of them had last seen her.

Hilary had been twenty when she married Rob Masters and had gone out to Hong Kong with him, but it must have been before then; her parents had split up earlier, it must have been around the time she was fourteen or fifteen. Her father had gone back down south where they had lived before moving to Calder Bay, and Hilary and her mother had stayed on for a while. I think they must have sold up and left Calder Bay about a year before Hilary married, therefore, at last reaching a more or less accurate date, it must have been some time in 1980, twenty-three years ago.

The same year I was first married, not that it lasted long; only two years and then I narrowly escaped what would have been another disastrous marriage, but had the sense to pull out in time, much to Charles' surprise and even when I made an attempt to explain to him why I couldn't go through with it, he continued to be dumbfounded. He had honestly believed that his wife could possibly live with him under the same roof as his awful sister; he just refused to face the fact that the marriage would have been doomed from the start. Beth Grayson's paranoid affection for him had been positively unhealthy. It had always amazed me that she tolerated him having his studio in the house, far less knowing he was often painting portraits of women, many of them in the nude. It hadn't bothered me; for all his faults, Charles was a professional and he was a good painter, there was no doubt about that.

By the time I met Godfrey, I was over thirty and didn't think I would marry again, but although fifteen years older than me, he was a kind and considerate man, and if he hadn't died two years ago, I'm sure we would still be together, but it wasn't to be. Godfrey had only been sixty-one when he died; no warning, no long illness to prepare either of us, just one massive heart attack and he'd gone. It had taken me until now to get my life back on an even keel and to stop wallowing in what was no more than self-pity and the last thing I wanted to disturb this healing process was to be asked questions by the authorities about an occurrence which presumably must have taken place in the grounds of my old home.

Chapter Four

HILARY

Aileen and I had hardly known each other, surprised she was able to recognise me so quickly. Although there were only four years between us, I had always been in awe of her. Even at eighteen she had seemed to have known instinctively the secret of elegance; the colours of her clothes blended perfectly, they never clashed; always, her shoes matched her bag; linen skirts and trousers simply never creased and I don't remember her ever wearing really casual clothes, not even in the height of summer. Her dresses, pure cotton, simple classic lines and if she wore shorts they would be tailor-made, mostly white or navy linen, never tee-shirts, instead, striped or spotted polo-shirts. I had been quite genuine when I told her she hadn't changed and in many respects she did look as I remembered her, although perhaps as a concession to the more liberal style of dressing of the twenty-first century, the hemline of the cream linen dress she had been wearing had been well below knee-length and in place of the traditional high-heeled sandals, her summer shoes were wedges, with the tapes tied around her ankles. She still wore her hair in a short page-boy style, but on her it didn't look dated at all. I noticed she hadn't been wearing a wedding ring, which could have meant anything, and presumably she would tell me when we met the next day.

Aileen had been the first of the family to leave "Carbisdale"; I don't know about the others because I had left Calder Bay when I married Rob and although Janice had written to tell me when she left home to live in the Lake District with her new husband, she never mentioned what the boys were doing. My parents had been divorced for three years by the time I met Rob; my father moving back to England and my mother and I remaining in the house in Green Lane. She sold up shortly after Rob and I went out to Hong Kong, and bought a bungalow in her home town and then, three years later, she was killed in a car crash. She had only been forty-seven. I came back for her funeral and to sort out her affairs, taking two year-old Kirstie with me. It had been the first time my grandparents had seen her and they spoiled her like mad. I'd like to think that having Kirstie there helped them through that terrible time. I phoned Janice, who by this time was living in Kendal, to tell her about my mother. She'd wept when she heard and said she wanted to be with us, but as she was eight months pregnant, we didn't think it would be wise. She sent a wreath; yellow and red roses and I placed it next to mine by my mother's grave in the cemetery on the hill looking over the town where she was born.

Aileen had also sent a wreath, this was made up of roses as well and I remember being reminded of those other flowers she had given me during our first summer in Green Lane. I don't know why seeing her again today should bring back this memory in particular, my brain had plenty of others from which to choose.

It had been at the beginning of the school holidays, around the time Charles Grayson was painting the portrait of my mother. I had spent what seemed to be like hours in the dentist's chair that morning having two molars extracted and had been curled up on the sofa in the lounge when Aileen had called in with an enormous bunch of scarlet roses; roses she had picked from the garden at "Carbisdale". They were for me, nobody had ever given me flowers before and I thought it was such a lovely gesture. She had only stayed a few minutes and after she had gone I think I must have drifted off to sleep, but it could only have been very shallow because I was disturbed by the sound of raised voices coming from the next room: " ..... she is an extremely pretty girl, Natasha; surely you can see that?" my mother was saying.

"I suppose so." Silence, and although I couldn't see my aunt, I could imagine her shrugging; she used to do that a great deal; it was her way of not wanting, or perhaps not admitting, there could be anyone more attractive than she was. As young as I was, I had no illusions about Natasha: she was vain, spoilt by my grandmother, but we all made excuses for her, even my father who never had much time for her: "Poor Natasha" he would say, shaking his head in despair.

My Aunt Natasha had been in the habit of spending a few weeks with us during the summer and this was her first visit to Calder Bay. She was nothing like my mother; apart from her being twelve years younger, I never could see any likeness between them. She did work, but not with any great enthusiasm, and often the jobs were only temporary which enabled her to take time off to spend weeks with one friend or another. Natasha, as she had told me to call her about a year earlier, made friends easily. I suppose she was rather shallow, but to an impressionable girl barely into her teens she was the epitome of glamour.

"Anyway, Marion," Natasha said, "I've made up my mind."

"Have you?" sounding bored, as though she had heard it all before.

"Yes," Natasha quick to answer back, "and there's no need to look at me like that."

"I wasn't aware I was looking at you in any particular way, but what is this monumental decision you've made."

"I'm going to marry Charles."

"Charles Grayson?"

"At this moment, Marion, there is no other Charles in my life; of course I mean Charles Grayson; who else?"

"Has he asked you to marry him?"

"Not yet, but he will."

"I wouldn't be too sure, Natasha."

"You've always tried to pull me down, haven't you? You're married, so why shouldn't I be?"

"Finding a husband, the right one, I mean, isn't like going into your dress shop and buying the first dress which catches your eye."

"What nonsense you talk, Marion. I wish I hadn't told you now."

Another silence, but shorter this time.

"Listen, Marion, in two years I will be thirty; I don't need to tell you that. For the last fifteen years I've flitted from one relationship to another, never short of boyfriends, or places to stay when I became bored with whatever mediocre job I was doing: exhibition work, showing housewives how to use an electric food mixer or some other kitchen gadget, which is a bit of a joke when you consider I hardly go into a kitchen; then there's pin-up modelling, slightly more pay, for third-rate crummy photography outfits, or the last job, if you can call it that, posing half-naked on the bonnet of the latest Ferrari at Earl's Court. I'm tired of it all. I'm not exactly proud of what can hardly be called my career path and that is why I'm going to make a supreme effort to settle down. Being married to Charles will suit me fine."

"Be careful, Natasha, I don't think Charles is the marrying kind."

"He's not gay is he?"

"No, he's not gay."

"Aha! So that's it! You're spending a lot of time over there; how many times, Marion?"

"I've had about six sittings I think."

"That seems to be a long time to paint a portrait; it *is* head and shoulders, isn't it?"

"This is a ridiculous conversation, Natasha. I'm going to wake Hilary up and take her down to "Marco's" for a milkshake; are you going to come with us?"

"No thanks, I'm going across the road; there's something I want to ask Charles."

Now that I had opened my mind to these old memories, I couldn't draw a halt there; I had to follow them through to their conclusion, something I had been trying to avoid since Saturday.

I had my strawberry milkshake and as I sat across the marble table in one of the booths in "Marco's" I looked closely at my mother's face, but it looked just as it usually did. I hadn't fully understood what I'd overheard, realising now that it had been way above my head. For instance, I had never heard the word gay used in that way before. On reflection, I think I must have been rather naive, young for my age, perhaps. Also, I was puzzled; I couldn't decide whether Natasha had been serious or not, and if there had been any hidden meanings, which there probably had been, I would certainly not have understood them. I believe I would have probably forgotten what they'd been saying, but two days later Natasha left. Janice and I had cycled up to the fruit farm outside Calder Bay in the afternoon to pick raspberries; anyone could do this and stay for as long as they liked; in our case, we waited until we had filled enough punnets to pay for tickets to see the latest James Bond film at "The Ritz", Calder Bay's cinema, and it was almost dark when we got home. When I asked where Natasha was, fully expecting her to be there, my mother said she had gone, adding something about meeting up with some friends who had a villa in the South of France. My father, who was watching a quiz show on television, didn't say anything, and sensing a strained atmosphere I didn't ask any questions, deciding to wait until the following day when I could speak to her on her own. As I prepared for bed I couldn't help feeling hurt Natasha hadn't told me earlier in the day, at breakfast when we had all been together, especially as she had promised to come and watch the fancy dress parade the following afternoon. I knew she could be unpredictable, but I thought she cared enough about me to have said goodbye. She had known what Janice and I were going to do and that it would be quite late when I returned, which made it all the more puzzling.

Those demons were back and I knew what they were up to; they were forcing me to face the truth, accept the frightening thought and one I wasn't certain I would be able to put into words the next time I spoke to Pete. Perhaps there would be no need; his pragmatic approach to life, not hampered as I was by emotional clutter, may enable him to reach the same conclusion, the one I was shying away from. There was another memory clambering for attention and for the first time in years I permitted myself to remember.

It was the time of my mother's funeral, the evening before Kirstie and I would be going back to Hong Kong. We had persuaded my grandfather to go along to his club; except for the day of the funeral, he hadn't ventured out any further than the garden, sitting for hours on the bench seat next to the lily pond, searching no doubt for some kind of solace. I had finished my last-minute packing and went to look for my grandmother; she was in Kirstie's room, seated beside the bed; Kirstie was sound asleep; both arms stretched out above her head as though in whatever dreams she may have been having, she was reaching out for something – or someone. Smiling, I put a hand on my grandmother's shoulder, as we both looked at her.

"She's a beautiful child, Hilary,' she whispered, 'I'm going to miss you both so much."

"I know, Gran, we're going to miss you too, but we'll be back."

She had gently placed a hand on mine. For reassurance? For the continuation – of what? It had been a poignant moment, both of us still grieving for the person we had loved.

"Come on, Gran," I'd said, "it's a lovely evening; let's have a glass of wine outside, I've opened a bottle."

The wine had been cool and refreshing and we had sat beside the old summer house on the wicker chairs they'd had for years, probably since they were first married and as far as I was concerned, like everything else in my grandparents' house, had always been there.

"I've lost them both now, Hilary." she had said, after taking a sip of her wine. Of course I had known what she meant, but not knowing what to say.

"First Natasha, and now Marion."

"We don't know about Natasha, Gran."

"No, that's true, dear, but a mother does know; she can sense it."

"What does Grandpa think?"

"Oh, he scarcely mentions her name, but when he does, only because I've said something about her, he says she'll be back."

"She might be."

"I have tried to find her, Hilary."

"I hadn't realised."

"No, you wouldn't have; I didn't tell your mother. In fact, apart from the Salvation Army, I didn't tell anyone, not even your grandfather."

"The Salvation Army?"

"Yes, I had remembered reading about someone who had asked them if they could trace a member of their family, and they were successful. I think it was the woman's brother, and they traced him as far away as Australia."

"That was amazing."

"I suppose it was, but the Salvation Army operates in many different countries in the world and they have what they call 'The Family Tracing Service' and apparently, thousands of people are traced every year on behalf of their relatives."

"I had no idea." instantly humbled. I had always recognised how clever my Grandmother was; she was extremely well read. I remember once, I must have been quite young, only about eight or nine, seeing the novel "War & Peace" by her bedside. Not for her, the mushy sentimentalism of a Mills & Boon.

"But they couldn't trace Natasha."

"And this is why you believe she's – "

" – no longer with us." finishing for me, "Yes, that's why. I don't see any logical reason why I should think otherwise."

"I don't know what to say."

"There is nothing anyone can say, dear;" she had smiled sadly at me, "there are some things in this life we have to accept and learn to live with, that is, if you want to remain sane."

And that had been nineteen years ago. My Grandmother had been right of course, but then obversely, so had my Grandfather for ever hoping, waiting for that moment when the back door would open and Natasha would walk in, asking what all the fuss was about: "Oh, Daddy," she would have said, "I've only been away on a lovely long holiday. There's no need to worry about me."

I don't know how long I had been sitting there, probably not so long, but with my thoughts fast back-tracking as they had been doing almost from the moment I arrived in Calder Bay, they had become a habit, an irritating one, wishing I had the ability to switch off and concentrate on something else. Perhaps it hadn't been such a good idea to have come back after all, but it was too late now. I could have simply decided to shorten my stay and start the drive back home in the afternoon, stay the night half-way and be in Oxford before lunch the following day, and if it hadn't been for making arrangements to meet Aileen, I believe I may have done just that. Stifling a sigh of the inevitability of it all, I leaned over for one of the bar menus. I would have something to eat, not too wholesome as I would be having a meal in the restaurant later, also I planned to walk round the bay and find a spot where I could sit and soak up the sun.

'Excuse me.' I said to the woman who had at that moment walked up to the bar.

'That's alright; allow me to help you.' she smiled, handing me a menu. When she smiled, I was instantly reminded of Janice; Janice as she would probably look now, but of course it wasn't her.

'Thank you. I'm sorry to stare, you must think I'm terribly rude, but for a moment you reminded me of a friend I haven't seen for years.'

'I'm told everyone has a double.' she said, taking two more menus from the pile.

'Frightening thought.' I laughed.

'I know;' laughing with me, spontaneously, a replica of the way Janice used to laugh, 'anyway, *bon appétit*' she added, walking away to a table by the open window. This time, I wasn't mistaken, recognising the man she was with. Charles Grayson. The article in the "Art Review" hadn't mentioned he was married, but then the focus had been on his career and his achievements in the art world, not his personal life. Strange though, the woman's resemblance to Janice; she was about the same age, her hair colouring also; a deep honey-blonde, a shade many women tried to achieve, but you could always tell whether it was natural or not, it didn't have that brassiness of the hair colorants.

It was so long since I had seen Janice, regretting the fall-off of letters and the occasional phone call; even having computers didn't make any difference. I knew she had one because she'd mentioned it in one of her later letters; why is it, I wondered, and not for the first time, that it's quicker to rattle off and send an email than to hand-write a letter, address the envelope and post it, but for some inexplicable reason people found this difficult; it didn't make sense. We had even exchanged email addresses, promising to send her one, but not yet. The haphazard way my mind was working would make it impossible to give her a family up-date. Of course, I could tell her about Kirstie returning to Hong Kong, her graduation ceremony, what Pete and I had been doing, but always I would be holding something back, and Janice would be astute enough to realise. Later, when it was all over. I refused to question what I actually meant; did I mean when the identity of the dead woman had been revealed? Or did I mean more than that. I was at it again, going round in circles; a child's roundabout, going round and round and getting nowhere.

Chapter Five

CARLA

'Do you believe everyone has a double, Charles?'

'Yes, I do; why do you ask?'

'Because the woman over there, at the far end of the bar, has just told me I reminded her of a friend she hadn't seen for a while; it wasn't only that though, I could tell by her expression she had for a fraction of a second, honestly believed I was that person. Eerie.' I shivered, in spite of the warmth of the sun streaming through the open window.

Charles looked over to where I had gone to pick up the menus, an inscrutable expression on his face; he took so long to answer me, I was beginning to wonder if was going to say anything.

'Is there something wrong?' I was forced to ask, feeling uncomfortable by his silence.

'No, no, Carla,' he said at last, 'there's nothing wrong. Sorry to sound so vague, I don't mean to be.'

'You know her, don't you?'

'You're a perceptive woman.' he smiled, the blue-grey eyes crinkling at the edges.

'I've never been told that before.' feeling myself blush. What on earth is the matter with me, I thought, I'm not the blushing kind and here is this man, someone I hardly know, making me feel like a schoolgirl.

'Well, all I can say is you should have been. The woman you were talking to used to live in Calder Bay; she was only in her teens then. She and her family used to live in England, I don't know where exactly, but they moved up here and bought the house opposite to mine. The family was called Robertson and her name is Hilary. She was friendly with the Hendersons, especially with Janice, one of the daughters; she and Hilary were about the same age.'

'And I reminded her of Janice?'

'I would say so.'

'How long have you known them, Charles?'

'I'd know Jack Henderson all my life.'

'You knew he was my father, didn't you?'

'Yes, Sadie told me, but not until after he'd died.'

'Oh, I hadn't realised.'

'It was ten years ago, from a heart attack.' he added.

'And I only knew of him a few days ago.' hoping he wouldn't hear the bitterness in my voice, but this knowledge was too new, too fresh in my mind for me to have reached any sort of understanding of why the relationship between him and my mother which had resulted in my birth being kept from me until it had been too late to discuss with her. The letter, addressed to me, had been inside her notecase beside her personal documents: birth and marriage certificate; the man she had married in 1956 when she had been nineteen and whom I always believed had been my father. There was no record of any divorce, or of his death certificate. She had told me when I must have been about four that he had died, but I had no memory of ever seeing him, with only a handful of old photographs to show me what he had looked like. Reading the letter had been painful, but worse was not having anyone to talk to.

'I'm truly sorry, Carla,' he said, resting a comforting hand on my arm and the gentle pressure was reassuring, all my energies being needed to hold back the tears, 'you should have been told.'

'She had her reasons, Charles.' and going on to tell him about the letter. He listened, his eyes never leaving my face, until I had finished and even then he was silent for a moment.

'How very, very sad,' he said, 'that you should have found out the way you did. Calder Bay is a relatively small town and the Hendersons at one time were well known, much respected as well, I'm sure.'

'You say at one time?'

'You will have seen where they used to live?'

'I have, yes, what there is left of the house of course.'

'A sorry sight; it was a beautiful old property; Edwardian, and had been in the family for two or three generations I believe, but within a matter of a few years, there has been a steady decline in their finances; on Jack's death, the company passed on to his oldest son; John he's called, and regrettably he is no businessman; he took enormous risks on the stock market in a vain attempt to recoup losses resulting in wrong company decisions being made, which ultimately led to bankruptcy.'

'How dreadful, and now with this latest news, well - ' not really knowing what to say.

'I know, and as the body was found in the grounds of the property, this will inevitably mean members of the family, including neighbours, will be interviewed by the police. They will eventually find out who the woman was, but it's bound to take time and meanwhile we'll all be living in a kind of limbo.'

'Not pleasant.'

'You're right. Shall we order, Carla?' he asked, looking at the menu for the first time.

'I think we should; I've not been in here at lunchtime before, so what would you recommend?'

'It depends on how hungry you are.' he smiled across at me. he really is an attractive man, I thought, looks a little like Robert Redford, that same quirky little smile that immediately transforms his features; also, he was easy to talk to; a good listener. It had been several months since I had spent any time with a man out of business hours; all too often lately the boardroom had been the main venue when anything discussed was company-related and where personal issues were non-existent.

'Oh, I don't know,' hesitating between the quiche salad and the lasagne, 'I think I would like the quiche salad; not quite as filling as the lasagne.'

'And I'll have the same.'

'How well do you know Calder Bay, Carla?' he asked me while we waited for our food to arrive.

'Hardly at all;' I admitted, 'I was away at boarding school from the age of eight, then college.'

'But what about holidays?'

'You'll probably think this strange, but mostly, I spent them with my aunt and her family, Sadie would always be there as well. Occasionally, but not very often, in the earlier years I would have been here, but as my school was in Cheltenham and had been the same one Sadie had gone to, plus the fact that my relations lived in Taunton which wasn't too far away, I think that was probably why, but now, Charles, as no doubt you can imagine, I'm thinking it could have been for a totally different reason. Anyway,' I added, 'it's pointless to dwell on the ifs and whys; that was the way Sadie wanted it to be, and I did have a happy childhood.'

'No shortage of friends?'

'Rather too many at times; have you ever been in a school dormitory?'

'No, thank God.' he laughed.

'There you are then; you've been spared that experience.'

'And now, Carla, no husband?' the question not surprising me for I'd noticed him looking at my ringless left hand.

'I was married,' I told him, 'but not anymore.'

'I'm sorry.'

'Oh, there's no need to be,' I said quickly, 'the divorce was amicable; we were both too young, far too young to carry the responsibility of being totally committed to each other, but what about you, Charles?'

'No, I never found a woman I wanted to spend the rest of my life with, or probably more accurately, I never found a woman who wanted to spend the rest of her life with me.'

'Oh, dear,' unable to stop smiling, 'you can't mean that.'

'I do as it happens; you would be surprised just how many women steer clear of men who paint for a living.'

'I knew you were an artist, actually; I've seen some of your work and then I read your profile in this month's "Art Review", also, I loved your portrait on the cover of the magazine.'

'Thank you.'

'Were you in love with her, Charles?'

'Why should you ask that?' a look of genuine bewilderment on his face.

'I apologise for being so forthright, I shouldn't have asked you.'

'No, please don't apologise; I'm intrigued by what you said, that's all.'

'There was something, something you had captured in the gentle way you had painted her; she was a lovely woman, but there was much more there than her natural beauty, as if you knew what she was thinking and as if you wanted to share those thoughts with her.'

'You saw all of that?'

'Yes, I did. Was that her name, Marion?'

'Yes, she was called Marion Robertson.'

Now it was my turn to be startled; I sat staring at him, my glass halfway to my lips.

'Marion Robertson,' I repeated the name, 'Hilary's mother?'

'That's right,' smiling at my deduction, 'I met her not long after they moved into their house and asked if she would sit for me. I instinctively knew I would be able to transfer her rather unique tranquil beauty on to canvas.'

'Once again, Charles, I apologise; I shouldn't have asked you whether you were in love with her, it was none of my business.'

'I don't mind you know, Carla. And yes, I was in love with her.'

'But not now?'

'No, not for a long time. You see, I'm quite old-fashioned in many respects; I believe in marriage and I would never knowingly come between husband and wife, even although a few years later Marion's husband left her and she and Hilary stayed on in Calder Bay.'

'Another sad ending.'

'Yes, it was.'

The quiches arrived at that moment, accompanied by fresh green salads and small side dishes of diced potato mayonnaise. Everything tasted delicious, the quiches exactly as they should be; the chef had balanced the proportions of ham and cheese well and the pastry was deep and crispy.

'Would you like a dessert, Carla?'

'No, thanks, but I would love a coffee.'

'You were saying you would be putting Sadie's house on the market.' he said, once the coffee had been brought over to our table.

'That's right; hopefully by Tuesday or Wednesday. I'm keeping a few pieces of furniture and some of her pictures and mirrors, but I've arranged for everything else to be collected by the auctioneers first thing tomorrow morning.'

'You didn't consider keeping on the house?'

'I did, as a matter of fact, but decided it would have been a bit pointless. I'd hardly ever want to stay in it, and I didn't want the hassle of renting; besides,' trying to explain without causing any offence, 'I don't have any feelings of belonging here; in spite of my background, I don't even feel Scottish.'

'I understand, I'd probably have thought the same way, in fact, I have a reverse problem in that however much I would like to move away from Calder Bay, my roots are too firmly embedded.'

'If you did move, Charles, where would you go; Edinburgh perhaps?'

'You've got your intuitive hat on again.' he laughed.

'I know; it's dreadful, but I can't help it.'

'Perhaps you're more Scottish than you think.'

'Being fey, you mean?'

'That's exactly what I meant, but seriously, I would choose Edinburgh; I'm fond of the city, always have been and it hasn't allowed itself to grow shabby in old age, as so many cities have done.'

'I believe I would enjoy living there,' I said, 'the centre of culture, and towering above everyone and everything, the iconic Edinburgh Castle. I remember reading somewhere what Robert Louis Stevenson once said –'

'– that Edinburgh is what Paris ought to be.'

'That's right, but ironically, I am one of the rare people who is not fond of Paris.'

'Neither am I,' he agreed, 'and not being fluent in the French language is something of a handicap.'

'They don't give you an inch, do they?'

'Only when it suits them!'

'I haven't even asked where you live in England, Carla.'

'In London, Notting Hill; I bought my house years ago in the then unfashionable and cheaper part of London with absolutely no inkling of how it would all change. A very ordinary mews house, a replica of so many others, with only the paintwork a different colour to differentiate it, costs the earth today.'

'You must find Calder Bay very quiet in comparison.'

'I do, but I rather like it. At least one has the space to think here, although in my case recently too much thinking.'

'When do you plan to go back?'

'By the end of the week, Charles; I've already extended the compassionate leave I was given and I'm getting the vibes, judging by yesterday's phone call that my directors are rapidly running out of compassion.'

'They sound tough.'

'I don't know about that, but they are extremely demanding.'

'What sort of company do you work for, Carla?'

'They're American; Gallagher Pharmaceuticals, but my office is based in London.'

'I've heard of them; they are one of the 'big boys', aren't they?'

'They are, yes; I was lucky, I suppose, to be taken on by them. They pay well, but they expect their staff to deliver.'

'It sounds stressful.'

'It can be;' I shrugged, 'but I've got used to it; I've been with them for over ten years now, so I've learned how to ride the punches.'

'I'm impressed.'

'Don't be, Charles; I merely do what I've been trained to do.'

'Which is?'

'I'm one of their corporate lawyers.'

'I've not had a lawyer as a friend before.' he smiled.

'I promise not to rip you off, then.' I laughed.

'Good, I'll remember that. Do you think you will have any spare time between now and when you go back?'

'I should have; why?'

'I was wondering whether you would like to come to Edinburgh with me on Wednesday; I have a meeting to attend in the morning, but it shouldn't last long and we would then have the rest of the day to ourselves. What do you think?'

'I'd like that very much; it's some years since I was there and while you're at your meeting I could have a walk round the Old Town, something I have been promising to do for so long, but never seem to get any further than Princess Street.'

'Fine, that's settled then, so I'll pick you up here at eight in the morning and we should easily reach Edinburgh before eleven in good time for the meeting.'

After Charles had left I spent a couple of hours sorting through my mother's papers which I had brought back to the hotel with me from the house. She had been a tidy person and everything seemed to be in order and after I had finished, read her letter again.

"My dear, Carla," she had written, "this letter is an apology and one which I hope with all my heart you will accept. I wrongly led you to believe you were the daughter of my husband, Ernest Northcot, but this was not true. Although we never divorced, Ernest and I separated a year before you were born; an aunt of mine had recently died and left me sufficient money to enable me to make a new life for myself. Many years earlier, I had visited Calder Bay and decided to come here. I met Jack Henderson shortly after I arrived; he was married with, at that time, one child; this situation should have prevented me from falling in love with him, but it didn't. Our affair was brief, but long enough for me to conceive. Jack Henderson is your father, Carla. Regrettably, he refused to acknowledge you, except he did make provisions for your education. I can never say I regret what happened between us; by doing so, would be to deny ever having had such a wonderful daughter. Thank you, darling Carla, for so many happy years and, please, don't think too harshly of me. The only regret I will carry to the end of my life is not having the courage to tell you, but I was afraid; I couldn't bear to have lost you. Your loving mother, Sadie."

I managed to reach the end without weeping this time. I think, talking to Charles had helped me a little towards understanding, in particular, what it must have been like for her; she had been so young, only twenty-one when I was born; living in what must have appeared to be an alien sort of place and abandoned by her lover. Of course, I accepted her apology, of that there was no doubt. It was my father's behaviour I was finding difficult to excuse. From how Charles had described the family, it would seem they had a certain social standing in the town; no shortage of money until recently, but back then, with no hint that their charmed life would one day come to an abrupt end, nothing would have been permitted to mar their elevated image, and the scandal of an unwanted child in their midst would certainly have made a few dents in that.

I folded Sadie's letter and put it back in the envelope; it was unlikely I would ever read it again. As Charles had so sympathetically said, it was very, very sad, but I had to live with it. At forty-five years of age that shouldn't be too difficult. There was one thing for sure though, I concluded, I had no intention of denying my parentage if any member of the Henderson family should see and make some comment on any resemblance. I wasn't being vindictive, perhaps it was my way, albeit belatedly, of making up for how Sadie must have felt during the time I was a child and I knew if it had been me, I certainly wouldn't have stayed on in the same town as the man who had made me pregnant and then promptly dumped me. Also, to have witnessed, as she must have done, his children growing up and living in presumably some luxury, must have hurt her, but why I asked myself didn't she leave Calder Bay? Was she being a martyr? Or, had she been so much in love with Jack Henderson, that knowing he was living so close, had been sufficient for her? There was no point in trying to apply any logic to any of this. The affairs of the heart deny logic. I didn't have any feelings of being deprived; I didn't miss having any brothers or sisters, I had cousins and that was enough for me.

I decided to eat early and had reached the coffee stage when the woman I had been talking to at lunchtime came into the restaurant. She didn't notice me at first, but once she was seated and was about to look at the menu the waitress had handed to her, she looked across and smiled. A very together sort of person, I thought, smiling back. It was about eight by now and the restaurant was beginning to get busy. It was a lovely evening, still warm with all the windows open; at the other end of the room from where I was sitting, double glass doors led out to a walled garden; a paved terrace overlooking a square of lawn, bordered by pansies and forget-me-nots, their petals a riot of colour; a trellis of wisteria, heavy with blue and purple flowers, created a dramatic backdrop and with brimming tubs of geraniums and begonias between the tables and chairs, it was all so inviting I just had to take my coffee out there.

There were a few people on the terrace; an elderly couple sharing a bottle of red wine, two women about my age, having an aperitif, presumably before going into the restaurant, and a man two tables away from me, sitting on his own. He had looked over when I had come outside and again, a couple of seconds later; the third time, with only the slightest hesitation, he stood up and walked over towards me.

'You *are* Janice, aren't you? I couldn't be sure at first –' words failing him as he realised his mistake, ' – I apologise, what must you think of me? I'm not always so crass,' he smiled, a boyish smile, and I wondered where he fitted into this mystery which appeared to be rapidly unfolding, 'but for a minute back there you looked so much like her. Sorry.' he repeated.

'It's alright,' I assured him, 'you're the second person today who has mistaken me for someone else; I'm beginning to get used to the experience.'

'I must say you're taking it very well.'

'Not much choice.' I shrugged resignedly.

'Are you in Calder Bay on holiday?' he asked. Surely he's not trying to make a pass, groaning inwardly, not in the respectable grounds of "The Royal", but perhaps he was merely being friendly. He looked harmless enough, but who could tell.

'Not on holiday, no,' giving him the benefit of the doubt, 'but my mother died a couple of weeks ago and I'm here to sort through her personal effects.'

'You're Sadie Northcot's daughter.'

It wasn't a question; he had worked it out for himself.

'Did you know her?'

'I did, yes; she was a lovely person and when I heard she had died I found it hard to believe. Very sad.'

'Why don't you sit down,' I suggested, 'and tell me who you are.'

'Thank you; I'll bring my drink over. Perhaps you would like one; I see you've almost finished your coffee.'

Wondering what I was letting myself in for, I said I would like a glass of wine, drinking the remains of my coffee.

'I should have introduced myself,' he said as soon as he came back with the wine, 'Callum Ogilvie.' he said, formally shaking hands with me.

'Carla Northcot.'

'Carla; that's Italian isn't it?'

'Yes, my mother's father came from Naples, but my mother was English, from Cornwall.'

'And do you speak Italian?' sounding as though he was really interested.

'Not well; apparently I was reasonably fluent when I was very young, but it soon disappeared when I went to school.'

'You must have been at boarding school, then?'

'Why do you think that?'

'Well, it would explain why I don't remember seeing you when we were all growing up.'

'You say 'we were growing up'; do you mean you and the Henderson family?'

'Sadie must have told you about the Hendersons.'

'No, I don't remember her ever mentioning them.'

'Well – well, perhaps not.' a flicker of discomfort on his face, and I wasn't going to let it rest; it was probably unfair of me to use him as a means of finding out as much as I could about the family. I didn't like loose ends; could be why I chose to study law, but Sadie had left me a legacy; a story only half-told and I wanted the full one.

'You know why she didn't, don't you, Callum?'

'Hell!' under his breath, 'Sorry, no need to swear, but you're too clever for me, Carla.'

'You are quite a few years younger than me, I think.'

'I'm thirty-nine.'

'And I'm forty-five, six years difference, so you weren't around when I was born.'

'Look, Carla, I shouldn't have said anything; besides it's none of my business.'

'Perhaps not,' I agreed, 'so we'll drop it shall we. Tell me instead about the Hendersons; how many children were there?'

'Five;' he said, obviously on firmer ground, 'the eldest, Aileen, she'll be a year older than you, Carla, then John, Janice of course, Bobby, he was my best friend, and the youngest Dougie, who's two years younger than me.'

'Big family; what about their mother, she must have had her hands full.'

'She died when Dougie was born.'

'So who looked after them all?'

'Oh, Mrs Baird; I never knew her first name, but she took on the role of housekeeper, but not exactly a disciplinarian; she probably had enough to do without checking up on us, therefore they all did more or less what they wanted.'

'Do you think now that this lack of discipline harmed them in any way?'

'I wouldn't have said so; I think it made every one of them more independent, even Dougie. He was the quiet one.' he explained.

'And Janice?' I asked, 'my double; what is she doing now.'

'She married years ago, lives in the Lake District somewhere.' he answered, giving me a quizzical look which I was finding difficult to interpret.

'You obviously haven't kept in touch with them.'

'No,' this time I could read his expression, wishing I hadn't asked, as for a fraction of a second his eyes clouded over, a look of deep sadness on his face, 'after Bobby was killed, there didn't seem to be any point.'

'What happened to him?'

'A motor bike accident, Carla; he was on the top road, between here and Arbroath, and the bike went out of control; he died instantly.'

'I'm sorry.'

'He was a great guy; we had some good times together.'

Bobby Henderson, my half-brother, I thought, and I had never known him and wondering about those other half-siblings, but made up my mind not to ask any more questions; also, I believed I had heard quite sufficient about the Henderson family for one day. We had another drink before he left; talking mostly about London where he told me he had been working for the last ten years and had only recently returned to Calder Bay.

The woman, whom I now knew to be Janice Henderson's old friend, was no longer in the restaurant when I walked through. If she had been, it occurred to me it was more than possible Callum would have seen her on his way out of the hotel. I was rapidly coming to the conclusion that Calder Bay was a bit too parochial for me, where it seemed everybody knew everybody else, being far more comfortable with the anonymity of living in a city.

Chapter Six

By eleven the following morning, an incident room at the Calder Bay police station had been set up for the police team, with Detective Inspector David McIntyre from Montrose Police Headquarters leading the murder enquiry

Inspector Howard Crawford, attached to Calder Bay Constabulary, had been assigned to the case, together with two of his officers, Sergeant Lilian Wood and Sergeant Alistair Dale, the Detective Inspector addressing their first meeting at four in the afternoon.

'We received the pathologist's report earlier today,' he was saying, 'the salient points being that the victim died from asphyxiation, possibly a travelling rug had been used, as shreds of green and red wool had been traced around the mouth and nostrils. While there are signs of decomposition, these have not been as advanced as one might have expected, considering the length of time the body had been confined in the wash-house; the reason being, the interior of the boiler had been dry and sufficiently air-tight. The age of the victim has been calculated to be of a female in her late twenties, slim build, five foot four, shoulder-length dark brown hair, straight with a fringe. Understandably, the time of death is proving difficult to establish in this early stage of the enquiry, but has been estimated to be between twenty-five and thirty years. First and foremost, we have to establish the identity of the victim; therefore, only one course is open to us which is to trawl back to that time. This will involve talking to people who were living in Calder Bay then, including members of the Henderson family.

' "Carbisdale", as you are aware, is in the process of being demolished; Inspector Crawford and I were up there on Saturday afternoon and very little remains of the house. The wash-house, however, is still intact and instructions have been given for all further work to cease on the site until Forensic have completed their search.

'Inspector Crawford and I will be interviewing each member of the Henderson family, also the immediate neighbours in Green Lane.

Sergeant Wood,' he continued, 'I would like you to focus on the clothes the victim had been wearing, namely the dress, jacket and shoes; find out, if possible, where they were purchased. They are in a reasonable condition, with fortunately the designer name eligible. I appreciate how arduous this will be and may prove negative, but it will be an initial attempt to find out whether she lived locally or not.

'Sergeant Dale,' turning to Alistair Dale, 'an identikit has been put together with what the pathologist has been able to provide; I admit this is a long shot, but we should try it on the off chance someone in the town should recognise the woman. We're dealing with a long period of time here I know, but what I want you to do is to visit the various establishments where she may have frequented, regularly if she had been a resident of Calder Bay; for instance, restaurants, bars, the main hotels and because she had been a smoker, the local tobacconists.'

'Almost thirty years,' he said to Howard Crawford after the meeting had been wound up and they were in the office he had been allocated for the duration of the enquiry, 'how many people can actually remember as far back as that, I wonder.'

'It depends, I suppose, on how good their memory is, sir.'

'That's true; well, for the time being, let's say we're talking about twenty-eight years ago which would make it 1975, and because of the flimsiness of the victim's clothes, it must have been during the summer, so shall we say between the months of June and August.'

'Calder Bay wouldn't have been a great deal different than from what it's like today,' Howard said, 'the town starts to get busy with holidaymakers as soon as the schools break up at the beginning of June. She may have been here on holiday; if so, would likely have been staying at one of the hotels, but even if she had, it would depend on whether any of the staff still worked there now, but that's something Sergeant Dale should be able to establish.'

'Yes,' David nodded, 'but if she had been, how did she manage to find her way up to Green Lane; tourists don't often venture any further than the town centre and the beach.'

'She could have known someone who lived in Green Lane.' Howard suggested.

'And this brings us to "Carbisdale" which at one time, before the demolition team arrived, had been a splendid example of Edwardian architecture owned for generations by the Henderson family. You've lived in Calder Bay all your life, Howard, haven't you; did you know any of them?'

'Only Janice Henderson, but that was at Junior School; I don't know where she went afterwards.'

'The office have prepared a list of them all, their ages and where they're all living now, which should prove useful.' he said, passing the sheet across the desk to him.

'I'll pencil in how old they would have been in 1975, shall I?'

'If you would, Howard. I've been thinking about that travelling rug; we don't know where she was murdered, whether in the grounds of "Carbisdale" or not, and the fact her body was discovered in the wash-house doesn't necessarily mean it happened in there. Because of the rug being used makes me think it had been pre-meditated, but why choose the wash-house to conceal the body?'

'Rather a big risk for a member of the family to take,' Howard said, 'there was no way of knowing how long it would remain undiscovered.'

'That's right, but whoever it was, must have had knowledge of that wash-house. According to Forensic, the door had been padlocked, although even as long ago as, say 1975, the whole structure wouldn't have been all that sturdy. "Carbisdale" including the wash-house, was built more than two hundred years ago, at a time when a property of that size would have been run by a number of servants, the wash-house used for laundering. Judging by the neglected state of the interior it would seem it had never been used by the Hendersons, not even for storage. Apart from the boiler and some ancient shelving, there was nothing else in there.'

'Talking about servants, sir,' Howard said, glancing again at the list of names, 'I notice that the mother died thirty-seven years ago, in 1966; Mr Henderson must have employed someone to look after them all.'

'That's a very good point; a housekeeper perhaps and if so, it was more than likely she would have been a local woman; she could be worth talking to.'

'I see that one of the sons was killed in a motor bike accident more or less exactly ten years ago.'

'I know,' he agreed, 'the same day as the father.'

'Strange.'

'It could be. How old were the children in 1975?'

'Aileen would have been eighteen, John a year younger, Janice, fourteen, Bobby eleven and the youngest, Dougie, nine.'

'And their mother died nine years earlier.'

'Could have been in childbirth, sir.'

'Possibly, Howard, but we'll check it out all the same.'

'I notice that only Dougie and his older sister are still living in Calder Bay.'

'We'll see them first then; they should be able to tell us where the other two are living. Gradually, we'll be able to build up a picture, recreate as far as we can what it was like in and around Green Lane during those summer months.'

'Charles Grayson, the painter, has lived next door to the Hendersons all his life.'

'You know him?'

'No, not personally,' Howard admitted, 'but my wife who's interested in art showed me an article in this month's issue of the "Art Review" and it mentioned he had continued to live in the house where he was born.'

'How old is he, do you know, Howard?'

'I do, yes; that was mentioned as well, he's fifty-eight.'

'So,' doing a quick calculation, 'in 1975 he would have been thirty. Married?'

'No, I don't think so.'

'Hmmph; could be interesting.'

'He had a sister; she died recently, just over a week ago, there was a small piece in Calder Bay's "Gazette" about her.'

'Another death,' David murmured, pursing his lips thoughtfully. 'Did she live with him?'

'Yes, she hadn't married either.'

'Presumably they would have known the Hendersons; been invited in sometime. He was much older than the children though, so perhaps not. What about his sister, was she younger or older than him?'

'She was four years older; I used to see her walking around the town, although it was years ago. She was a strange-looking woman; we kids thought she was a witch; this was because of her hair, long and black, very striking I suppose, although I don't think she could ever have been described as pretty, too severe looking.'

'I wonder what she did for a living.'

'We never knew and not having seen her for such a long time I always thought she must have become something of a recluse. Probably kept house for him.'

'Possibly.' The beginnings of the picture were starting to appear; as yet formless, merely impressions, but as they steadily progressed, he knew they would move forward and into place. David McIntyre always enjoyed the initial stages of a murder investigation, rather like having a plain canvas placed in front of you and lightly tracing in a line here, a curve there and another, and a final loop to join them together. Thinking of canvases, he made up his mind to talk to Charles Grayson first.

'"Carbisdale" didn't have many close neighbours,' Howard was saying, 'and what few there were, all in Green Lane.'

'That's right, and with the church and the vicarage at the other end of the property which paradoxically is the front, the only other neighbour. I did notice when we were there on Saturday that the entrance in Green Lane leads directly into the grounds with no gate, although the entrance from Carlogie Road does have one, but without a lock.'

'They weren't very security minded, sir.' Howard commented dryly, 'Calder Bay isn't immune from break-ins; you would have thought the family to have been more circumspect.'

'I agree; complacency, I suppose, thinking that sort of thing would never happen to them. But, going back to how the body was brought into the grounds, it would have been considerably less conspicuous to have used the main entrance, especially as the wash-house is at the back of the house.'

'Presumably it would have been dark wherever the murder took place and unless the killer had brought her there by car, what had she been doing in Carlogie Road in the first place?'

'Exactly; once again we return to that travelling rug. Where did it come from, Howard, and perhaps more importantly, who did it belong to? It could be significant it wasn't found in the wash-house.'

'You mean if it had been, it could be relatively easy to find the owner?'

'Yes, if he or she had been one of the Hendersons, or a neighbour. Incidentally, Howard, I've been trying this morning to trace the names of the people who owned the house immediately opposite, but it would seem there have been quite a number of different owners over the years. In 1975, a couple called Robertson, moved in, but the house was sold four years later. This may or may not be significant, but nevertheless, I think we should make every effort to trace them.'

***

Not exactly prepossessing, David thought, pulling into the gravel driveway of Charles Grayson's house in Green Lane on Tuesday morning and looking up at the ivy-covered facia indicative of several years of neglect. The front door was wide open to reveal a sunless hall, made even more dreary by heavy oak furniture: a high-backed settle with faded upholstery, so much so the original colour and design were impossible to make out, and one of the largest dressers he had ever seen. Dickensian wasn't in it, he decided, wondering how anyone could exist in such a place.

'Good morning;' a voice called to him from the side of the house. He had been so engrossed, he hadn't noticed the man now striding towards him, 'I take it you're Detective Inspector David McIntyre?'

'Yes, that's right; good morning, Mr Grayson.' recognising his voice from when he'd phoned him the previous day.

'I expect you're somewhat taken aback by the dilapidated state of everything,' Charles Grayson said, 'but thank God it is all about to change; by the time the renovations are completed nobody will recognise the place. Anyway,' he went on quickly, making him wonder whether this was the way he normally greeted anyone or was it caused by nervousness, 'we'll go round to my studio which I think you will find more aesthetically pleasing.'

He was right; the studio, a large light and airy room; white painted ceilings and walls and sliding glass doors leading out on to an Italian-tiled terrace. A grassy area continued as far as the dividing fence, with, he couldn't help noticing, several spaces where the wood had rotted and broken away.

'I've made some coffee, Detective Inspector,' he said, pointing outside to the cafetière and china mugs on the wrought-iron table, 'would you like some?'

He was courteous, polite, and now they were away from the front of the house, appeared calmer; this was obviously his domain, David thought; his place of work, having already seen the easel, the paints and a number of canvases, some of them incomplete; presumably the gallery Howard had told him about must be in a separate room.

'As I said on the phone, Mr Grayson,' David said, once the coffee had been poured and they had both taken their first sips, 'we are conducting a murder enquiry into the death of the woman whose body was discovered in the grounds of the property next door to you.'

'"Carbisdale",' he said quietly, 'yes, quite shocking.'

'Indeed. Our first step is to find out the identity of the victim; from there, hopefully, we should be able to arrive at the motive which should lead us to the killer and step by step we will. I have here,' he went on, opening his brief case, 'an identikit which has been prepared from the pathologist's findings.' handing it over to him, at the same time watching his reaction as he looked at the closest likeness they had been able to put together, but he couldn't detect any noticeable change in his expression.

'She was young.' he said, without looking up.

'Yes, in her late twenties.'

'Her hair; it would be considered slightly old-fashioned today.'

'We believe she was murdered sometime between the mid-nineteen-seventies to the end of that decade and are using 1975, at least initially, as a starting point.'

'Yes,' he nodded, 'young women around then did wear their hair long and the Audrey Hepburn fringe was very popular then.'

'You have a good memory.'

'Not particularly,' he smiled briefly, 'but I'm an artist and I'm trained to be observant, especially in respect to peoples' features and mannerisms.'

'And do you remember seeing anyone who looked like her around the time we're talking about?'

'No, I can't say that I do, Detective Inspector; I would have been thirty in 1975, there were many pretty girls in Calder Bay, but I don't recall anyone in particular. Sorry.' handing the identikit back to him.

'How long have you known the Henderson family, Mr Grayson?'

'Oh, all my life I suppose.'

'You would have been older than the children.'

'I was, yes; it was Jack Henderson, their father, I was friendly with, we often played chess together.'

'Would this have been in "Carbisdale"?'

'Always,' he smiled again, ruefully this time, 'Beth wouldn't have approved.'

'Beth?'

'My sister; I suppose you would have described her as extremely disapproving and for whatever reason she didn't like Jack very much and seeing us sitting for hours over a chessboard would have not pleased her, so to avoid any aggro I always went next door.'

'I understand your sister died quite recently.'

'Yes, she did.' his lips tightening, making it apparent he was reluctant to say any more about her, but David persisted.

'Was she friendly with the family?'

'Not with the family, I don't believe she was, but she got on with their housekeeper, Mrs Baird, and would often go round there for a cup of tea with her in the afternoons.'

'Do you know whether Mrs Baird is still alive?' David asked him.

'I really couldn't say; she wasn't all that old when she worked for them, probably in her mid-forties.'

'And she lived in Calder Bay?'

'Oh, yes; I remember Jack telling me that she had moved into a flat about the florists in the High Street; this was shortly after her daughter married John Henderson.'

'Had the daughter been friendly with the family in the nineteen-seventies?'

'I don't think so; actually, I don't remember ever seeing her.'

'You've been helpful in filling in a few gaps for us, Mr Grayson; there is only one more question I have to ask.'

'Yes?'

'Did you know the people who owned the house across the road from you; I understand they were called Robertson.'

'I didn't know the husband, but Marion Robertson sat for me and, if I remember rightly, this was in the summer of 1975.'

He damn well knew it had been 1975. For the first time David spotted a change in him; it had been just before he casually mentioned the year, also the edginess he had noticed earlier had returned, accompanied by a tiny nervous tic below his right eye; he must have realised this because he put a hand up to cover it, but it was a wasted effort. Charles Grayson was displaying every sign of discomfort, but whether this indicated guilt remained to be seen. David refused to believe that so early on in their investigation they had arrived at the crux of the whole business; experience had taught him never to take anything or anyone at face value. There were never any shortcuts, no lucky breaks in a murder enquiry. Charles Grayson may have known the murdered woman, may have recognised the identikit of her and for whatever reason had said nothing.

That reason didn't necessarily indicate he had killed her, but what did it indicate? There was something here and David felt the vibes too strongly to dismiss them, recalling what Charles Grayson said only seconds earlier, that Marion Robertson, who had lived across the road, had sat for him in the summer of 1975. Was it merely a coincidence he had painted her around the time a woman, yet to be identified, was murdered, possibly within yards of where he lived? He disliked coincidences and didn't trust them; they were all too easy to accept and, at times, difficult to ignore. David's knowledge of art was confined to knowing, and sometimes recognising works of the old masters, but apparently Charles Grayson was a respected and accomplished artist, with many of his paintings exhibited nationally. Marion Robertson must have possessed some exceptional quality to inspire him to paint her. Could there possibly be a link between the two women, he wondered.

'I believe they sold up a few years later.'

'Yes, they did,' he said, 'I think this was in 1979, not long before Hilary got married.'

'Hilary?'

'Their daughter.'

'I see,' David nodded, 'presumably she would have been fairly young in 1975?'

'About fourteen or fifteen.'

'Was she friendly with the Henderson children?' It was likened to getting blood from the proverbial stone, he thought, but he wasn't disappointed, having noted how sparing he had become with his responses.

'She was, yes, especially with Janice Henderson; they were the same age.'

'Quite the extended family.'

'You could say that, Detective Inspector. Hilary was an only child, probably thought of them as her brothers and sisters.'

After asking him how long his other neighbours had lived in Green Lane, he brought the interview to a close, but not ruling out a further visit.

'Detective Inspector?' he asked as he walked back to the car with him, 'Do you suspect that the woman was murdered by someone living in Green Lane?'

'It's too early in our enquiry to form that conclusion, but what we do believe, Mr Grayson, is that she was known to someone living in this area and whether that person is responsible for her death or not, he or she would require to have had a motive to take such a drastic action and that may prove more difficult to find.'

'You think it was pre-meditated?'

'Yes, we do think that, Mr Grayson.' he answered, but without elaborating. He could have mentioned the travelling rug, but had decided to hold back on that for the moment. There would be time later, once the initial interviewing had been done and the various reports had come in from Alistair and Lilian. Meanwhile, he wanted to pursue the leads Charles Grayson had given him; the woman he had painted during the summer of 1975, the nervousness he had shown when this had been mentioned, the obvious reluctance of wanting to expand on what little he had said about Marion Robertson, followed by his attempt at vagueness of when she and her family had sold up. There had to be an explanation; it defied logic otherwise and avoiding the easy option of assuming, he had to find one. A link. A connecting link between Marion Robertson and the dead woman? Charles Grayson had mentioned the daughter and that she had been a friend of Janice Henderson. They had yet to learn where Janice Henderson was living, but there was the rest of the family and, according to what he'd just said, Hilary Robertson had also been friendly with them.

David was still mentally running through the various options open to them when he drew into the allocated parking space in front of the police station. Howard had left a copy of "Art Review" on his desk for him and picking it up looked at the portrait of the woman on the front cover; on the bottom right-hand corner he read Charles Grayson's name and further along, in the centre, the title of the portrait. "Marion". The

Marion Robertson they had been talking about less than fifteen minutes ago? It had to be; no artist would give the same title to any of his other of his paintings. He looked closer at the portrait, holding the magazine up to the light to get a clearer view of her features; she was certainly a lovely looking woman; a delicate kind of beauty, unusually slanted eyes and a mass of deep auburn hair and the way she had been looking, beyond the easel, possibly out towards the terrace, assuming there had been one there at the time. It wasn't easy to put an age to her; a few years older than Charles Grayson who had said he'd been thirty in 1975, also that Hilary had been either fourteen or fifteen, but possibly fourteen if she had been the same age as Janice Henderson, David reckoned she would have been in her late thirties. Had he been in love with her? Artists did fall in love with their subjects, not quite understanding why he should feel so certain and then he remembered why; the style of painting was similar to that of Sir James Gunn, in particular to the portrait he had painted of his wife which he had called "Pauline in the Yellow Dress". Was this the reason for Charles Grayson's agitation? Had he been in love with Marion Robertson and been reluctant to talk about her? It was one explanation, but David believed there was much more than that.

***

Aileen Hope, as she was now called, lived in one of the new villas around the bay, and while not exactly welcoming when Howard arrived shortly after eleven, she did offer him some coffee which he accepted, not because he wanted one, but thought it may help in making his visit appear less official.

'Of course, Inspector,' she said, having taken him into her spacious and ultra-modern kitchen; gleaming chrome and sparkling royal blue cabinets and working tops, 'what has happened is absolutely dreadful and quite frankly if, as the television newsreader said, the body had been in the old wash-house for years, I don't see how you are going to find the person who killed her.

'I agree; it's not going to be easy, but with hard slogging and talking to as many people as possible we will solve the case.'

'But how can people help you?'

'The main problem at this stage is to find out the woman's identity. I would like you to have a look at this identikit which we have had prepared, Mrs Hope.' placing a copy of the identikit on the table in front of her.

He watched as she looked at it, heard the sharp intake of breath, noticing how pale she had become: 'Mrs Hope,' stretching over to take the paper away from her, 'try not to distress yourself -'

'No – no, it's alright, Inspector, I'm fine. I could be wrong, of course, and I hope to God I am, but -'

'- you think you've recognised her?'

'I think so; oh dear, this is really awful.'

'Who was she, Mrs Hope?'

'If I'm right, Inspector, it could have been Natasha; I never knew her surname, but she was Hilary Robertson's aunt. She didn't live with them, but she was staying there on holiday one summer.'

'Can you remember when?'

'Yes, just a second; let me work it out, it had been my birthday about a week before I met her and as it was my eighteenth, my father had given me rather a large party, so that would have been in 1975; my birthday is on the 30th June.' she added.

'You say Hilary Robertson; they were living across the road to you, weren't they?'

'Yes, that's right; Hilary was always over at "Carbisdale"; Janice and she were the best of friends.'

'How old would she have been then?'

'The same age as Janice, fourteen.'

'And how many times did you meet her aunt, Mrs Hope?'

'Only the once; I'd taken some flowers over for Hilary to cheer her up; she'd spent the morning at the dentists and didn't feel all that great and her mother and Natasha were there; I didn't stay long and I never saw her again.'

'So, she was Mrs Robertson's sister?'

'Yes,' she nodded absentmindedly, 'Inspector, this is going to be a dreadful shock for Hilary.'

'I'm sure it will be, but before getting in touch with her, we should be able to get further corroboration that the dead woman was her aunt.'

'How?'

'You will not be the only person who will remember seeing her, that is if they, like you, should see the resemblance from this.' pointing to the identikit, 'There's Hilary's parents too; they will need to be contacted.'

'I don't know about her father, Inspector, but Hilary's mother died almost twenty years ago.'

'You've kept in touch with Hilary?'

'Not for quite a number of years; Janice and she used to write to each other, but Hilary was here in Calder Bay this weekend; we bumped into each other on Sunday and met up for a drink last evening.'

'Was she visiting?'

'In a way; she had been in Edinburgh on Friday and had seen her mother's portrait in the "Art Review" magazine while she was there and decided on the spur of the moment to come up here for a couple of days. She was driving back home to Oxford this morning.' she added.

'Had she heard about the body being found?'

'Yes, she had; by the way,' she said, 'she's called Hilary Fisher now. I trust you're not going to try and contact her today, Inspector, she's going to be tired after the drive, also, her husband who is away on business at the moment, will not be back until tomorrow.'

'Don't worry, Mrs Hope, we'll bear that in mind.' attempting to convey they weren't entirely without sensitivity, 'It would be helpful to us if you also have the contact numbers of your brother and sister as we understand they're not living in Calder Bay now.'

'Of course; I'll get their telephone numbers for you.' going over to one of the cabinets and opening a drawer, 'I've not been in touch with either of them recently, so I don't know whether they will have heard the news.'

'If they had,' Howard asked, 'wouldn't they have called you?'

'Certainly Janice would have done, but I doubt very much whether John would. I'm sure you are aware, Inspector, that with the collapse of the family business, resulting in the loss of quite a number of jobs in the area, followed immediately by he and his wife making a hasty exit from Calder Bay, he wouldn't be exactly welcome here if he should wish to come and see us at any time and it would seem the occasional telephone call comes under this category.'

'I see.' Howard said, and seeing quite clearly; Aileen had no time for her brother or his wife either, recognising the bitterness in her voice. After the company's bankruptcy and the subsequent sale of "Carbisdale", rumours had been rife in the town for several weeks. No doubt Aileen Hope considered herself to be somewhat exposed, being left to literally face the music of what the local residents were calling the scandal of the Henderson family, wondering whether Dougie Henderson felt the same way.

'You were all very young when your mother died, weren't you?'

'We were; she died when Dougie was born and there's nine years difference between Dougie and me. I was a boarder at Cheltenham Ladies College from the age of eleven up to when I became eighteen, which meant I didn't see a great deal of them all during that time.'

'You must have had someone looking after you, though.'

'We had an *au pair* for Dougie up until he went to school, but Mrs Baird, our housekeeper, had been with us for as long as I can remember.'

'Is she still alive?'

'Very much so; she retired about eight or nine years ago, but I see her now and again in the town.'

'She's living in Calder Bay?'

'Has done all her life.'

'Do you have her address, Mrs Hope?'

'All I know she's living in the flat above "Margaret's Flowers" in the High Street, but I doubt whether she ever saw Hilary's aunt, Inspector.'

'Perhaps not, but it's always possible she may have done. Finally, Mrs Hope, who looked after the grounds, which from what I could see when I was there on Saturday, are quite extensive?'

'Jimmy McIntosh was our gardener, with over the years a series of young boys from the town to help out, but he died a few years ago.'

'Had you ever been in the old wash-house?'

'Certainly not; I had no need to go in there, besides Jimmy always kept the place locked. As far as I ever knew nobody ever used it; there were two sheds for storing all the gardening equipment and for us children we had the summer house when the weather was good.'

'Well, Mrs Hope, I must thank you for your time.'

'That's alright, Inspector; it's all most regrettable and I trust everything can be resolved as quickly as possible, but quite frankly, after all this time, I doubt if it will.'

Chapter Seven

The town hall clock was striking three as David rang the bell of 14b High Street; jugs of roses and delphiniums lined the pavement in front of the florist's window; their blooms a riot of colour and, where they had recently been sprinkled with water, glistening in the brilliant sunshine. Mrs Baird didn't take long to answer, her voice sounding clearly on the intercom and, as soon as he answered, followed by the metallic click of the lock. One flight up and she was waiting for him at the top of the stairs: a tall thin woman, upright and, he noticed, seeming not to need the aid of a walking stick as she greeted him, leading him into her kitchen; a bright sunny room, two windows looking down on to the busy street below and over towards the bay. She offered him some tea as he had fully expected her to do and, not wanting to offend her, accepted a cup and watched as she nimbly prepared it; placing china cups and saucers on the table and in the centre, a plate of "Abernethy" biscuits.

'I wasn't too surprised when you rang, Detective Inspector,' she said when she had poured out the tea and was sitting down opposite to him, 'such a dreadful thing to happen.'

'It was, Mrs Baird, and it's to be hoped we will be able to solve the case as speedily as possible.'

'Do you know who the woman was?'

'Not yet, but I'm sure we will. The pathologist has put together an identikit of the victim and, provided she hadn't just been passing through the town when she met her death, it is more than possible that someone seeing it will recognise her.'

'Have you brought this identikit with you?' she asked, her eyes bright with interest.

'I have, yes; here you are.' handing it to her.

She studied it closely before saying anything.

'She must have been a pretty woman,' she said at last, 'but I'm sure I've never seen her. I think I would have remembered if I had; it's the hairstyle, or I should say the fringe; you don't see many fringes nowadays, do you?'

'No, I don't suppose you do;' he agreed, 'although we believe she was killed in 1975, very likely in the summer of that year.'

'1975;' she repeated slowly, taking another look at the identikit, 'that was a long time ago.'

'Yes,' David nodded, 'and it's for this reason a good part of our investigation has to depend on people's memories and that's not easy.'

'No, indeed, it won't be, especially when you reach my age, Detective Inspector; on looking back, the years are inclined to roll together with only notable events separating them; the second world war, of course,' she went on, 'the late king's funeral and then, other royal occasions, but as for 1975, I can't think of anything; to me it seems to have been a summer like any other summer.'

'You would have been working for the Henderson family then?'

'Oh, yes, I'd been with them since 1960 that was the year my husband died and with a small daughter to bring up I had no choice but to find work and when I was offered the job of housekeeper it was truly a godsend. Myra Henderson had her hands full; two young children and another on the way. She was a lovely person; the same age as I was, also we were at school together. I was devastated when she died, she had only been forty-one, you know.'

He was making no attempt to curb her reminiscences, working on the premise that something relevant might emerge and perhaps provide another slant to their enquiries. If he was going to get any solid background on the family, she was the right person to talk to.

'What sort of man was Jack Henderson, Mrs Baird?'

'As to that, I couldn't say;' she answered, too quickly he thought; he hadn't missed the slight tightening of her lips when his name was mentioned, 'he appeared to spend a lot of time at work; I don't think the family saw a great deal of him, but I must say he could be very charming. Liked the ladies, too,' giving a dry chuckle, 'and he wasn't without his admirers, but he never married again, which I often thought was a pity; those children needed a mother to keep them in hand.'

'Were they unruly, then?' he asked her.

'Not unruly exactly, but the boys would get into scrapes at times, not so much Dougie, he just tagged along, but John and Bobby were a handful, only boyish pranks, nothing more than you would expect when you consider they had virtually no supervision, especially Bobby, you never knew what he and Callum would get up to next.' sighing, presumably remembering what happened to him.

'We know about the motor bike accident.'

'I thought you might, Detective Inspector. That was a terrible day; I'll never forget it. The shock was too much for his father; nobody had known he had a weak heart and within a matter of hours of hearing about Bobby, he suffered a fatal heart attack.'

'Very sad.'

'Oh, it was; the family seemed to fall apart after that; John had already been working for his father for a number of years, but even although he is my son-in-law, he was no businessman and of course the company started to fail and now there is nothing, not even their lovely old house.'

'A few minutes ago you mentioned the name Callum; was he a friend of Bobby's?'

'Yes, Callum Ogilvie; they were in the same class at school, they practically grew up together; he was an only child, so probably that was why he treated the family as his own; a bit like Hilary –'

'Hilary Robertson?'

'Yes, that's right; she lived across the road from "Carbisdale"; the family didn't stay long in Calder Bay, but during the time they were living in Green Lane, she and Janice were inseparable.'

'Did you know her family?'

'I knew Hilary of course, but not her parents, only to say hello to, that is.'

'I was talking to Charles Grayson this morning,' David said, 'and he mentioned that your daughter was married to one of the Hendersons.'

'Did he; I don't know Charles very well, but his sister often came over for a cup of tea in the afternoons and even after I left "Carbisdale", she would call in here to see me, but sadly Beth is no longer with us.'

'Had she been ill, Mrs Baird?'

'No, I don't believe so; she had only been in her early sixties; that's not considered old these days.'

'He was telling me that a friend of his had also died recently.'

'I suppose you mean Sadie Northcot?' again the tightening of the lips which told him quite plainly that she had not liked Sadie Northcot.

'Yes, I do; apparently she had been living in Green Lane for several years.'

'I don't wish to speak ill of the dead, Detective Inspector, neither do I want to be accused of tittle-tattling, but not many people liked her.'

'Why?' deciding it was time to come straight to the point, having by now gauged her mettle; Mrs Baird was a strong woman and he didn't think much would faze her.

'Because,' a speculative expression in the way she was looking at him, 'she was pretending to be something she wasn't, but most of us saw through her alright more or less from when she moved into her house in Green Lane, and I remember it was shortly after Myra had her first baby, which was in 1957. She told people her husband, who apparently was called Ernest, worked abroad and she was only able to see him a couple of times a year, although there were rumours not long after she arrived of Jack Henderson making a number of visits. I refused to believe this at first, but within a year of these rumours, she went away for a few months and when she came back she had a young baby with her and then, it must have been two or three years later, she mentioned to the few people she had become friendly with that her husband had died. I know this sounds very old-fashioned in this day and age, when illegitimacy is accepted as a way of life, but it wasn't like that forty-five odd years ago.'

'And did the child grow up in Calder Bay?'

'In a manner of speaking she did, although from the age of eight she became a boarder at a school down south; in Cheltenham, I think it was, and afterwards she was at university, so you could say she hardly knew Calder Bay and if she had ever visited her mother, I don't think I would have recognised her if I had seen her.'

'Did you know her name?'

'She was called Carla.'

'Unusual, sounds Italian,' David said speculatively, 'and were the two women friendly; Sadie Northcot and Beth Grayson, I mean?'

'Goodness me, no; Beth disliked her intensely.'

'Why so strongly do you think, Mrs Baird?'

'It does sound a bit dramatic, doesn't it,' she smiled half-apologetically, 'but as to the reason, I really don't know, but Beth was a strange woman; she felt everything so deeply; there were no white or grey areas with her, she either liked a person a great deal or, as with Sadie Northcot, the dislike could be extreme. It could have been jealousy.'

'Jealousy.' David repeated, trying to fathom out the implications of what she had just said, recalling Charles Grayson telling him that his sister hadn't liked Jack Henderson and now he was hearing that according to the housekeeper, Beth hadn't liked Sadie Northcot either, the woman who it was believed had had a child by him. Was Jack Henderson the pivot? Beth Grayson had never married, had always lived in Green Lane with her brother, where Jack Henderson had been their closest neighbour and, on reaching that point, the phrase: "Hell have no fury like a woman scorned" came into his head. The irony of this didn't escape him; the three people who could have provided him with an explanation were no longer alive: Jack Henderson, who died ten years ago and more recently, within days of each other, Sadie Northcot and Beth Grayson.

'Do you know of any reason why she should have been jealous of Sadie Northcot, Mrs Baird?'

'I've never tried to work it out,' she answered slowly, 'it didn't seem all that important.'

'How long do you think Beth had disliked her; since they first met, or later on?'

'I think it must have been some time during the first year Sadie was here.'

'And then when she returned with her baby?'

'Beth simply refused to talk about her; no doubt you can imagine the sort of things people were saying, but she never said anything and I don't ever remember her mentioning Sadie Northcot's name again, not to me anyway.'

'When was the last time you saw her?' he asked.

'About a week before she died; she called in to see me one afternoon about this time.'

'And she appeared well?'

'Just the same as she always did,' she answered, 'very pale, but then she never did have much colour in her cheeks, even as a young woman, and she seldom wore make-up, but when she did it hardly improved her appearance, if anything it seemed to emphasize her gauntness. There was something, though; I've just remembered.'

'Yes?' gently prompting her.

'I think there must have been something on her mind that afternoon, she appeared preoccupied; I asked her if she was worried about something, but she didn't say anything, just shook her head, but whatever it had been she didn't want to talk about it, but then she could be like that; she wasn't the type of woman to take you into her confidence, it hadn't been the first time since I had known her, and I had learned not to press her, and then the next time I saw her, she had been fine.'

'Did she have any boyfriends when she was young?'

'I don't think she ever did, you know. In many respects, Beth was a shy person; spent too much time on her own, I always thought. There was only one man I ever saw who was able to bring her out of herself and that was Jack Henderson; I think she had what would have been described back then as a crush on him. She was still in her teens, so I don't really think it was more than that and I doubt whether she ever told anyone; kept it all to herself likely.'

'It happens.' was all David said; what she had supplied him with went a long way to fill out the character of Charles Grayson's sister. It sounded to him that she had been a complete introvert, plagued by shyness and envy for those who attained what she knew would have been impossible for her. Sadie Northcot had arrived in Calder Bay in 1957 and the following year she had a child; Beth would have been about sixteen at the time. No doubt she would have heard the rumours circulating about Jack Henderson's visits and with the appearance of the baby, this had in her imaginative mind been sufficient to convince her that Jack Henderson had chosen Sadie Northcot instead of herself. The fact that he was married probably didn't enter her head or that she was only sixteen and no more than a schoolgirl. Far-fetched? Perhaps, but the more he learned about these people, the more he was beginning to think the whole set-up was far-fetched. A body discovered in the grounds of an old mansion where it had been for almost thirty years; a well known and accomplished artist living with his spinster sister in a crumbling property next door; the spinster sister harbouring feelings of envy and hatred; a child from a liaison between a woman whom nobody liked in Calder Bay and the owner of the mansion across the road and now, yet another question, what was the reason for Beth Grayson's abstracted manner a week before her death? What else, David wondered; it was more than far-fetched, it was positively bizarre and, thanking Mrs Baird for taking the time to talk to him, made his way back along the High Street to the office.

***

It was after six before Howard was able to see Dougie Henderson; he and David had spent the last hour going over what had transpired during the day. Not surprisingly, Lilian had drawn a blank with the clothing and with her copy of the identikit, although Alistair had more success on his rounds of the various businesses in the town; the first being at the tobacconists where the owner, who had been there for over thirty years, remembered seeing a young woman resembling the victim; he hadn't known her name, but told Alistair she had been in a few times to buy cigarettes; he could even remember the brand, which was *du Maurier*. Alistair, not being a smoker, hadn't heard of the name, but Lilian had been quick to enlighten him, describing in detail the somewhat uniquely shaped packet and, heartened, Alistair had continued along the street until he had come to "The Shipwreck Hotel" and, having spent many a pleasant evening in the bar, had become friendly with the staff. Although most of them were too young to have been working there in 1975, there were a few whom he thought may have been with the hotel then. Gerald Winters, the head waiter, was supervising the preparations for lunch when Alistair went into the restaurant.

'Good morning, Alistair;' he smiled, 'but perhaps I should be calling you Sergeant as you're obviously on duty.'

'No, Alistair will do fine, Gerald. I'm working on the enquiry into the discovery of the body in the grounds of the Hendersons' old property.'

'A nasty business,' he shook his head, 'you just don't expect that sort of thing to happen in Calder Bay; they said on the news the body had been there for several years.'

'Yes, we believe it was in 1975; were you working here then, Gerald?'

'I was; I've been with "The Shipwreck" for exactly thirty-five years; I came straight from school.' he added.

'That's what I was hoping.' taking a copy of the identikit from his folder and handing it to him.

'An identikit; that's clever.' Gerald said, holding it up to the light, 'I believe I do recognise her, Alistair; at least I'm fairly sure. I'm trying to think back to that year; it would have been in the summer, about this time of the year in fact; she used to come in quite often for a meal.'

'Did you know her name?'

'Sorry, Alistair. She never made the reservations, I think it was always the people she was with who used to phone up.'

'I realise it's a long time ago,' Alistair said, 'but can you remember who they were?'

'Mostly, she accompanied Mr and Mrs Robertson and I did get the impression they were related in some way; only an impression, mind you. She could have been Mrs Robertson's sister, not that they looked alike, but the two of them were often together; if not in here, but in the bar.'

'You have a remarkable memory, Gerald.'

'Well, both women were worth remembering,' he smiled, 'especially

Mrs Robertson; there was just something about her which stood out, if you know what I mean?'

'Star quality?'

'That's it exactly; star quality, yes, she had that alright. It wasn't as if the other woman wasn't attractive because she was, but there's always been pretty girls in Calder Bay, but Mrs Robertson was different; she would, I'm sure, always stand out in a crowd.'

Alistair had gone next to the tea room at the far end of the High Street, but the proprietress, although she'd had the business for years, wasn't any help, neither were the dry cleaners a couple of doors along, although he had more luck at "The Kinloch", a quieter hotel than "The Shipwreck" and where he knew the barman; as with Gerald, Nick Edwards had worked for them for years and had immediately recognised the woman in the identikit, but again hadn't known her name.

'She was only in here a couple of times,' he explained, 'and I'm fairly certain it's the same woman, Alistair.'

'You must have seen any number of pretty girls coming in here;' remembering what Gerald had said, 'was there something about her which made her so different?'

'There was as a matter of fact,' he answered, 'it was her eyebrows, and it's the same in the identikit, have you noticed how one is a fraction higher than the other?'

'You're in the wrong profession, Nick,' Alistair said, 'but you are absolutely right; one is higher.'

'There's also the fringe; a lot of girls round about then had fringes, but they were always straight, but hers was short and curled under.'

'What do you mean?'

'Well, a bit like the pageboy style, nobody wears their hair like that these days, but it was as if her hair was naturally curly and she had brushed it under because if she hadn't it would probably have been all over the place.'

'I must say you're very knowledgeable.'

'My wife's a hairdresser, Alistair, so I suppose I've picked up a few things over the years, but the woman reminded me of Audrey Hepburn; her fringe was exactly the same.'

'You say you only saw her in here twice; was she on her own?'

'The first time she was, but the second time she was with one of the Henderson boys.'

'But in 1975, they were all very young; this woman was in her late twenties.'

'Was she; well, she didn't look it; anyway, it was John she was with then. He told me he was eighteen and I believed him, Alistair; there was no reason not to, the licensing laws weren't as strict twenty-eight years ago and as it happened he only had a soft drink.'

Alistair hadn't pursued the conversation after that, not wanting to appear to be so interested in that she had been drinking with a member of the Henderson family, although the barman would presumably have seen the implication when it would appear everyone in Calder Bay, either from the news or by word of mouth, would know the body had been discovered on the premises of "Carbisdale". He had done well though, Howard was quick to acknowledge; Alistair Dale was a good officer, having been with the Force for six years now and had a keen eye for detail, also the ability to think things through to their logical conclusion, all of which should stand him in good stead for early promotion.

Dougie Henderson lived half-way along Carlogie Road in one of the houses which had been converted into flats, his being on the top floor with a panoramic view from the floor-to-ceiling window in the lounge of the private residents' garden; a wide expanse of manicured lawn bordered on each side by bushes and shrubs; clumps of rhododendrons and azaleas vying for attention in the late afternoon sun.

'Would you like a beer, Inspector?' he asked, walking over towards the open-plan kitchen.

'Sounds good, yes please.'

'This is my favourite time of the day,' he commented, taking two cans of lager from the fridge, 'to get home and relax after a hard day's slog, although I don't suppose your hours can ever be described as regular.'

'Put it like this,' Howard smiled, 'some days are longer than others.'

'How do you think I'll be able to help you;' he asked, pouring his lager into a glass, 'from what I've been hearing, the body had been in the old wash-house for years.'

'We've calculated as far back as twenty-eight years and as far as we can pin-point to when, it looks as if she was murdered sometime at the beginning of July in 1975. We realise you were only a boy then, but young boys have been known to be observant, also to have good memories.' and for the second time that day taking the identikit from his folder and handing it to him.

'I'm not sure,' he said thoughtfully, after studying it for a couple of seconds, 'but it could be the same woman; she did look a bit like her.'

'Did you know who she was?' Howard asked him, allowing him time to think back and remember.

'Yes, I never met her, but Bobby said she was Hilary's aunt.'

'Hilary Robertson?'

'Oh, yes of course, presumably you will know all about us and naturally this will include any of our friends and neighbours, but you're right, her aunt had been staying on holiday with Hilary and her parents.'

'You say you didn't meet her?'

'No, I only saw her the once; this is all somewhat embarrassing, Inspector,' he started to explain, 'but why I should feel like this I don't know, I was only nine, although when I think about it now, all these years later, I have to admit I cringe with what can only be called embarrassment.'

'Well,' Howard helped him out, 'if you tell me where this was, we can take it from there.'

'Fine.' taking a deep breath, 'I can tell you exactly when this was, which was the 30th June of the year you're talking about; it was a Monday, the school holidays of course, and my elder sister's birthday, her eighteenth and there was to be a party for her that evening, no ordinary party with a handful of friends, but quite a do with a marquee on the front lawn and all the rest of it. The caterers arrived during the morning, the marquee was being erected and there seemed to be people all over the place; it soon became clear even to us that we were in the way, so Bobby suggested we make ourselves scarce. I thought he meant we were going down on the rocks to catch whelks which we often did during the summer, but he had a different idea.'

'Only you and Bobby?'

'No, Callum Ogilvie was with us, but then he always was in those days.'

'I've heard he was a good friend of your brother's.'

'He was, yes; anyway, Bobby's idea was for us to squeeze through the fence into the garden of the house next door.'

'Why?'

'A good question,' giving a dry chuckle, 'and that was exactly what I asked him, but he just laughed, accused me of being chicken and that it wouldn't be the first time he and Callum had been in there. You see, at the end of the front garden at "Carbisdale" there was a small orchard and that's where the dividing fence was and after a bit of manoeuvring, we pushed our way into next door's garden and to the back the house where Charles Grayson had his art studio. I've no idea whether Bobby or Callum knew he would have someone with him in the studio; they didn't tell me everything, said I was too young.'

'Only a couple of years younger than they were.'

'I know, but when you're only nine and the youngest of a large family, everyone seems much older.'

'I'm sure you're right.' Howard commented, wondering what was going to come next, although beginning to get a very good idea.

'There were no blinds or curtains at the studio window and Charles Grayson had his back to us; he was at his easel painting the woman who was sitting a little bit further back in the room. I think I must have stood there with my mouth wide open; the scene was so unexpected and my first instinct was to get away from there as quickly as possible, but not the other two, they thought it was great. You've probably guessed she was naked.'

'Well, yes,' Howard admitted, 'and you think she had been Hilary

Robertson's aunt?'

'I think so, Inspector.'

'Did you know her name?'

'Bobby said she was called Natasha, I don't think he knew her surname.'

'We know he was killed in a motorbike accident, Mr Henderson.'

'I rather thought you might.'

'How did he learn who she was; do you think he'd ever met her.'

'I'm sure he hadn't, but I have no idea how many times he'd seen her in Charles' studio, but he said it had been John, my other brother, who had told him.'

'And Charles Grayson didn't know he had an audience?'

'No, but his sister saw us.'

'Where was she?'

'She came round from the side of the house, I think she had been there all the time, and this was when we started to make our way back to "Carbisdale".'

'She didn't call out to you?'

'No, she just stood there staring at us. Even Bobby found that scary, but she was a very forbidding sight; we kids used to call her a witch; cruel I know, but she did look rather fearful; long black hair and the whitest skin I've ever seen.'

Chapter Eight

JOHN

'I can do without this intrusion, Karen; the last I want is to be dragged back to Calder Bay, a town from where I have spent the last ten years doing my damndest to escape, only to be interrogated by some hick copper.'

'He said he was a detective inspector, John, unnecessarily reminding me; Karen always did take everything I said so literally, 'and that we needn't go to Calder Bay to be interviewed; he would come here.'

'Do you think I want anyone from there to see how we live; you have to admit, Karen, it isn't quite in keeping with that of an ex-managing director of a company which fairly recently had gone bust.'

'I don't see what you're getting so heated about, John.' accompanied by one of her pouting shrugs.

'I shouldn't need to remind you, but I was going to anyway, I left under a cloud and believed by everyone in Calder Bay to be personally responsible for the collapse of J. Henderson & Sons.'

'Probably because they all lost their jobs.'

'Most of them were damn lucky they'd had those jobs; what nobody seemed to realise the company was top heavy with managers, useless personnel officers and shop floor workers trying to function with outmoded equipment and had been long before father died. It was only a matter of time, Karen, before the whole outfit would crumble and was already beyond redemption when I took over.'

'I'm sure you're right, John;' now entering her placating mode, and one she had used for years and had never accepted it just didn't work, 'perhaps you should try to be less dramatic.'

'Dramatic! Karen, you're married to a Henderson and drama has always been synonymous with us; we've thrived on high drama, but NOT to the extent of dead bodies being found on the premises!'

'Poor woman.'

'What do you mean; poor woman?'

'Well, being murdered; I'm sure she didn't ask for that, John.'

'Nobody *asks* to be murdered; they merely *get* murdered, but as far as this one is concerned, whoever killed her and decided to half-bury her body on *our* property had a bloody nerve! And now the remaining members of the family have the indignity – and inconvenience – of having to be questioned by the police as if we were all bloody suspects!'

'Would you like a drink, dear?'

'To calm me down you mean? Alright then, Karen, go on; I'll have a stiff whisky.'

I had to admit that she was right; my reaction to hearing about what they'd found in the old wash-house was probably extreme and for the first time since the call came through from Calder Bay police station, I began to seriously wonder who the dead woman had been. The officer I'd spoken to had said they believed she had been murdered at the beginning of July in 1975. Twenty-eight years ago. I'd been seventeen, remembering that was the year Aileen had her birthday party, the last day in June; an extravagant affair and must have cost a packet, but back then, there never appeared to be any shortage of money, but apart from the party, nothing else of any note stood out. I didn't go away that summer, spending the couple of months in Calder Bay: swimming and playing tennis, picnics in the dunes around the bay and lazing about with nothing of any real importance to concern myself with before I started at Aberdeen University in the September. There had been the usual crowd of us, boys I had known from junior school and there had been the girls, one or two I fancied, but no-one special; that was until Natasha appeared on the scene. Natasha was something else. Fantastic figure, good-looking, everything I thought a girl should be, the only snag being she wasn't a girl, she was a woman, a good ten years older than me. All the same, for a few weeks I fooled myself that the large age gap didn't matter. It didn't to me, but it didn't take me long to realise that, to her, I was an amusing past-time while she was on holiday and then, in true will-o'-wisp fashion she had gone, her parting words on the last afternoon I saw her being that she was joining some friends in the South of France. That had been what I needed to finally penetrate my arrogance and make me realise I was way out of her league and by the time I caught up with her, if I ever did, she wouldn't be the same; those ten or eleven years would have begun to show. I hadn't given her a thought since then, but now being forced to think back to the summer of 1975, it was only inevitable that I would.

That night, I had a nightmare, the memory of which stayed with me for most of the following day. If Karen noticed my pre-occupation as we drove up north, she didn't make any comment and, apart from stopping for a coffee at one of the service stations on the motorway, we didn't exchange more than a dozen words. Like most people, I suppose, I'd had nightmares before, but not as horrendous as this one.

I had been in St. Paul's churchyard, walking along one of the gravel paths, until I reached the oak tree when I became aware of no longer being on my own; father was there, walking slowly towards me, a hand raised, not in greeting but to ward me off; Bobby was behind him, but appeared not to have noticed me. On the other side of the path, behind a row of gravestones, a group of people had gathered, some of them I recognised; old friends I had long forgotten. There was a complete silence until Natasha called out from behind me. I swivelled round, but I couldn't see her, then my eye was caught by a flash of scarlet; her dress, the same one she had been wearing the last time I saw her. She *was* out there, darting between the graves, playing games, teasing me. She called out to me again, her voice becoming louder: "Come on, John ..... John ..... It's time ..... We've a long way to go ..... John ..... PLEASE, JOHNnnnnnnn ....."

I hauled myself out from where I had been, aware of Karen shaking my shoulder, her face gradually coming into focus.

'Come on, John,' she said, 'it's time to get up; we've a long way to go today. Please, John, wake up.'

'Oh, God,' I groaned, momentarily surprised to see everything looked as it normally did; our bedroom, the canopied four-poster, the Queen

Anne dressing-table with the gilt-framed mirror and the bay window overlooking the fields of the neighbouring stud farm; the half dozen thoroughbreds grazing peacefully. This was England, the outskirts of Chester, not Calder Bay; there was no graveyard, no ghosts and no Natasha taunting me. 'I've had a dreadful nightmare, dreadful.'

'Do you want to talk about it?' Karen asked, a look of concern on her face.

'No, best to forget it, Karen.'

'They're nonsense anyway, they could never happen, you know.'

My perceptive wife. How did she know nightmares couldn't happen in real life? That one had certainly seemed real enough, giving an involuntary shudder as I climbed out of bed.

Karen had reserved a room for us at "The Royal" and after booking in and freshening up we went into the bar for a drink. It seemed strange to be in Calder Bay again; neither of us had been back since we'd moved out of "Carbisdale" and although it was almost two years now, it only seemed like yesterday since we drove out of Calder Bay on the way down to Chester where we had decided to settle and I could return to the profession for which I had spent years of training only to fall in with what father really wanted from me; a front-of-house yes-man, with a seat on the board, but with no say in the running of the business and, a carrot dangling, of the future prize of finally taking over from him which, perhaps fortuitously, was earlier than any of us had expected. He had been determined that the company should remain in the family and had concentrated all his efforts and considerable charm in persuading me to switch careers; there had been no-one else; Bobby had never shown any interest in the business, but father, as he invariably had done with him, indulgently excused him. And, as for Dougie; he had shown himself to be a force to be reckoned with, which had surprised us all at the time; Dougie, the youngest, the quiet one, appearing content to follow, but when it came to his career, he had literally stuck his heels in; he wanted to be an architect, nothing else held any appeal for him and he would not be swayed by father which had, not only puzzled him, but he had taken

Dougie's refusal as a personal slight.

'Are you going to get in touch with any of your family, John?' Karen asked, tuning into my thoughts, when we were in the bar with two large gin and tonics in front of us.

'I might give Dougie a ring, but I don't see why I should. Neither he nor Aileen bothered to let me know about what's been going on up at "Carbisdale" and they must have known since the weekend when the body was discovered. What about you, Karen; do you want to see your mother while we're up here?'

'I thought I would pop in and see her some time tomorrow before we go back.' but without any great enthusiasm, her mind obviously elsewhere, 'I keep thinking about this meeting we're having with the police, John.'

'Yes?'

'I can't understand why they should want to see us; it all happened such a long time ago and we were only kids then.'

'Not that young, Karen.'

'What do you mean?'

'Except for Dougie, we were teenagers and all at an age to be observant. I expect the police will be trying to resurrect the scene of the crime so to speak and they'll want to speak to everyone who had been living close to "Carbisdale", not just the family.'

'Oh, I see; seems a hopeless task to me.'

'That is what they're trained to do, remember. Apparently, they've made up an identikit of the victim and probably that will be the first thing they'll want to know; whether we recognise the woman and if so, when we last saw her; questions like that.'

'I can't say I'm looking forward to tomorrow morning, though.'

'Nobody likes being interviewed by the police, Karen,' I emphasised, 'so why should you be any different?'

'Good Lord! What are you doing here, John?'

'I hadn't noticed Aileen coming in, watching her now as she walked towards us. While realising it was probably inevitable we would see each other over the next couple of days, I had hoped to avoid her.

'Aileen,' I said, standing up to plant the obligatory kiss on her cheek.

'You are always full of surprises, aren't you, John. Karen,' turning to Karen, 'how are you?'

'I'm fine, thank you, Aileen; a bit weary after the drive though.'

'I take it you do know about what's been going on?' she asked me, any further interest in Karen's welfare forgotten. Why was it, I wondered for the umpteenth time, Aileen had this irrational dislike for her. I knew the answer of course, but had chosen over the years not to admit to myself that my sister was a social snob. As far as she was concerned, I had married our housekeeper's daughter and while this was technically correct, Karen's background was equally as socially acceptable as any member of our family. In many respects, in spite of losing her father when she had been too young to remember him, she hadn't lost out as we had in being lovingly brought up by a parent who had always been around. Growing up, she'd had her own circle of friends and we had seldom seen her. Mrs Baird had been our housekeeper, but not a mother substitute; that hadn't been her role; to keep us all in check, in fact, there hadn't been anyone. Perhaps, trying to rationalise Aileen's antagonism towards Karen, was because she resented her for that reason. Aileen had been nine when mother died, old enough to have remembered what it had been like to have a mother. It could be an explanation.

'I do know, Aileen,' answering her, 'but not until we got the call from Detective Inspector McIntyre. Anyway, aren't you going to sit down and have a drink with us?'

'Oh, alright, John, that would be nice.' obviously remembering her manners.

'We have an appointment with the Detective Inspector tomorrow morning.' I told her, once her drink had been brought over.

'A long way to come.' she commented, looking at me above the rim of her glass.

'I suppose it is,' I agreed, keeping my voice level; she always did have the knack of zooming right in with her poorly disguised opinions, 'but I thought it was time I paid a visit to Calder Bay.'

'Why?'

'What do you mean, Aileen; this is my home town, a place where I was born, went to school and lived in for over forty years; Karen, also, had lived here all her life, so why shouldn't we return when we feel like it?'

'People in Calder Bay have long memories, John; I'm sure you realise that.'

'Quite frankly, that doesn't concern me.'

'Perhaps it should, especially at the moment.'

'I can hardly be blamed for the body of a woman being found in the grounds of "Carbisdale".'

'All I'm saying is this is probably not the best time for a nostalgic visit.'

I took a deep sip of my gin and tonic, deciding her remark wasn't worth a reply. What could I say? Nothing. And I didn't want an argument.

'There is something you should know,' she said, lowering her voice, although there was no-one close enough to hear, 'but I think I know who the woman was.'

'Don't tell me you've been asked to make an identification?'

'Not a physical one, but I was shown an identikit yesterday which the authorities had put together and, while I can't be one hundred per cent certain, she bore a fairly close resemblance to Hilary's aunt.'

'Natasha?'

'You met her?'

'Once or twice; she had been staying on holiday with the Robertson as you probably know,' rationing how much I wanted to say; I had almost forgotten Aileen's keen perception which could at times be likened to a terrier, knowing she wouldn't let go of a topic until she had literally stripped it bare.

'I only met her once,' she was saying, 'but what really disturbs me is Hilary's reaction, should it turn out that I'm right.'

'They will be bound to ask her to identify the body and that will be a gruesome experience for her.'

'I know, and that's what makes all of this so much worse somehow; that somebody we knew had been murdered so close to where we were all living at that time. The irony is, John,' she went on, 'Hilary was actually in Calder Bay this weekend; she's living in Oxford now and drove back yesterday morning.'

'She would have been here when the body was found.'

'Yes, that's right; we had a drink together on Monday evening; she'd heard about it on the news on Saturday, we didn't discuss it at any length, but like me, she was shocked. I don't think Janice and she could have been in touch for a number of years; she didn't know about Bobby, or about father dying. She had taken a walk up Green Lane and discovered what was happening to "Carbisdale", so we spent most of the evening talking about when she and her parents had been living here, just catching up with things generally.'

'Is she still married to Rob Masters?'

'No, they divorced years ago. This happened when they were living out in Hong Kong, she told me her daughter had been eleven and then about four years ago she re-married.'

'I'm surprised the marriage lasted as long as it did.'

'Why do you say that?'

'From what I remember of Hilary, she was a very self-contained person, lived at times in her own little world. Janice told me she was an illustrator of children's books, whereas Rob was totally the opposite, brash, super-confident, always had a lot to say for himself.'

'Well, all I can say is, she seems happy and actually hasn't changed all that much.'

'What made her come back to Calder Bay?'

'She'd seen a portrait Charles Grayson had painted of her mother in a magazine; this had been when she was in Edinburgh attending Kirstie's graduation and thought as she was reasonably close to Calder Bay she may as well spend a couple of days here.'

'I didn't know about the painting; when was this done?'

'Not long after they moved into their house in Green Lane in 1975.'

'A coincidence.'

'In what way?'

'No particular reason, Aileen.'

'You don't like Charles very much, do you?'

'Neither do you, Aileen.'

'I neither like nor dislike him; I had my reasons all those years ago for breaking off our engagement.'

'Ah,' unable to keep the smile off my face, 'the witch.'

'Who's the witch?' Karen asked.

'The witch, Karen,' Aileen said, including her in the conversation for the first time, 'was the nick-name we gave to Charles' sister; she was a very strange woman and incredibly possessive towards him; if I had married Charles, I realised that my life would have been hell, so I called it off.'

'Has she died, then?' I asked, picking up on the past tense.

'Yes, a few weeks ago.'

'She couldn't have been all that old.'

'In her early sixties, I think.'

'Did she have cancer or something, then?'

'Not as far as I know; she just died.'

'Aileen,' Karen said, managing to stifle a splutter of amusement, 'people don't just die; there's always a reason.'

'Is there,' actually looking surprised, whether by Karen's logic or by the fact being pointed out to her, it was hard to detect, 'well, does it matter; the woman's gone and that's that.'

'Harsh words.'

'So they might be, John, but I did not like Beth Grayson; quite frankly, she gave me the creeps.'

'Okay,' I said quickly, 'point taken. Anyway, what is this Detective Inspector like?'

'I haven't met him; it was Inspector Crawford who came to see me.'

'They've got quite a task on their hands.'

'Perhaps.'

'What do you mean, perhaps?'

'Well, John, surely once the body is formally identified as Natasha that will help them in finding the murderer.'

'Theoretically, I suppose you're right, but then it might not be her.'

'What you're saying is, that a complete stranger to Calder Bay, and to anyone who was living here then, was murdered by someone who had happened to know a likely place to dump her body; namely, our old wash-house. No, John that is just not an acceptable theory; whoever that woman was, her killer must have known about the wash-house.'

'You seem to have worked it all out,' I said to her, 'who do you think killed her, then?'

'That is a daft question; you might as well ask me to pin the tail on a donkey blindfold.'

Aileen didn't have another drink with us; making the excuse she was meeting some friends for a meal. It may have been the truth, but either way, I wasn't sorry to see her go. A little bit of my elder sister goes a very long way; her brash assertiveness unpleasantly reminding me of father. In his opinion, he had always been right; never pausing to consider another person's view and once he had made up his mind, I had never known him waver.

'She's hard work.' Karen said, breaking into my thoughts.

'You can say that again.'

'Has she always been so self-opinionated?'

'Probably, but don't let her manner get to you, Karen; she can't help the way she is.'

'No, I won't; of course I've always realised she doesn't like me, but it's a pity she makes it so obvious each time we're in her company.'

'Which fortunately isn't often.'

***

It was no surprise to me the following morning to find that Aileen had been right; the identikit handed to me by Detective Inspector McIntyre did bear a close resemblance to Natasha. I'd had enough time since talking to Aileen to think over the possible consequences should the dead woman turn out to be Hilary's aunt, that the confirmation of this didn't have the impact it might have had otherwise.

'How well did you know Natasha Paton, Mr Henderson?'

'Not very well; I didn't even know her surname.'

'But you knew her as Natasha?'

'Yes, and that she was Hilary Robertson's aunt; she was staying with them on holiday.'

'This was in the July of 1975?'

'That's right.'

'Can you remember when you last saw her?' the question surprising me.

'I don't think I can.'

'You've said you didn't know her well, but how friendly were you?'

'Sorry?'

'I'm trying to find out what sort of friendship you had with her.'

'Oh, well, we were friends, that's all.'

'When you saw each other, where did you meet?' recognising the catch; he was attempting to trip me up, but it wasn't going to work; I had read the signal to be on my guard.

'Nowhere in particular,' I said, 'around the bay mostly, when we would be swimming or sunbathing.'

'Were you ever on your own with her?'

'No, the others were always around.'

'These were your friends?'

'Yes, boys from school.'

'Were you and Natasha Paton lovers?'

'I was only seventeen, Detective Inspector, and Natasha was years older.'

'Neither are deterrents to a sexual relationship.'

'Perhaps not.'

'You haven't answered my question,' he said quietly, 'were you lovers?'

'And the answer is no, we weren't.'

'Did you find her attractive?'

'She was an attractive woman.'

'Did you have a girlfriend around that time?'

'No-one special.'

'Therefore,' he was increasing the pressure, 'you were emotionally free to enjoy a light summer romance with an attractive woman still in her twenties, possessing a sophistication which to a young man of seventeen might have been irresistible.'

'She would hardly want to waste her time with me, would she?'

'Probably not. You can't remember when you last saw her, Mr Henderson, but can you remember when you first saw her?'

'It was in Green Lane; she was coming out of Hilary's house.' realising as soon as I spoke, I had slipped up and could tell by the slight narrowing of his eyes he'd noticed my too-speedy response.

'Did you see her often?'

'For a short while, fairly often.'

'And then, what?'

'I'm afraid I don't know what you mean.'

'What I mean, Mr Henderson, did she suddenly disappear from where you usually saw her, or did she tell you she was going?'

'Oh, I see; no, she told me she was leaving.'

'Did she tell you where she was going?'

'She did, actually; to meet up with some friends of hers who had a villa in the South of France.'

'I see, and where were you when she told you this?'

'I can't remember, in the bay, I suppose.'

'Did she tell you when you were together having a drink one evening?'

How the hell did he find that out? Metaphorically kicking myself for not mentioning the one and only time Natasha and I had met openly in public, although I had particularly chosen the bar in "The Kinloch", feeling sure that no-one I knew would be coming in, but presumably I was wrong, realising I shouldn't have under-estimated the long memories of the Calder Bay residents.

'I couldn't have been drinking, Detective Inspector, I was under age.'

'I realise that, Mr Henderson, but you and Natasha Paton were seen in the bar of "The Kinloch Hotel".'

'Okay, okay, so I was in the bar with her; it had slipped my mind.'

'And on that occasion she told you she was leaving?'

'No, it wasn't then; she had already told me and suggested we have a drink together.' and that was the best I could do, for the first time since being shown into his office, thinking of Karen and wondering how her interview with Inspector Crawford was going; it certainly wouldn't match the grilling to which I was being subjected.

'One last question, Mr Henderson,' he said, 'can you recall what she had been wearing that evening?' Was this another trap and how could whatever I told him have any possible bearing on their investigation?

'A dress, sleeveless and bright red, scarlet I think you would have described the colour. Can you tell me, Detective Inspector, the reason for you wanting to know?'

'I expect it did sound a bit puzzling, but as we do know what she had been wearing at the time of her death and, on the off chance it had been the same dress until such time as her niece is able to make any formal identification, it could further prove that the woman had been Natasha Paton.'

'You've asked Hilary?'

'Yes, we have, she and her husband will be here tomorrow.'

'Not very pleasant for her.'

'Indeed it won't be, Mr Henderson. It never is.'

Chapter Nine

CALLUM

The message, asking me to get in touch with the Calder Bay police station, was on my answering machine when I got back home on Thursday. I had spent the last three days in Glasgow installing a new computer software system for one of the major engineering companies there. While away, I had scarcely given a thought to what was happening in Calder Bay, although as soon as I drove into the town, it took only seconds before I was reminded, having seen Charles Grayson outside the tobacconist talking to Carla Northcot, so deep in conversation they didn't notice me. I hadn't realised they knew each other, then remembered Sadie telling me Charles had often called to see her, especially after his old friend, Jack Henderson, had died, and wondering now whether Charles knew about Carla. Sadie may have told him; she never said anything to me, but then she didn't have to; I had, years before, drawn my own conclusions when I'd noticed a couple of framed photographs of Carla in her house and thinking how much she looked like Janice. I never mentioned this to anyone, not even to Bobby; I wasn't sure how he would have reacted if I had, and now of course it was too late, but I couldn't help thinking if he had still been alive and saw Carla, he would spot the resemblance. Somebody else had though, recalling Carla telling me I was the second person to have mistaken her for someone else, trying to think who it might have been. Perhaps Charles Grayson, that is, if he didn't already know about her, but if not, there were still a few more likely people who may have seen her during these last few days when she had been in Calder Bay.

I had told Carla I had known her mother, but I hadn't elaborated on the friendship. Sadie had acted as a confidante, someone I was able to talk to, knowing that whatever I said wouldn't go any further. In a way, I suppose, I used her in the way Americans consult a psychiatrist; Sadie never asked any questions, just sat quietly, usually we were in the kitchen, but sometimes on warm summer evenings, outside on her terrace, while I poured out my woes. I don't know how I could have coped when I came back to live in Calder Bay if it hadn't been for her support; I was at an extremely low ebb, narrowly escaping, I'm sure, a nervous breakdown, but merely by listening to me, I came out of the mental quagmire I'd fallen into. During the time I'd been working in London I had come back to Calder Bay a number of times, but I found being constantly reminded of how life used to be too painful; it was a very long time before I was able to reconcile myself to Bobby's death and even now, ten years later, a day hardly went by when I didn't think about him. Perhaps it was time to let go, not to hide away as I had been doing, but to renew my friendship with the Hendersons. I wasn't so sure about John's reception, but I didn't believe Dougie, or even Aileen, would be averse to seeing me.

I was shown into Inspector Crawford's office the following morning, surprised to find it looked like any other office: the desk with computer and printer, metal filing cabinets, a couple of book shelves, strip lighting and the sash window with horizontal blinds slanted to show slices of the moving vehicles in the High Street. The Inspector looked vaguely familiar, but I couldn't remember where I'd seen him before; he was about my age, so it could have been from school.

'Good morning, Mr Ogilvie,' he said, standing up to shake hands, 'thanks for coming in.' and going on to explain he was involved in the murder investigation, in particular with establishing the identity of the victim.

The identikit of the woman wasn't all that well defined, not in the way a photograph would have been, but nevertheless, the general impression was sufficient for me to be fairly sure I recognised her.

'I think it could have been a woman who was here on holiday around the time you've mentioned, Inspector.'

'Did you know her?'

'No, but I saw her a few times, but not to speak to; she was Hilary Robertson's aunt and she was staying with them in Green Lane. I think Hilary said she was called Natasha, but she didn't mention her surname.'

'You're not the first person we have spoken to over the last few days who has seen the resemblance to her and we should by the end of the morning have confirmation of whether the victim is the same person or not after the outcome of the formal identification.'

'You've found someone to identify her?'

'Yes, we have,' he answered, obviously giving nothing away; it was like getting blood from a stone, I thought, but perhaps that's the way police officers operate, having had no previous experience of being interviewed by one, 'it's our understanding,' he was going on, looking at me steadily across the desk, 'you were a close friend of the Henderson family?'

'Yes, that's right; I was in the same class at school as Bobby.' even to say his name out loud after all this time was painful, making it difficult to make me act naturally.

'Who was killed in a motorbike accident ten years ago?'

Was he doing this deliberately? Did he have some sort of second sense, knowing how much distress he was causing by mentioning that awful day, one that I had done my utmost to, if not forget, but to push right to the back of my mind.

'Yes.' was all I could manage to say.

'You may find this reference to your friend irrelevant to the current murder enquiry, Mr Ogilvie, as it may well be, but in an investigation of this kind we have to be as thorough as we possibly can in working our way through the background of the people who were living in and around the area where the body was discovered.'

'Bobby and I were close friends, like brothers I suppose you could say, and I found it hard to accept what happened to him.'

'I understand.' and maybe he did; there was a slight lessening in his manner which I'd thought to be heavier than warranted, 'Would you have said he was a competent cyclist?'

'Extremely competent; he was twenty-nine, Inspector, no longer a kid; if the accident had happened twenty years ago and not ten, perhaps I could have understood, because up to his teens, he was a bit of a daredevil, but once he'd been to university he settled down. I'd often been on the bike with him and I never knew him to take risks.'

'He'd matured?'

'I believe it was more than that,' I said, and for once didn't mind talking about him, 'you see, there was this boy at university, he was older than us, and we all thought he was great, a bit of hero worshipping, I suppose. His family must have been fairly well off, because he had his own sports car and drove like an idiot; the inevitable happened, he crashed on the motorway. He was killed, of course, but it was as if his death acted as a slap in the face to us both really, but especially to Bobby.'

'Tragic.'

'Yes, it was.' I agreed, not sure whether he meant Bobby's or our friend's accident.

'You probably knew "Carbisdale" very well?'

'I did; I spent more time there than in my own home. Hilary was the same; in fact we were treated as though we were part of the family.'

'Do you remember the old wash-house?'

'Of course; I would see it every day I went to the house.'

'You didn't live in Green Lane?'

'No, in Carlogie Road, about two hundred yards up from St Paul's therefore I always used the main entrance and had to pass the wash-house to reach the front door.'

'Did you ever see inside it?'

'No, thank goodness,' giving an involuntary shudder, 'but Bobby and I did try to once; we were in the middle of prising open the padlock when Jimmy McIntosh -'

'- the gardener?'

'Oh, you've heard of him;' they were certainly being thorough, 'yes, he'd worked for them for years; anyway, we thought he was in the orchard, but he wasn't, and when he saw us he yelled out saying no-one was allowed to go in there.'

'Why do you think he said that?'

'I don't know, only that Mr Henderson had given him strict instructions that the door must never be opened, only by him.'

'Can you remember when this was?' he asked.

'Not exactly; it was in the summer, I know that, and I think we were younger than eleven, but I'm not sure.'

After what seemed like hours, but couldn't have been any more than forty-five minutes, I emerged from his office feeling as though I had been subjected to the third degree, but one with a twist; Inspector Crawford had an unnerving way of delivering the simplest of questions, he'd given me the impression there had been a different meaning behind each one of them. I was thinking of when he'd asked if I had ever been in the wash-house, but I now realised that wasn't what he had wanted to know at all; it had been his way of arriving at a possible clue, a relevant lead in their enquiry, not whether two eleven year-olds had ventured inside the place and, unwittingly, I had supplied him with something he would no doubt latch on to, trying again to remember when this had been. When he'd asked me, I had said without any hesitation it hadn't been in 1975, but how could I have been so certain? All I really remembered was that it had been in the summertime, probably during the school holidays and around that age surely every summer had been more or less the same. We had so much freedom from when we were about seven or eight, it never seemed to rain during those long summer holidays and we used to spend most of the time in either the garden or the orchard with only Jimmy McIntosh to tell us off if we got too rowdy or took more fruit than we should have; we hardly ever went round to the back of the house, except that one time. The lock on the wash-house door was, I remembered, quite high up, which meant we couldn't have been much less than eleven because we had been tall enough to reach it, but it was no good, my memory wouldn't stretch any further than that. And now, Inspector Crawford would be thinking he might have a suspect. I couldn't in my wildest imaginings see Jack Henderson as a murderer; the idea was just too crazy, not that the inspector would be thinking in that way, probably anyone with a possible motive would be considered suspicious. And, why had she been murdered? I could only think of one credible reason, but was it strong enough for such a violent act; she could have been having an affair with him and had started making demands which he couldn't or wouldn't handle, but would he have put the body in an outbuilding, only yards away from the house? It could be argued that this was the reason why the wash-house had been out of bounds, but it still didn't make any sense to me, grateful I had chosen a less stressful career which didn't involve the solving of crimes where the final outcome could have a detriment affect on people's lives whether they were guilty or not.

It was now after midday and, although I hadn't dealt with that morning's mail, decided to have a beer first; I had already lost half a day, another couple of hours wasn't going to make much difference.

The bar of "The Royal" was already filling up with lunchtime customers, some I recognised from the various offices in the town and a number of tourists with the tell-tale cameras slung around their necks, their faces reddened by the sun. I was half-way through my beer when Hilary Robertson came in; I would have known her anywhere, although I hadn't seen her for years. I didn't recognise the man she was with; I knew she had married Rob Masters, but it wasn't him. And then I realised; she must be the person the Inspector had meant when he'd said he had found someone to identify the body, but she didn't look as though she had been through such an ordeal; a bit serious, I suppose, but as soon as she spotted me, her expression changed and she smiled, exactly as she used to; a shy smile which seemed to light up her whole face.

'Callum,' she said, 'how nice to see you.'

'Hello, Hilary; as they say, it's been a long time.'

'It certainly has; Callum, this is my husband, Mike Fisher.'

'Hello, Mike;' I said, shaking hands with him, 'can I get you both a drink; what would you like?'

We took our drinks over to the window and sat down.

'I believe I know why you're in Calder Bay,' deciding it would be best to come straight to the point, 'I've been with Inspector Crawford this morning.'

'- yes, Detective Inspector McIntyre introduced him to us as we were leaving the police station a few minutes ago and he told us that you'd noticed the likeness to Natasha in the identikit.'

'It was her, wasn't it, Hilary?'

'Yes.' she nodded.

'I'm sorry, Hilary; I really am; it must have been dreadful for you in there.'

'It wasn't as bad as I'd expected; also, I had Mike with me.' touching him lightly on the arm.

'That was good.' was all I could find to say.

'You see, Callum,' she started to explain, 'I was actually in Calder Bay last weekend; it was a spur of the moment decision; Mike was away on business and I came up to Edinburgh to attend Kirstie's graduation ceremony at the university there and, well, it's a long story, but anyway, after I had booked in here, I took a walk up Green Lane, for old times' sake, I suppose, more than anything else.'

'Of course; presumably you didn't know about "Carbisdale" no longer being in existence?'

'No, that was a bit of a blow, I must admit, but not as much as learning about Bobby.'

'Yes, poor Bobby.'

'I'm truly sorry, Callum, I know you were great friends; you must miss him.'

'It's taken me a long time, ten years in fact, to come to terms with his death.'

We chatted for a while, skirting away from what happened to Natasha. Mike Fisher was alright and I was interested to hear about his work as an archaeologist and about the dig he'd been on in southern Italy. Also, Hilary's work as an illustrator; I had already known she had chosen a career in art, Janice having given us a number of updates in the early years when Hilary and Rob had been living in Hong Kong. It was refreshing to think and talk about something else rather than the depressing topic of murder which had taken hold of the people of Calder Bay for almost two weeks now. She showed me a photograph of Kirstie, the first I had seen, and I was immediately struck by her delicate features and the rich auburn hair; the likeness to Hilary's mother was uncanny.

'I know,' Hilary smiled when I mentioned this, 'but her temperament doesn't extend to my mother's; Kirstie is an extremely assertive young woman.' going on to tell me of how immediately she had graduated she had flown out to Hong Kong and only the day before they had received an email from her to say she now had a job in publishing.

'Did you meet Hilary's mother?' I asked Mike.

'No, sadly, she had died by the time Hilary and I met,' he explained, 'of course I've seen many photographs of her, also the portrait which Charles Grayson painted.'

Hilary picked up on what he'd said by telling me that she had seen this in a copy of "Art Review" while she'd been in Edinburgh and that had been why she had decided to come back here for a few days.

'I think I may have mentioned he was doing a painting of her, Callum.'

'I remember you did.' my memory instantly back-tracking to the day of Aileen's party when the three of us had sneaked into the Grayson's garden, hoping Hilary would never know; if she ever did, it wouldn't be from me. The undisputed fact that I now knew that the woman we had seen in Charles Grayson's studio, adopting what I learned much later was the famous Christine Keeler pose, had probably within a matter of days been murdered, was unpalatable to say the least.

'I've never seen the painting, you know, Callum, which is a pity.'

'It could be being exhibited; I've heard he has become quite famous in the art world.'

'I hope so, or it could be in his gallery.'

'I didn't know he had one.'

'The magazine article mentioned he had one at home as part of his studio.'

'It's true I haven't been up to Green Lane recently, but the last time I saw his house it was exactly as it was when we were all kids; needed some serious renovation.'

'Well,' she laughed, 'it looks as though it is about to get its facelift; I took Mike up there earlier this morning and the whole frontage is covered in scaffolding.'

'Not before time.' and having a reasonable idea of why the remedial work was now being done; this must have something to do with his sister dying; we all knew what the "witch" had been like; she had been some years older than him and, presumably, the house had been bequeathed to her when their parents died and she had forbidden any changes, whether for the better, to be made to the place. But, I decided, this was something else there was no need to tell Hilary; she had enough to think about at the moment than the demise of a woman for whom nobody had a good word to say.

Chapter Ten

CHARLES

By midday on Thursday all the ivy which had been strangling my house for longer than I could remember, had been pulled and dragged away from the stonework and before the builders had finished for the day, the scaffolding was in place in preparation for the following morning when the initial stages of the renovations would start.

Meeting Carla and having the chance when we spent time together in Edinburgh to get to know her, had acted as a fillip; for the first time in my life I was seriously considering making what to me would be a radical change. Although I guarded my studio jealously; a place which had proved to be a haven and conducive for painting, I didn't enjoy being in any other part of the house, possibly because of Beth; even now, when she was no longer there, I continued to feel her presence, my impression intensified when I went upstairs to her bedroom. Carla and I had been having a drink in "Browns" in George Street when I mentioned this to her and she had understood immediately what I meant.

"I've always believed that houses do give off vibes; it's as though the walls have somehow absorbed everything that's happened within them over the years and then, when given the chance, it oozes out to form what we usually call an atmosphere. What do you think?"

"It's a good way of describing it and when you mention when they are given the chance, perhaps they didn't have that chance while Beth was alive."

"Possibly." she had smiled at me, a slow sympathetic smile.

"I don't mean to be so uncharitable towards her, but she wasn't an easy person to have around, but then I don't suppose she ever was, and latterly I found her continual brooding presence intolerable."

"It's an odd feeling when someone dies though, isn't it; I felt most uncomfortable going back to my mother's house. Everything seemed so alien to me as if I shouldn't be there, but of course I had to be to sort everything out."

"That's something I have yet to do," reluctant to admit such weakness, "Beth's clothes and things, I mean."

"Would you like me to help you?" she had been quick to offer.

"I can't expect you to do that, Carla."

"Look at it this way; I didn't know your sister, therefore I would be impartial."

"Thank you; I have to admit it would be a relief, I was beginning to wonder whether I would ever get round to doing it."

"That's settled then; will Friday morning suit you, Charles; I will have finished everything I have to do by then, so it will be another free day."

We had a long leisurely lunch in the brasserie, both of us choosing the pan-fried chicken with duck confit, maple syrup and a lemon and tarragon syrup which was delicious, rounding it off with a chocolate mousse with French kirsch cherries. Before going back to the car, we strolled through Princes Street Gardens, surprisingly quiet although so close to bustling Princes Street.

"I love this city." Carla said.

"It has that affect on people, I think; apparently it is the city of Enlightenment and I've heard it described by many to be the 'Athens of the North'."

"I can believe it, Charles; certainly it has inspired dozens of famous people, the list is endless."

"Including JK Rowlings."

"Including JK Rowlings." she had laughed.

She was fun to be with and I couldn't remember having such an enjoyable day; Edinburgh a perfect backdrop and, as we drove out of the city my mind was made up; once all the renovations were completed, I would put the house on the market and move to the 'Athens of the North'. I didn't mention this to Carla, wanting to hug the idea to myself for a little while, confident I would see her again.

The foreman of William Lowe & Sons was the first to turn up on Friday morning shortly before eight, followed by the stone-makers and the carpenters in their own transport, the name of the company printed on the side panel of the van; now, I thought cynically, word will go round that long overdue improvements to the Grayson property are underway. I had already noticed the woman from across the road where the Robertsons used to live, taking a peep through a gap in the curtains, giving every appearance of an avid interest in the unusual activity going on in Green Lane.

Carla arrived at eleven, having walked up from the High Street; I took her round to the back entrance which led directly into the studio, not wanting to subject her to the neglected chaos of the hall. I'd made some coffee which we drank before going upstairs and I led the way along the landing to the bedroom Beth had once occupied and had done all her life.

'I apologise for the mustiness, Carla, but with the workmen outside it won't be possible to open the window.'

'Don't worry, Charles, I'll cope.'

'I'm sure you will;' I smiled wryly, feeling ashamed at having to bring her into such a dismal room, 'some of her clothes may be alright for the charity shop, but I think most them should be binned.'

'Okay, Charles; I'll separate them and see what's worth taking along there.'

'What would you like me to do?' feeling totally useless.

'Nothing.' she smiled, opening the wardrobe door, 'I don't expect it will take me long; there's not a great deal in here.' she added, looking inside the dark cavity of the wardrobe.

'If you're sure?' making to go back downstairs.

'I'm sure; you go back down to the studio, I'll come and find you when I've finished.'

I couldn't settle to do any painting although there was one canvas which was waiting for me to add the finishing touches in time for it to be collected at the beginning of the following week, therefore instead, I spent the next half hour or so tidying the desk and answering the last two days' mail.

'Charles?' Although I had kept the door open, I hadn't heard her coming downstairs and looked up to see her standing in the doorway, a puzzled expression on her face.

'Is something wrong?' jumping to my feet and going over to her.

'I don't know, but I found some things, they had been pushed right to the back of the wardrobe; I don't think they could have belonged to your sister.'

We went back upstairs together, Carla this time going first.

'There they are, Charles, on the bed; they were inside the bag.' pointing to a dark green travel bag, unzipped, with the contents piled up beside it. Summer clothes; brilliant colours, colours that Beth never wore; shoes and sandals again hadn't belonged to her, but it was the other bag, much smaller, bright red with a shoulder strap, which made me catch my breath in horror. Natasha's bag! I knew without having to look inside that it had been hers; she'd had it with her each time I'd seen her. The clothes would have belonged to her also and as the sheer enormity, the implication of what had turned up, literally hit me, I couldn't move; I couldn't take one single step forward to what was on the bed, what had been hidden in the wardrobe for all those years.

'Charles,' Carla's voice coming as though from miles away, gradually reached me and I felt her hand on my arm, and heard the concern in her voice, 'take it easy; we'll go back to the studio, shall we, get away from here? Please.'

She took my hand and like a child I let her guide me out of the room and downstairs; she didn't speak again until we were back in the studio, the door firmly closed behind us.

'First things first, Charles;' she said, 'do you have any brandy?'

'Yes,' I managed, surprised to find my voice sounded as it always did, 'in that small cabinet beside the desk.'

'I'll pour us both one and we'll take them outside on to your terrace, shall we? You need some air.'

'Thank you, Carla.'

'You don't have to thank me, Charles; you've obviously had a dreadful shock, but wait until you've taken a sip before saying anything further.'

The combination of the soothing liquid and the warmth of the sun had an instant healing affect; the numbness was beginning to diminish, allowing me to think and act rationally.

'You were right;' I said at last, 'they didn't belong to Beth.'

'But you know who they did belong to, don't you?' she asked gently, her expression still concerned.

'Yes, I'd have to check inside the handbag, but I believe they were Natasha's.'

'Was that the name of the woman who was murdered?'

'Yes, I wasn't sure before, because there had been no formal identification, although by this time there may very well have been, but seeing those things of her, I don't really think there is any doubt.'

'But your sister had them.'

'It would seem so; nobody else would have put them in there.'

'How awful, Charles; no wonder you were so shocked.'

'I've had a visit from the detective inspector conducting the murder enquiry, this was on Tuesday morning, and I dare say others will have as well: Aileen and Dougie, perhaps Callum, he was Bobby's friend, and no doubt they would have been in touch with John and Janice, but I don't know; I haven't been in touch with any of them.'

'Did you know the woman?' she asked; a question I was expecting and wondering how she would view me when I told her.

'I knew her, Carla; she was Hilary Robertson's aunt and had been staying with her family on holiday.'

'Hilary; she's the woman who mistook me for Janice.'

'Yes, that's right. Carla, I want to be entirely honest with you; I realise we've only very recently met, but already I would like to consider you as a friend and someone I would like to remain friendly with and hopefully see again.'

'I want that also, Charles,' she said quietly, 'and as you say, we haven't known each other for very long, but I enjoy being with you and we will see each other again, although London is rather a long way from Calder Bay.'

'I wasn't going to mention anything about this, but I've decided to sell this house and move to Edinburgh.'

'That's a good decision; Edinburgh will suit you, Charles.'

'I hope so, but to get back to what I was about to say, Carla, about Natasha.'

'Yes?'

'Marion Robertson was sitting for me at the same time as Natasha arrived in Calder Bay and as soon as she learned I was an artist was insistent I paint her also.'

'Forward.'

'She was, yes, very. However, I agreed, and that was my first mistake. She was adamant she wanted to be painted in the nude. Being an artist, I had painted nudes before, so although I wasn't all that keen because of her, shall we say, her precociousness, I agreed.'

'What was your second mistake?' a tiny smile hovering on her lips.

'You've guessed, haven't you?' wishing I could share her smile.

'You made love to her.'

'Mystic Meg.'

'I know; I'm dreadful, aren't I? Sorry, Charles, it's wrong of me to be so flippant. Go on.'

'There's not a great deal more to say, except she took that one lapse of mine as a signal that I was serious about her and started making demands for me to marry her.'

'Good Grief; she didn't sound real.'

'I think that was just the way she was, she'd probably been thoroughly spoilt; she had been the youngest of the family, Marion was eleven or twelve years older than her and Natasha had obviously been used to getting what she wanted.'

'And she wanted to be married to you.'

'She increased her persistence, took to coming here at all times, until after about a week of this, I suggested as I was going to spend a few days in a property I have in Cap d'Ail in the South of France, she could accompany me. I suppose you would say that could be classed as my third mistake, but I will say it was my last one as far as she was concerned. I had already discovered that Natasha loved change, she loved new people, travelling, all the so-called glamour of life, but my idea had been she would soon get bored with my company and it would give me a chance to talk some sense into her. Anyway, she jumped at coming with me. I know this is now going to sound very melodramatic, but if you remember, I always had Beth in the background, continuously breathing down my neck, I decided not to tell her I was going away, so I was to pick Natasha up outside the church in Carlogie Road, this way, I knew Beth wouldn't see her in Green Lane as she was bound to do otherwise. Well, when I drove up she wasn't where we'd arranged; I waited for a while, but not for too long, I didn't want to look conspicuous in case anyone should get suspicious about me hanging about and when she still didn't arrive, I carried on; down to Portsmouth and took the early morning ferry over to France. I've told you the truth, Carla.'

'I know you have, Charles and thank you for telling me. What do you plan to do now?'

'First, I need to check the contents of the handbag; there should be some means of identity inside and then I'll have to get in touch with the police. I haven't got a choice, Carla, and quite frankly, if Beth had anything to do with what happened to Natasha, I don't want to carry that weight around with me for the rest of my days.'

'I understand; I would feel the same way.'

'I realise they will suspect me; that will be inevitable.'

'Initially, perhaps,' she said, 'but surely they will question themselves that if you were guilty you would have got rid of her luggage.'

'I would hope so.'

'Also, as they were found in your sister's bedroom, they have to suspect her. From how you've described Beth, I'm beginning to build up a picture of her personality.'

'I thought you may have done.'

'I'm thinking of motive; if you tell them what you've just told me, it wouldn't supply them with one, but if they were to consider Beth as being guilty, it shouldn't be too difficult for them to arrive at the motive, also why she didn't dispose of Natasha's belongings.'

'Why, Carla?'

'I'm sorry, Charles, Beth was your sister after all, and I don't mean to be rude, but she didn't sound a well-balanced woman.'

'Far from it.'

'There you are then; when does an unbalanced person become seriously and mentally disturbed; don't you think it's a very thin red line?'

'Yes, I'm sure it is.'

'Most murderers, unless they are insane, would want to get rid of any evidence which would link them to the crime, not hide it away in their wardrobe and forget it was there. It just isn't rational behaviour.'

'I'd better go up and bring the bag down.'

'No, I'll go, Charles I'll go up and get it. There will be fingerprints, mine of course because I took it out of the travel bag, but yours won't be on it, so it's best you let me go through it.'

'But, Carla,' I said aghast, as the thought occurred to me, 'this means you'll be involved.'

'I am already, Charles, my dear,' she said firmly, 'I'm not going to sit back and watch you being wrongly accused of something you didn't do, also, I am related to the Henderson family, whether I like it or not.' leaning over and kissing me gently on the forehead.

I sat then for the few minutes she was away, my face turned up to the sun and my brandy remaining unfinished, and thought of my good fortune in meeting someone like her, someone who had the spontaneous capacity to care; a rare gift, and in many respects was not all that dissimilar to Sadie. Carla was a fascinating woman, I decided, hearing her footsteps crossing the hall.

'There was a label on the travel bag,' she said, placing the handbag in the centre of the table, 'I hadn't noticed it before and it has her name written on it, Charles.'

'That clinches it then.'

'I think it does;' she nodded, tipping out the contents, carefully touching only the edges of each item as she spread them out on the table, 'passport, wallet, two credit cards, some bank notes, cheque book, make-up purse and a bunch of keys, one of them a Yale and that's all.'

Although lunchtime, Detective Inspector McIntyre was in his office and listened without interrupting while I told him what we'd found and within fifteen minutes he was pulling up outside, alongside the builders' van. I had already walked round to the front as I had done the first time he'd been to the house and took him along to the studio. I introduced Carla to him, explaining she had been the daughter of the late-Sadie Northcot who used to live in Green Lane and I didn't miss the slightly perplexed expression as he looked at her. He must have noticed the way I was watching him, because he quickly explained.

'I thought for a moment, Miss Northcot, I had seen you before, but I was mistaken.'

'That's alright, Detective Inspector,' and as I looked at her, wondering whether he had spotted what was now becoming familiar to me; her teasing little smile, 'it would seem I have a double in this town; your reaction is not the first since I've been staying here these last couple of weeks.'

He didn't stay long, only five or ten minutes, enough time to place everything from the handbag into the plastic bags he'd brought with him. I thought he would have wanted to look at those other things upstairs, but he said he would leave that to forensic and that one of their officers would be along shortly to do a fingerprint check, adding we would have to give him ours. As he was leaving he asked us not to go back into the room until forensic had finished what they had to do, which suited me fine, coward that I was; I never wanted to see that bedroom again.

After he had gone, I made some fresh coffee and we went back outside on to the terrace to wait for the forensic officer to arrive. I think we had both exhausted the subject of how and why Natasha had been killed, agreeing there really was no more to say; it was in the hands of the police who were far better equipped to, hopefully, reach the right conclusions in their investigation.

'When will you be going back?' I asked her, realising it must be soon.

'My flight is booked for midday on Sunday.'

'From Turnhouse?'

'Yes, that's right; I hired the car when I arrived there, so I'll hand it in when I reach the airport. I wish I didn't have to go just yet, Charles,' she added, 'but I'm afraid I will have to.'

'I understand, Carla, of course I do.'

'When will they have completed the renovations?' she asked.

'They've estimated four weeks, but the interior also needs some serious attention, mostly painting, but that can start before the builders have finished, so all in all, I think it will be ready to be put on the market by the end of August.'

'You're determined to move, aren't you?' she smiled.

'More determined than ever now, Carla. I'll keep on the studio and gallery up to when I leave Calder Bay; fortunately nothing needs to be done in here, but I'm going to dispose of all the furniture in the main house, by auction or whatever, and spend the last few weeks either in "The Shipwreck" or "The Royal".'

'And you've decided on Edinburgh?'

'Definitely.'

Chapter Eleven

The report from Forensic was on David McIntyre's desk by three in the afternoon. It was concise, but informative in that prints on both bags matched those taken on several items of clothing belonging to Beth Grayson. The only other prints in the room, apart from hers, were Charles Grayson's, but these were only on the door handle.

'What do you make of it, Howard?'

'I wouldn't like to say it was conclusive evidence, sir, there's something missing.'

'I agree; not only is it that elusive motive, but how was she able to carry out the killing and how did she get hold of the two bags? That's perhaps what we should be asking ourselves.'

'I think we can safely assume by the packed travel bag, also the passport, that Natasha Paton was on her way somewhere.'

'And with someone.' Howard suggested.

'More than likely, given what we've learned so far about her, but we can't even assume that, at least for the present. According to Hilary Fisher, it had been her mother who'd told her that Natasha had left to meet up with friends in the South of France.'

'And the family never heard from her again?'

'Apparently not; from what she was saying, I think they thought she would turn up as it hadn't been the first time she'd gone away, sometimes for months at a time before getting in touch with them.'

'Therefore, they weren't unduly worried.'

'Hilary's grandmother was; she told Hilary she had tried to trace Natasha, but without any success; this was years later, at the time Hilary's mother died. I got the impression Hilary was holding something back, although I may have been mistaken and as she was visibly shaken at having to identify her aunt, I didn't press her. Incidentally, Howard, I'm seeing the last member of the Henderson family tomorrow morning.'

'Janice Henderson.'

'Yes; she may be able to throw a different perspective on what we've learned so far about the various people who were around here at that time. I have to admit what we have managed to glean is a bit of a jumble, but I'm sure we will be able to untangle it all.'

'Where do you think Charles Grayson's friend fits in, sir?'

'Perhaps only as far as being related to the Hendersons. I didn't mention it before but when I called to see Mrs Baird on Tuesday there was a framed photograph on the sideboard of the two Henderson girls, Aileen and Janice, taken on the steps outside "Carbisdale", she'd written their names below the photograph and although I haven't met either of them, I took the younger one to be Janice; Carla Northcot looks remarkably like her.'

'I wonder whether she realises.'

'It's possible, but Charles probably does; he would have been thirteen when she was born, too young probably to have been aware of the rumours circulating then, but he had been friendly with Jack Henderson who may have told him.'

'Charles Grayson is rather an enigma, isn't he?'

'I would say so.'

'He had been quick to recognise those things as Natasha Paton's.'

'Yes, he slipped up there, considering she still had to be formally identified.'

'Which goes to prove he did see the resemblance in the identikit.'

'He probably thought we would suspect him of being her killer.'

'He could be of course, Howard.'

'In spite of Beth Grayson's fingerprints?'

'There could be an explanation for her fingerprints being on those bags. It's only a theory, Howard, and not really a feasible one, but he could have murdered Natasha and put her things where he knew Beth would find them and she had, and to protect her brother, she'd stashed them out of sight, at the back of her wardrobe, once she had wiped away any traces of his fingerprints.'

'It would have given her an even stronger hold over him.' Howard suggested.

'It appears that influence was a strong one; she hadn't liked his friendship with Jack Henderson for instance, who else didn't she approve of, Howard? It was quite interesting to see when I was up there today that only a few weeks after her death, the builders are carrying out extensive renovations to the house.'

'Could have been a relief to him; she couldn't have been an easy person to live with.'

'I'm sure you're right; nobody knows what goes on behind closed doors, do they?'

'A truism, sir.'

'So, Howard, let's do a quick recap; who do we have?'

'In the way of suspects, you mean?'

'Well, we can start with them; Beth Grayson, and her brother, Jack Henderson and John, and someone else, as yet unknown.'

'We still come back to the bags and clothes with Beth Grayson's fingerprints, don't we?'

'I know we do. So far, we haven't considered Jack Henderson as a possible suspect, but perhaps it is time we did and, as for his son, although he was only seventeen at the time of the murder this doesn't exonerate him; he would have been physically strong enough and have the knowledge of the wash-house, possibly the necessary wiles to plant everything inside Beth Grayson's wardrobe, a woman he probably disliked and considered deserved to get the blame.'

'Do you think there could be any significance in Mrs Baird saying Beth Grayson had appeared distracted the last time she saw her?' Howard asked.

'I think we should try and find out the reason for that; I'm not happy about those two deaths, you know, Howard, both of them occurring within days of each other.'

'Sadie Northcot and Beth Grayson; we don't even know the cause of death in each case;' Howard commented, 'it won't take long to find those out, though.'

'That would be a start, Howard, and then there was Sadie Northcot herself; apart from her having an affair with Jack Henderson, we know precious little about her, who she may have been friendly with, for example.'

'Apparently, Beth Grayson wasn't one of them.'

'No, Mrs Baird was quite adamant about that, but the dislike Beth had for Sadie must go further than the old jealousy about Sadie's relationship with Jack Henderson. I feel that another meeting with Charles Grayson is imminent; while I'm in Kendal tomorrow, Howard, do you think you could go along and see him and if it's possible, have a word with Carla Northcot. We don't know how much longer she'll be staying in Calder Bay; presumably she is only here to attend to her mother's personal effects.'

'This case does seem to be expanding somewhat.' Howard remarked dryly.

'You're right; I don't know about you, Howard, but do you get the impression that practically everyone we've interviewed appear to be keeping something back; they may not be lying necessarily, but evading the truth. There's only two who can't do that of course.'

'Jack Henderson and Beth Grayson.'

'Potential suspects, yes, also we have another two who can't talk; namely Sadie Northcot and Bobby Henderson.'

'You did say the other day, sir, that there were too many deaths.'

'Touché.

*****

David left early the following morning, well before eight, wanting to reach the motorway before the bottleneck of holiday traffic joined the route to the coast. It was almost eleven when he left the M6 at the junction for Kendal with the River Kent following him for most of the way until he turned off for Hill Farm, the road becoming narrower as he approached the double gates, finally pulling up in the cobbled courtyard in front of the two-storey stone-built farmhouse. He recognised the woman standing in the open doorway from Mrs Baird's photograph and as he stepped out on to the cobbles she came down the steps to greet him, two black and white collies on either side of her, closely hugging her heels.

'Hello, there;' she called out, 'you must have left Calder Bay terribly early, Detective Inspector, and such a long journey.'

'I've known worse,' he said, shaking hands with her, 'this is a lovely part of the country, Mrs Craig.'

'It is, isn't it, but please call me Janice; everyone else does, even my children.' she smiled, and that was when her resemblance to Carla Northcot became more pronounced, remembering the way she had smiled at him the day before. The two women were of the same build and height, also their facial features were similar, but the strong likeness ended when it came to their personalities: the woman now walking in front of him back up the steps to the door had, he thought, a totally different disposition from the rather serious and quiet Carla Northcot who had struck him as a typical career woman, while Janice Craig was outgoing, a farmer's wife with a family; she was quite natural and didn't, like Carla, give the impression of weighing up each word before she spoke. She was taking him across the enormous hall, wood-panelled with a long highly-polished oval table in the centre with a vase of red and yellow roses, their sweet scent following them as they reached the kitchen.

David had been in several farmhouse kitchens and they had all looked the same; stereotyped, scrubbed wooden table, bench seats on either side, wooden dresser with hanging mugs, free-standing oven alongside an Aga and a double sink, but in this one, there wasn't an Aga in sight, no hanging mugs and no wooden dresser; instead, it was ultra-modern: fitted units, royal blue with a cherry red trim, gleaming chrome fitments, but the main feature was the end wall, with floor to ceiling sliding glass doors leading out on to wood-decking; in the distance, the rolling fells of the Lake District and in the forefront, lush green fields where cattle were grazing.

'We're a dairy farm;' she explained, 'until I came here, I had never seen so many cows!'

'You wouldn't have seen many in Calder Bay?'

'No,' she laughed, and as if remembering why he was here, her expression changing, 'Not a very happy place at the moment. Have you discovered who the woman was yet, Detective Inspector?'

'We have, but not until yesterday,' not looking forward to breaking the news to her, 'she's been identified as Natasha Paton.'

'Natasha!' a look of disbelief on her face, 'you don't mean Hilary's aunt?'

'I'm afraid so.'

'Oh, no! Poor Hilary. Does she know?'

'Yes, she was the one who identified her.'

'How dreadful that must have been for her, but of course, I don't suppose there was anyone else. Was she terribly upset?'

'She was upset, although she had her husband with her.'

'Thank goodness for that. Shall we have some coffee, Detective Inspector, or perhaps you'd prefer a beer after your drive?'

'As much as I would like one, I had better not, coffee will be fine.'

While she busied herself he walked out on to the decking, considering it best to give her time to absorb what he'd just told her, rather than wade in with the questions he planned to ask. It was peaceful standing there, even the air felt cleaner, fresher than it did at home, reminding him he hadn't had a break for too long and now with this case on their hands, it seemed unlikely he was going to be able to get away for some weeks yet.

'We can have our coffee out here if you like.' she said, coming to stand beside him. I love it out here.' she added, looking across the fells towards the horizon.

'Pity we couldn't bottle it up.'

'I know,' she smiled gently, 'but if we did there would be nothing left.'

She poured out the coffee and they sat down opposite to each other at the wrought-iron table.

'Detective Inspector,' she said slowly, 'I've been thinking about what you've told me and I've been trying to fathom out how anyone could be so evil to do what they did to Natasha; all we know is that this happened a number of years ago, which of course it must have done because she only came to Calder Bay once and that was the first summer Hilary and her parents moved into the house across the road from "Carbisdale" and I'm trying to remember what year it must have been.'

'We've been able to narrow it down considerably since we started our investigation, mainly thanks to your friend.'

'Hilary remembered? Mind you,' she went on, 'she always did have a marvellous memory, so when was it?'

'In July 1975 and apparently Natasha told Hilary's parents she was going to the South of France to stay with friends, this was on Thursday, the tenth; the day before Calder Bay's fancy dress parade and I understand it is always held on the tenth each year.'

'She's quite right, I remember Hilary telling me on the morning of the parade, this was when we were making our costume, and she was quite upset at Natasha for not telling her she was going. Even when we actually won first prize, I knew she was still thinking about her.'

'You mentioned costume in the singular.' genuinely interested to know what it must have been.

'Oh, sorry,' smiling, presumably as she remembered, 'it was quite ingenious actually; I think it had been Bobby's idea for us to enter as the Loch Ness Monster and got Hilary and me to stitch the travelling rugs together which everyone, except Aileen and John of course, crawled under and made our way along the High Street down to the bay and all people would be able to see of us were our feet.'

'Travelling rugs.' David murmured; was this what he'd been looking for, the missing link.

'Yes, that's right. Mrs Baird wasn't too happy about us taking them out of the house, far less stitching them together and even then we found we were one short; she had been absolutely sure we had five, but there were only three in the linen cupboard, so we had to make do.'

'A bit of a tight squeeze.' he commented.

'It was, and terribly hot.'

'Have you been back to Calder Bay, Janice?'

'Not for a long time; when the children were young we hardly went anywhere and naturally there's the farm making it difficult for Sam to get away; probably feeble excuses, but after my father and Bobby died, although Aileen and Dougie are still there, I just didn't have the heart somehow and now, Detective Inspector,' she went on quietly, her expression sad, 'with this terrible discovery, Calder Bay is spoilt for me, also I simply couldn't bear seeing where "Carbisdale" used to be.'

'Hilary was there last weekend; she told me yesterday it had been a spur of the moment decision.' going on to explain how she had seen the painting Charles Grayson had done of her mother.

'She really was a beautiful woman, you know; I hope Charles did her justice.'

'I understand the Graysons had been your neighbours for years; how well did you know them?'

'I suppose I knew Charles fairly well; he was very friendly with my father and as far as his sister is concerned, I don't think anyone knew her.'

'I'm told she was something of a recluse.'

'That's one way of describing her; she's a very strange woman, Detective Inspector, very strange. When we were young, we found her quite frightening, we'd convinced ourselves she was a witch. She used to ride a motorbike and I remember Bobby saying it should have been a broomstick! Aileen certainly had a lucky escape there.'

'In what way?'

'Because she was once engaged to Charles, this would have been about twenty years ago, I think, but when she realised that Beth would be living with them, she knew it would be a disaster. The woman disliked anyone he was friendly with, utterly possessive, and would have made Aileen's life hell if she had married him, so she called it off.'

'You may or may not be interested to hear that Beth Grayson died fairly recently.'

'Did she really; well, I honestly thought she was indestructible. She couldn't have been all that old; still in her sixties. So,' she went on, 'Charles will be free, although I could never understand why he didn't leave home years ago. How he can live in that awful house, I do not know; it's a miracle it's still standing.'

'I've spoken to a number of people who were living in and around Green Lane at the time we've been talking about, including Mrs Baird.'

'She worked as our housekeeper for a long time, even before my mother died; I often think about her, she was such a hard worker, nothing was ever too much trouble.'

'She was telling me that Beth Grayson had kept in touch with her.'

'I'd forgotten they knew each other; I don't think you would have described them as being friends exactly, but Mrs Baird was a kind soul and I never knew her to criticise anyone; I expect she merely accepted Beth Grayson the way she was. I remember being surprised to see her in our kitchen one afternoon having a cup of tea with Mrs Baird, but as soon as she saw me, she completely clammed up and just sat there glaring at me as though I had no right to be in my own kitchen.'

'Perhaps Mrs Baird felt sorry for her.'

'She probably did, but I think in Beth Grayson's case it was undeserved. I apologise if I sound so uncharitable towards her, but I didn't like the woman. She was terribly mischievous, you know.'

'How?'

'Difficult to explain, but she could be quite vindictive if she thought anyone had annoyed her; Bobby often caught the brunt of her wrath. It wasn't as though she ever said anything to him; she was far more subtle than that, she would go behind his back, set little traps for him. For instance, Bobby and his friend, Callum, had started breaking into the Grayson's back garden, out of pure devilment I expect, but she spotted them once and complained to my father.'

'Not very courageous of her.' David commented mildly; what she was saying was helping to broaden Beth Grayson's character.

'It wasn't, but then she was like that; however, in that instance, it back-fired on her, not that she would have known anyway. You see, in my father's eyes, Bobby could do no wrong, so apart from telling him to stop going in there, nothing more was said. Of course Mrs Baird wouldn't have heard about this and I rather doubt whether Beth Grayson would have told her; she wasn't the confiding type. I expect you know that Mrs Baird's daughter is married to my older brother?' she added.

'Yes, I met them both this week.'

'You visited them?'

'I would have done, but they drove up to Calder Bay instead.'

'Now that does surprise me; he did leave under rather a cloud after the collapse of the business as far as many people in the town were concerned, but then John always was pretty thick-skinned.'

***

Howard left a message on Charles Grayson's answering machine when, after a couple of attempts to call him had failed. They didn't know where Carla Northcot was staying while she was in Calder Bay, but on the off chance she may be at her mother's house, he decided to walk along there and find out. As David had said yesterday, Charles Grayson's property was in the midst of what appeared to be extensive renovations and, now that all the ivy had been removed, already showing signs of improvement. The only vehicles parked outside belonged to the builders which could mean he was out. Across the road and further along was Sadie Northcot's house and, opening the gate, he walked up the short path to the front door and rang the bell. It's strange he thought how an unoccupied house always gave the impression of being empty; even the bell resounding in the hall had a hollow sound, but to make sure, he walked round to the back garden; an attractive patio facing a long stretch of grass which so soon after she'd died was looking neglected and in need of cutting.

'Excuse me,' the voice calling out to him from the other side of the hedge which separated the house from the one the Robertsons used to live in, 'but I don't think Miss Northcot will be coming back.'

'Has she left Calder Bay?' Howard asked, walking over towards the woman.

'She told me yesterday she would be going back to London tomorrow as she's done all she can in the house and I understand it's now on the market.'

'I was hoping to see her before she left; do you happen to know where I can find her?'

'Well, she's been staying at "The Royal".' she was quick to tell him, 'It was very sad about her mother, wasn't it; we haven't been living here very long, but I was just beginning to get to know the lady; she was such a nice person and quite a character. We had no idea she was ill, she always looked so well.'

'I didn't realise she had been ill.' Howard remarked.

'Perhaps she hadn't been, we weren't really sure and I haven't liked to ask Miss Northcot, but I was only talking to her the day before she died, so I must admit it was a shock when we heard.'

'Who found her?'

'Her cleaning lady, actually,' she answered, 'but I've no idea when she died, but it must have been in the early hours of the morning because she had quite a few telephone calls that evening, so she must have been alright then. I was in the garden and her lounge window was open; that's how I know.' she added as if expecting him to ask her.

He managed to extricate himself without offending her; she had given every impression she would have been happy to have stood there chatting indefinitely; obviously bored with her own company, he decided, but what she had just told him was interesting and could be worth following up on, retracing his steps back down Green Lane towards the High Street.

The girl on reception at "The Royal" told him that Miss Northcot was in the coffee lounge. There was only one person in there, a woman sitting on her own by the open French window, a cup of coffee on the table in front of her. Mid-forties, Howard reckoned, and for a second as he stood in the open doorway, she reminded him of Janice Henderson as he remembered her from school. Her hair was similar; thick and blonde, and the high brow and the upright way she was sitting. It was uncanny, wondering what Janice would look like now. She must have sensed him looking at her, because she looked across, a questioning expression on her face and a hint of a smile hovering on her lips, as though she found his interest amusing.

'Sorry to stare,' Howard apologised, 'but you reminded me of someone I used to know.'

'Oh, dear,' the smile widening, 'this is becoming repetitive; now I know what it must be like for celebrities being constantly recognised.'

'I'd better introduce myself, then,' he said, showing her his warrant card.

'Inspector Howard Crawford,' she read out, 'and were you looking for me?'

'If you are Miss Carla Northcot, yes.'

'I'm Carla Northcot; what must you be thinking of me, Inspector, but you see you're the third person in this town who has told me I reminded them of someone else.'

'They say everyone has a double.'

'So they say; won't you sit down and tell me why you wanted to see me.'

Here's a woman, he thought, used to making decisions, trying to guess what profession she was in, but no doubt he was about to find out.

'I understand you have already met my superior, Detective Inspector McIntyre?'

'Yes, I have.'

'He would have presumably told you that we are conducting the investigation into the murder of a woman who was called Natasha Paton.'

'That's right and that it occurred twenty-eight years ago. How do you think anything I say will be of help to you, Inspector?'

'I'll explain; as you've just said, this murder happened twenty-eight years ago when you and I, including a number of people we've talked to during this past week, would have been teenagers. What we are trying to do is to try and establish Natasha Paton's movements during those days leading up to her death; where she had been in the habit of going and any friends she may have made and in particular whether anyone had seen her on the night she was killed.'

'This would have been in 1975.'

'Yes, the beginning of July.'

'I would have been eighteen on the first of September and I wasn't in Calder Bay at all that year, so I'm not going to be much help; that was my last year at school and I spent the holidays as I always did with my relations in Taunton.'

'A long way from Calder Bay.'

'I know; I'd been a boarder at Cheltenham Ladies College from a very young age. It was my mother's old school and she used to travel down to Taunton at the end of each term to be with me.'

'Your mother was English?'

'Yes; I'm rather a mixture as a matter of fact,' she smiled, 'an English mother and a Scottish father and an Italian grandmother.'

'And yet, Northcot is, I believe, an English surname.'

'I rather think you know who my father was, Inspector Crawford,' looking at him, her head tilted slightly to one side, an inscrutable expression on her face.

'We don't make guesses, Miss Northcot; we work with hard proven facts, but we have it on what we believe is from a reliable source that your mother had a child by the late-Jack Henderson and that she was called Carla.'

'I won't argue with that, 'but I will say it wasn't until very recently when I read the letter my mother had left me to say Jack Henderson had been my father; up to that time I had always believed Sadie's husband, Ernest Northcot, was my father.'

'I appreciate you telling me this; it must have been quite a shock to you.'

'At the time it was.' shrugging dismissively, although making it plain she was reluctant to discuss it any further.

'Before I came in here,' Howard said, 'I called at your mother's house to see if you were there; it was your neighbour who told me where you were staying.'

'Oh, I see; I did wonder how you knew where to find me.'

'She mentioned something to me which I feel may have some relevance to our investigation, but first I would like to explain why we should be thinking along these lines.'

'Yes?'

'At first, it appeared this was going to be a straightforward murder case, but a number of anomalies have occurred which are, quite frankly, disturbing in that a number of people who were living in Calder Bay at the time of the murder have since died and while we appreciate that twenty-eight years is a relatively long period of time and it would be natural for some people to have died during that period, it is the times of these deaths which appear to be somewhat out of the ordinary.'

'How many people are we talking about here, Inspector?'

'As far as we know, there are five: two members of the Henderson family, their gardener, although apparently he was an old man indicating there is nothing suspicious about his dying, and two others.'

'You're including Sadie?'

'Yes, we are.'

'Before you tell me what her neighbour has said, why are you questioning the other three deaths?'

'The first two;' he started to explain, 'Jack Henderson and his son Bobby, although Bobby's death occurred first as a result of a motor bike accident ten years ago, his father dying within hours of hearing the news, the verdict being he had a heart attack. The third person is Charles Grayson's sister, who died two days after your mother.'

'This all sounds rather incredible.' she remarked coolly, but with no noticeable change in her expression.

'I agree it does, and it may transpire on further investigation that we have no grounds for suspecting anything untoward, but it does need to be checked out.'

'Alright, I understand. Are you saying that Sadie's death wasn't a natural one, Inspector?'

'I'm not saying that, but this is where you could provide us with a couple of answers. As you are aware, Miss Northcot, your mother's death certificate states that the cause of death was due to heart failure.'

'It does, yes.'

'Did you know she had a weak heart?'

'I had no idea, but then she wouldn't have told me anyway.'

'So you wouldn't know whether she was taking any form of medication.'

'I didn't, but I've just realised,' pausing for a second, her eyes thoughtful, 'I found a doctor's prescription in her wallet; it was such a scribble and I couldn't decipher it and naturally it is in medical terminology; I still have it, but all I could make out was the date and that it was for a six months' renewal period and would have expired at the end of October this year.'

'It would have been still current at the time of her death,' Howard remarked, 'and was there any medication in the house?'

'No, there wasn't; I did look, but couldn't find any.'

'If you would let me have the prescription, I'd be grateful; we will then be able to contact her doctor.'

'She may, I suppose have been on the point of renewing the prescription, but somehow I don't think so.'

'Why do you say that?'

'Because,' this time her smile was sad, 'Sadie was a meticulous person; if she was on medication she wouldn't have run herself short, she would have made sure she overlapped with the renewal times. Also' she added, 'having gone to her doctor in the first place, she would have continued with the dosages, otherwise why bother going to him?'

'I'm sure that will quickly be sorted out.' he assured her, 'According to your neighbour, your mother took quite a few telephone calls that evening.'

'How the heck did she know?'

'You may well ask;' his turn to smile; mainly at the look of astonishment in her expression, 'because she was in the garden and your mother's lounge window had been open.'

'Oh, I see, and you think there is some relevance to these calls?'

'There could be, but again, as with the doctor's prescription, not difficult to check. Which phone would she have been using?' he asked.

'She didn't have a mobile; therefore it would have been the land phone.'

'That's fine; we'll get in touch with British Telecom if you'd like to give me the number.'

'Of course, I know it off by heart; I'll jot it down for you.'

'Thank you; I hope what I've been saying hasn't added to your distress over losing your mother.'

'Surprisingly, it hasn't; perhaps I've become immune from unpleasant shocks, but I will want to know anything you may find out, Inspector, so I'll give you my card.'

***

'Forensic have confirmed, Mr Grayson, that apart from your prints on the door handle of your sister's bedroom, all the others matched hers.'

'I didn't expect otherwise.' he commented dryly, his expression unreadable, although Howard was getting the distinct impression that Charles Grayson was on the defensive. He had greeted him cordially enough, but Howard couldn't help noticing the guarded expression on his face as though he was bracing himself. For what? Could it be that he realised now he had slipped up the day before and was waiting to be asked how he had known the dead woman had been Natasha Paton? Perhaps.

They were in the studio and as David McIntyre had described it to him, he had known what to expect, although the difference between Charles Grayson's working area and the grim interior of the main house was quite staggering. In comparison, it would seem no money had been spared in the decorating and furnishings in here and the stylish terrace, the latter bathed in brilliant sunshine.

'When you were shown the identikit of the victim by Detective Inspector McIntyre, you said you were unable to recognise her as anyone you had seen in Calder Bay around the time Natasha Paton had been murdered.'

'That's right, Inspector; to me she looked like many other young women, not to anyone in particular.'

'And yet, you were able to identify those items from Miss Grayson's wardrobe as belonging to the dead woman.'

'Well, yes; her passport had been in the handbag.'

'And you put two and two together?'

'You could say that.'

'A good guess, Mr Grayson; the body was formally identified yesterday, possibly at the same time as those items were discovered.'

'It was, wasn't it?'

'I believe you knew before you looked inside the bag,' watching him closely, 'possibly you recognised the clothes, or one of the bags.'

'Alright, Inspector, in some respects you're right; it was the handbag I thought I recognised, but it wasn't until I read the name in the passport I knew for sure.'

'Because you had known Natasha Paton.'

'For a short time during that summer she was here on holiday.'

'How well did you know her?'

'Not very well; I only saw her a few times before she left.'

'But well enough for you to paint her.' Howard could have imagined the infinitesimal intake of breath, but he didn't think so; he was probably wondering where that piece of information came from.

'I'm a professional artist, Inspector Crawford;' he answered giving him a withering look, 'I have painted a number of women during my career and there has never been any need for me to get to know them; it's the human form, the beauty, or the non-beauty, of each sitter which interests and inspires me; Natasha Paton was no different from any of my other subjects.'

'Had you finished the painting before she left Calder Bay, Mr Grayson?' ignoring what he considered to be contrived indignation.

'Almost, but I had sufficient on the canvas to enable me to add the final touches.'

'Did she give you any reason why she was going?'

'No, she didn't, but I wasn't unduly concerned; as I've said, I'd almost finished the painting and that was only what mattered to me.'

'I see,' Howard said, 'and your sister, Miss Grayson, did she ever meet her?'

'Not as far as I know, and I rather doubt it; Beth kept herself very much to herself and very seldom ventured into the studio, especially when she knew I was working.'

'And yet, 'Howard persisted, 'Natasha Paton's belongings have, presumably, been at the back of your sister's wardrobe for the last twenty-eight years.'

'You say *presumably*,' he emphasised, showing the first signs of irritation, 'you don't think I put them in there, do you?'

'Someone put them in there, Mr Grayson; I realise that the evidence provided by Forensic indicates those prints were hers, which of course they were, but we cannot rule out the possibility of any original prints being wiped off.'

'Do you know, Inspector Crawford, I find what you are suggesting to be quite unacceptable; the implication I'm reading into it is that you suspect that I was responsible.'

'You believe your sister murdered Natasha Paton?' side-stepping any comment.

'I honestly don't know what to believe; why on earth should Beth do such a thing, it doesn't make sense.'

'One can always come up with a possible theory; a reason why anyone should feel so intensely, so strongly, to go to such lengths as to dispose of another human being.'

'Well, in Beth's case, I can't.'

'I realise she died quite recently,' Howard said, 'and is unable to defend herself, therefore in a situation such as this, we have to do our utmost to work out what must have happened and why.'

'Dead men can't talk, Inspector, or I should say in Beth's case, dead women can't talk.'

'That's true. We understand from the death certificate that Miss Grayson died as a result of a heart attack.'

'She did, yes.'

'But it would appear it wasn't as straightforward.'

'What do you mean?'

'She didn't die here, in her own home, but she was found unconscious on the beach and taken to hospital where she suffered the final heart attack.'

'I know that, but what is so mysterious, Inspector? Beth had a heart attack and died and that was that.'

'Because of the unusual circumstances of where she was found, an autopsy had to be carried out; it was discovered there was a considerable amount of sea water in her lungs, not sufficient to kill her.'

'I know; Beth was a strong swimmer.'

'The time of death, according to the coroner's report, was at nine-thirty at night, Mr Grayson.'

'I honestly don't see the point of bringing all this up, I really don't. My sister was a strange woman; in recent years she had become something of a recluse, seldom going out during the day, but she enjoyed swimming and was quite impervious to the cold and had taken to having a swim in the evenings. The doctor thought she may have had cramp, but had had sufficient strength to swim back to the shore, and then the shock of it all had been too much for her.'

'This only happened a couple of weeks ago; can you remember whether she seemed depressed around this time?'

'I was actually asked the same question, you know, by your Chief Inspector and the answer is the same; she was no different than she was normally.'

Chapter Twelve

CHARLES & CARLA

To save time in the morning, I packed my travel bag before going down to the bar to meet Charles. I wasn't sorry to be leaving; I was starting to feel uncomfortable here and couldn't help wondering who the next person would be to think I was a member of the Henderson family, although I suppose technically that was true; I certainly didn't feel any familial ties and the undisputed fact that my biological father had chosen to ignore my existence, perhaps unfairly, didn't exactly endear me to any of them. When I'd said to the Inspector it had been a shock to learn about my true parentage I had been exaggerating, when what I had felt was deep hurt and disillusionment in losing the person I had believed for forty-five years to be my father, even to the extent of having his name, although any memories I may have had of him were hazy. What kind of man had Jack Henderson been anyway? Charles appeared to have liked him; they had met regularly, played chess together, therefore, they could be described as friends with a common interest, but it would seem their friendship didn't extend to Jack Henderson confiding in him, the way Sadie had done. It's a pity; I thought uncharitably, her confiding hadn't extended to her daughter. Yes, I decided, snapping shut my bag, it is time to leave Calder Bay; all this uncharacteristic introspection was not good.

Charles was already in the lounge bar when I went in; sitting at the same table we'd had the last time.

'Hello,' he smiled, pulling out a chair for me, 'you look lovely; lilac silk and lace, the colour suits you, Carla.'

'Thank you; it's one of my old favourites; I'm a hoarder, Charles,' I admitted, 'and find it extremely difficult to throw clothes away, even when they become out of date as this dress has.' realising that the one I had chosen to wear this evening must be at least fifteen years old; I'd bought it in a little French boutique in the King's Road and thought then it was very Parisian.

'What would you like to drink, Carla?'

'I'd love a campari and soda; is that what you're having?' looking at his glass.

'Yes, I thought it would make a change from my usual lager.'

'What sort of day have you had?'

'It started off well; I spent an hour working, but because of the noise the builders were making, plus the incessant clanging from the JCB next door, I decided to take a couple of hours off and drove along the bay as far as Montrose, had a coffee in the town before coming back, only to find a message on the answering machine from an Inspector Crawford saying he wanted to see me.'

'About those clothes?'

'Partly; he wanted to know how it was I had recognised them as belonging to the dead woman when her body had only been formally identified yesterday morning. Police officers must be born with suspicious minds, because he didn't appear particularly convinced when I told him, reluctantly mind you, that I recognised the handbag as being the one I had seen Natasha using.'

'Why do you think he didn't believe you?' Indignant on his behalf.

'Because he's probably thinking I murdered her, that's why; suggesting that it may not have been Beth who put those things in the wardrobe. He also appeared sceptical when I told him I hadn't known Natasha very well, saying I had known her well enough to have painted her.'

'How on earth did he find that out?'

'I don't know, Carla; that's been puzzling me.'

'Could he have seen the painting, do you think?'

'It's unlikely; it was exhibited in the Glasgow Art Gallery, but not for long as it was quite quickly sold. I have a record of the purchaser, but as far as I can remember he was a private collector, from London, I think.'

'It doesn't really matter though, does it, Charles?'

'I suppose not,' he agreed, 'and now it looks as though they are viewing Beth's death as suspicious -'

'- but you said she had died of a heart attack, so where are they coming from?' I interrupted, confused; recalling what the Inspector had said about Sadie. Is this the way they worked, by tossing conflicting ideas and possibilities in the air, rather like the infinity juggler, in the hope they won't all tumble down meaninglessly?

'She did, but apparently it's the circumstances leading up to that which they find unexplainable.'

'In what way?'

'You see, Beth had been having a swim that evening; not for her behaving as everyone else. She didn't walk along to the bay during the day, find a sheltered sand dune and take a swim when the water was warm; instead, she used to wait until much later when she knew the beach would be deserted. She was a loner, Carla, basically anti-social and was likely considered to be more or less a recluse by many people in the town. However, as I was saying, she'd been swimming and was found lying unconscious by the edge of the water. A couple of lads who had been fishing on the rocks further along spotted her and rang for an ambulance. She partially regained consciousness, but later that night suffered a heart attack which proved fatal.'

'And the police are thinking there's something suspicious about that?'

'It would seem so. Also, because of the nature of the death there had to be a post mortem of course and the pathologist's report stated she may have had cramp as there was a considerable amount of water in her lungs, so she must have gone under at some stage, but had managed to make it back to the shore, probably because she was a strong swimmer.'

'It all sounds quite feasible to me, Charles. A tragic accident; poor woman, to die like that and on her own.'

'Knowing Beth, I don't believe she would have wanted it any other way.'

'Tough woman.'

'She was tough alright; it was just her nature I suppose.'

'I haven't told you yet,' I said, 'but this morning when I was in the coffee lounge Inspector Crawford came in.'

'Especially to see you?'

'Yes, but not about yesterday; he wanted to ask questions about Sadie's death.'

'Sadie's death? What bee have they got in their bonnet now?'

'You may well ask,' unable to stop smiling at his expression of outraged surprise, 'but they are looking into at least four other deaths which they're considering may not have been natural, Sadie's been one of them, your sister's another which ties in with what you've just been telling me; the third being Jack Henderson and the fourth, Bobby.'

'This is beginning to sound too incredible for words, Carla. What do you think?'

'Quite frankly, Charles, I don't know what to think, but it transpires as far as Sadie's death is concerned they may have hit on something which is, well, odd to say the least.' and going on to tell him about the prescription I had found in the house and the absence of any medication, also the phone calls she had apparently taken on the evening she died.

'Who in this world would want to harm Sadie?'

'Again, it's another I don't know.'

'There's far too many of them.' managing a smile.

'No doubt they will sort everything out; I know this is a trite remark, Charles, but that is what they're paid for.'

'Inspector Howard Crawford certainly had a busy morning.' he said dryly.

'That's what I was thinking. Incidentally, he was another person to look at me as if he'd seen me before.'

'I expect you'll be glad to leave Calder Bay.'

'Before I become totally paranoid?'

'I would say you were the least person to become paranoid.' he said, smiling broadly.

***

Carla did look lovely; she wore little make-up, her peaches and cream complexion had a natural glow and her hair, light brown with blonde highlights and cut quite short, framed a heart-shaped face. I was going to miss her. She was comfortable to be with and while I recognised her strength of character, I also detected a softer, warmer side to her and one I didn't think she would readily reveal. I was trying not to put too much hope in us furthering our friendship, fearing that once she was back in her own habitat she would become immersed in her work, presumably answerable to the various demands made upon both her time and energies. She was twelve or thirteen years younger than me; a wide gap which may prove to be too much for her to handle.

'You're looking very thoughtful, Charles; you're not worrying about all this business, are you?'

'Not worrying exactly, just finding it disturbing I suppose and I can't help wondering what else is going to turn up.'

'I know what you mean, but whatever it is, it can't affect us anymore than it has done; within a matter of hours we've learned that both my mother's death and your sister's may not have been from natural causes and if it turns out that the police are right, we will just have to live with that.'

'You're right of course; let them get on with it.'

'As the song goes, Charles;' she sang softly, *'whatever will be, will be; que sera, sera!'*

'A truism.' smiling in delight and wishing the evening would last forever, 'Shall we have another drink before going into the restaurant?'I asked.

'Yes, please.'

I was bringing our drinks over to the table when I happened to glance out of the window, the one facing the car park, and saw Aileen driving in; reckoning she would likely use the side door into the bar and would be bound to see me. It wasn't as if I was hoping to avoid her, but I was thinking of Carla, of how she would react at meeting her.

'I hope you're ready for this,' I said, putting the drinks down, 'but I've just seen Aileen Henderson outside?'

'Really; don't look so worried, Charles. I don't mind, a pity it wasn't Janice and then I could judge for myself whether I look like her.'

I hadn't seen Aileen for years, but she didn't look much different from when she had been in her teens; as elegant as ever, but comparing her with Carla, I realised how contrived this elegance was, how everything she was wearing was neatly colour-co-ordinated: ankle-length navy dress; white bolero-style jacket, navy and white shoulder bag and navy and white court shoes. Hard to believe, I thought, looking across to where she was standing in the open doorway and looking round the bar, that we had once been engaged; twenty years ago and she had been the one to break off the engagement, her reasons, which at the time I had found bewildering, now almost forgotten. I would like to think that if we had gone through with the marriage and she had found Beth's presence unacceptable, I would have had the strength of character to oppose Beth and to suggest we lived elsewhere than in Green Lane, but that's something I can't answer, not that it mattered. Aileen and I are ancient history.

She had seen me and from where Carla and I were, I couldn't make out whether this pleased her or not, but nevertheless, she was coming over.

'Hello, Charles;' she said, 'how are you?'

'I'm fine, thanks;' polite, cordial and lacking any real warmth, 'Aileen, let me introduce Carla Northcot to you. Carla,' I went on, turning to look at her, 'Aileen Henderson.' and watching as the two women shook hands.

'Carla Northcot,' Aileen repeated, but if she had noticed the strong family resemblance she made no sign; there was no change in her expression; the smile, socially polite, remained in place, but her eyes, as though transfixed, remained on Carla; her face, hair, figure and clothes as though she was systematically cataloguing everything she could about her. 'I've been waiting to meet you for a long time.'

'Have you?'

'Would you like a drink, Aileen?' I asked, more to break the tension, not emanating from Carla whose manner hadn't altered, but from Aileen; there was a heightening of colour in her normally pale cheeks which he remembered seeing before, years ago; it was an indication she felt compromised in some way, that Carla wasn't as she expected perhaps.

There was no doubt in my mind that Aileen was fully aware of Carla's background, how, is anyone's guess; it could have been she had heard the rumours which had been circulating around the time when Sadie had first arrived in Calder Bay.

'I'd like a gin and tonic please, Charles.'

As I moved away from the table Aileen was asking Carla how much longer she intended to stay in Calder Bay, but I didn't catch Carla's reply, although I didn't particularly like the note of acerbity in Aileen's voice, recalling how at times she could adopt an autocratic manner when she wanted to display her superiority; however, when I returned with her drink they were talking about, of all people, Sadie.

'I hadn't realised you knew Carla's mother.' I said.

'Why should you have known, Charles; I knew Sadie very well and had done for years.'

And indeed, I thought, quenching an unreasonable feeling of resentment. Resentment? Why on earth should I be reacting in such a negative way? Could I be resentful Sadie hadn't told me of her friendship with Aileen? There was no reason why she should have done; our relationship, purely platonic, had been based on mutual respect and while not necessarily a meeting of minds, we had discovered we held similar views, in particular, our interest in the arts. She told me once she had done a bit of acting; her word, but I found out quite by chance from an old stage magazine that she had taken the lead role in Noel Coward's 'Blythe Spirit', not in the West End, but in the provinces. She had been a self-effacing woman and I had admired her a great deal. She had secrets, of course she had, but unless they are paragons of virtue, who doesn't have slices of their lives they prefer to keep to themselves? Why should she have been any different? And now, focusing on what Aileen was saying, I didn't know what to think. There was an undercurrent here which I was finding slightly disturbing.

'You probably knew her better than I did, Aileen;' Carla said lightly, 'spending years away at school and then later at University meant we saw little of each other.'

'At least your mother was alive during those years; I was only nine when mine died, but then, my father was always around.' she added, quite unnecessarily I thought.

'You were lucky.' Carla said quietly.

'Yes, I was, wasn't I; I can't imagine what it must be like not to have had a father.'

I was fully expecting Carla to come back with something, anything to put an end to whatever it was Aileen was trying to instigate, because that's what it seemed like, but she didn't. Instead, she turned her head away from her and looked at me.

'Did you know Hilary Robertson was here last weekend, Charles?' Aileen asked, breaking the silence.

'Don't you mean this weekend?' puzzled, when I knew she had been in Calder Bay yesterday, presumably at the request of the police.

'No, I don't; she actually arrived on the same day they found that woman's body which as probably everybody in Calder Bay knows was last Saturday. Also, I had a drink with her on Monday evening before she left.'

'She must have had two trips then.' I said, for a moment having completely forgotten about seeing Hilary in the churchyard, going on to tell her that Hilary had identified the body.

'Well, perhaps now that the policed know who the woman was, they'll be able to solve the case and the quicker the better as far as I'm concerned. This is all very bad for our family; as if things weren't grim enough, thanks to John's ineptitude in ruining the business.'

'I'm sure they will, Aileen.'

'They are certainly questioning an extraordinary amount of people; even our old housekeeper. Imagine,' raising her eyebrows, 'how could she possibly help them! Also,' she went on, 'I had a call from Janice this afternoon to tell me that Inspector Detective McIntyre had actually driven all the way to the Lake District to interview her! All I can say is, they appear to be working in a most haphazard way.'

Fortunately, she had finished her drink by this time and said she had to go.

'Thanks for the G & T, Charles;' she said, followed by another long appraising look at Carla before standing up, 'nice to have met you at last, Carla.'

'Phew!' Carla breathed, as soon as she had gone.

'Exactly.'

'What's bugging her?'

'Loss of face, I would say; she's always been very concerned about her social status and the fall of the family's fortunes has probably hit her quite hard and, of course, with this latest business, no doubt she thinks it's drawing attention back to them all. I haven't mentioned this before, Carla, but Aileen and I were once engaged.'

'Really?' her eyes widening in surprise.

'This was twenty years ago, but she decided not to go through with it because of her strong dislike for Beth.'

'Poor excuse.'

'I never thought of it like that before, but you could be right. Anyway, it's all in the past and long forgotten.'

'Judging by what she's like now, I would say you had a lucky escape!'

'I couldn't agree more.' I chuckled.

'All those *double entendres*, Charles; I was left wondering when she said she had been waiting to see me whether Sadie had told her of having a daughter, or it had been her way of implying that she knew about Jack Henderson being my father. And, then the rather biting comment about being lucky to have had a father.'

'You kept your cool though.'

'I didn't see the point in being any other way, Charles. You'll be surprised to hear that I had seen her before; years ago, but I'm fairly sure it was her.'

'Where was this?'

'At school; I think I told you I went to Cheltenham Ladies College –'

'– Aileen did go there; I remember her telling me.'

'She had been in the year above me and,' smiling, 'she had been the prefect.'

'Not head girl then?'

'No, she was likely pipped at the post.'

'She wouldn't have liked that,' I commented dryly, 'but from what you've just said, there's every chance she would have known who you were, also –'

'– my resemblance to Janice.'

'That's what I was thinking and I've also been wondering about the friendship with Sadie; that rather surprised me.'

'Perhaps she wanted to know what sort of woman her father had been attracted to.'

'You could be right. Now we've worked that out, shall we go into the restaurant?'

'And talk about something other than the Hendersons.'

'Any suggestions?'

'Yes, I have actually,' looking at me over the rim of her raised glass, 'when we're going to see each other again.'

Chapter Thirteen

CALLUM & DOUGIE

I had not seen or heard from Callum for years, therefore was surprised to get a call from him on Sunday morning. It was almost as if the discovery of the woman's body at "Carbisdale", which had now been officially identified as Hilary's aunt, was acting as some sort of catalyst in bringing those people who had known each other all those years ago to the forefront to what could be described as the scene of the crime. First, I'd heard that John and Karen had been here, although they hadn't been in touch with me, which I suppose wasn't all that surprising, then Aileen telling me Hilary had actually been in Calder Bay on the weekend when the body was found and now, Callum, who'd been working in London for almost ten years, had come back to live here and had sounded keen to renew our old friendship. I have to admit I wasn't all that keen to see him again, nothing I could put my finger on, but I'd always found him pretty heavy-going, intense and taking everything so seriously; not so much when we were all young, but later, after we'd left University. Perhaps the truth is, I was always a bit jealous of him; when he was around, which seemed to be all the time, Bobby would ignore me, those two years between us seeming much more. There were times when I was sure neither he nor Callum even noticed I was with them.

We'd arranged to meet for a drink in "The Shipwreck" and, instead of taking the car, I walked down to the town; mainly for the exercise, but I wanted to spend these few minutes before I saw him again, to think back to when we were kids, in particular to that time when the three of us were more or less caught spying on Charles Grayson, and wondering whether the police had been in touch with Callum. More than likely, I decided, by now in the High Street and about to cross the road to "The Shipwreck".

I saw Callum before he noticed me, catching his reflection in the mirror behind the bar. He looked older than thirty-nine, as if those years during the time he'd been away had taken their toll, realising with a jolt, it had taken me a few seconds to recognise him.

'Hello, Dougie,' he said as I walked over to join him, 'good to see you again.'

'Hello, Callum, how are you?'

'Physically, I've never felt better, but quite frankly this business has shaken me up somewhat. I don't really know why it should have; something that happened twenty-eight years ago, but it isn't a pleasant thought.'

'I know what you mean;' hoping the next hour or two wasn't going to be spent hacking over the whys and wherefores of what was being called by the local press as the Natasha enquiry, 'anyway, I'm thirsty, what about you, Callum, ready for a refill?'

We took our beers outside to the terrace, already filling up with the regular Sunday lunchtime customers. I've always preferred "The Shipwreck" to "The Royal", the pub looked the way pubs should look; in this case, a traditional seaside tavern, and although the fishing décor and paraphernalia may appear to be contrived, looked fairly authentic to me.

'Did you know Hilary had been in Calder Bay?' he asked me, as soon as we sat down on one of the wooden benches.

'I did, yes, Aileen told me; she had a drink with her last Monday, this was the day before she went back to Oxford.'

'I bumped into her in "The Royal" on Friday; she told me she had to make a return trip to identify the body.'

'How did she seem?'

'Alright, as it happens; her husband was with her.'

'She must have married again after the divorce then?'

'Yes, she did; he's called Pete Fisher, seems a nice guy.'

'That's good; never could understand what she saw in 'bull in the gate' Rob Masters.'

'They didn't stop for long; I think they were making their way back to Oxford in the afternoon.'

'I'm sorry I missed them, I would liked to have seen Hilary again. So, Callum,' I asked him, making an attempt to steer the conversation in another direction, 'what made you decide to come back to Scotland?'

'I guess you would say I had reached a kind of watershed in my life; only a matter of months before I reached forty and realising I didn't have a great deal to show for it; a job in the City which was taking me nowhere and a relationship going sour on me; the whole gamut, Dougie, and enough to make me pack up and leave before I finally cracked up.'

'I'm sorry to hear that, about the relationship, I mean.'

'Thanks; it's okay now.' but I could tell by the dull look in his eyes that whatever had occurred in his life was not okay; Callum Ogilvie was a much-troubled man, finding his unburdening somewhat embarrassing, uncertain what sort of response I should make or be expected to make, 'Yes,' he was going on, 'Jeff found someone else; it was as simple and prosaic as that, Dougie.'

If he had suddenly given me a punch in the solar plexus, I don't believe I could have felt more winded, but now I knew the reason for my reluctance to meet up with him; not that I even suspected he was gay, but there had been something, possibly lying dormant in my brain for years, which had been struggling to make itself heard amongst all the rest of the accumulated mental clutter. How long had he known, I wondered. Five years, ten, or further back? Had Bobby known? And as soon as I thought of him, tiny, iridescent bubbles, similar to those blown by children through a wire hoop dipped in washing-up liquid, materialised until one by one they burst above my head: Bobby and he had been inseparable, from when they first met in primary school, through secondary school and university, right up to the night of Bobby's accident; Callum's devastated reaction, his uncontrollable sobbing during the funeral service. Attempting to catch those bubbles floating too far away from me, I wanted to learn more and there was more; I was certain. Girlfriends. As far as I knew, neither Bobby nor Callum ever had girlfriends, even when there had been a crowd of us on the beach during the summer, when there had been girls there, those two had never singled any of them out the way we others did. And now, the inevitable conclusion: Bobby had also been gay. With the idea firming up inside my head and taking hold, I was asking myself, who else had known. About Callum? About Bobby?

'Shocked?' he asked.

'Not shocked, no, just surprised; I hadn't realised.'

'Even in these enlightened times, in certain circles, it is still considered a stigma to be gay, therefore I wouldn't have been offended you know.'

'I like to think I'm sufficiently liberated, even although I've spent most of my life in such a parochial town as Calder Bay where the majority of people are conservative in their views and are opposed to change of any kind, whether it's to an extension to the town hall or the acceptance without criticism of whether a person is gay.'

'Fair enough, Dougie. It is only the beginning of the twenty-first century; I can see a time when general attitudes will relax, but there will always be a strong element of disapproval which in a democratic world those people are, of course, entitled to feel.'

'Changing the subject, Callum,' I said, determined this time to do just that; I'd had my say and was doing my best to see him, not as an old friend because in my mind, he no longer existed, but as a person who vaguely reminded me of someone I used to know, 'did you hear that Beth Grayson had died?'

'I had, yes, but I don't expect there will be many who'll do much mourning for her.'

'She scared me rigid when I was a kid, but I think she was to be pitied really.'

'Why?' a puzzled frown appearing, 'Why pity, Dougie?'

'Well,' trying to explain, although realising I was probably wasting my breath, 'she had no friends, only a brother, but I don't think he much cared for her from what I've heard around the town. I suppose you could say she was her own worst enemy, appearing to go out of her way to antagonize people.'

'She was not a good person, Dougie.'

'Why do you say that?'

'You remember that time years ago when we broke into the Grayson's garden –'

'- don't remind me; it makes me cringe when I think about that day.'

'I don't see why it should,' he grinned, 'and for a fraction of a second, looked like the young Callum, 'we only did it for a laugh.'

'Beth Grayson wasn't laughing though; I can see her now, standing at the corner of their house, like something out of a horror movie, staring at us –'

'- that's the point I was coming to, Dougie,' he interrupted, 'you probably didn't know, but she reported our trespassing to your father.'

'If she did, why didn't he say anything to us?'

'He did, but only to Bobby.'

'Was he mad?'

'No, just said to him that we mustn't go in there again, that was all.'

'Why didn't she approach us at the time, yell at us, or something?'

'Because, as I've said, she was not a good person.'

***

Poor Dougie. He looked pole-axed when I told him I was gay; he really had not expected to hear that. In a purely selfish way, I'd found that telling him had been therapeutic, reminding me of those talks Sadie and I used to have and which had been curtailed so cruelly. Dougie and I didn't make any arrangement to see each other again; I was about to suggest it, but there was a wariness in his expression which put me off, deciding he probably needed time to absorb what I'd said, come to terms with what he must have by now realised about my true relationship with Bobby. That wasn't going to be easy for him. Dougie was a straight-forward kind of guy; he always had been, although I recognised a toughness, an assertiveness about him which had never been evident in the early years. Perhaps this hadn't been such a good idea to try and pick up old threads again, wondering whether to get in touch with Aileen or not. It isn't as if I really knew her all that well, the thought suddenly occurring that wanting to renew the ties with the Hendersons was a pathetic attempt to get closer to the memory of Bobby. I was at it again; going round in circles and arriving nowhere new.

I hadn't expected Dougie to have mentioned Beth Grayson and I wished he hadn't. I had meant what I'd said to him about her and could have added quite a bit more because if I had, it would only have reminded me of the last time I saw Sadie and I didn't want that.

Normally I would have given Sadie a ring to ask if it was alright if I could call in, but on that day I didn't. It was still early, only six in the evening; I had spent most of the day in Montrose, making a presentation of new computer software, and it had been a spur of the moment decision to visit her and before driving up Green Lane, I stopped at the florists to buy some freesias for her, parking outside her house. It had been another warm evening and I reckoned she would be out on her terrace. I was half-way along the side path when I heard voices coming from that direction and learning she wasn't on her own, thought it best not to interrupt, but it wasn't until I made to turn round when I recognised the voice of her visitor.

"Now you are here, Beth," Sadie was saying, "why don't you sit down and tell me the reason for your visit?"

"I haven't come for a social chat, Miss Northcot; what I have to say will only take minutes."

"As you wish."

"I object most strongly to your relationship with Charles and I want you to stop seeing him."

"How extreme you're being, Beth."

"Did you hear what I said?"

"Oh, yes, I heard you quite plainly," Sadie had replied calmly, "and as I've just remarked I consider your manner to be extreme, meaning I have no intention of furthering this unpleasant conversation and would ask you to leave."

"Charles is spending too much time in your company and I strongly object; I don't want him to have anything to do with a woman like you."

"I've asked you to leave, Beth."

"I'll go when I'm ready, Miss Northcot -"

"- I'll correct you there, Beth; I'm a married woman, my name is *Mrs*

Northcot."

"Pah!" at least that's what it sounded like to me. I had always disliked Beth Grayson, but I hadn't realised just how unhinged she was, shocked at what I was hearing. I should have intervened, but I held back, possibly because I believed Sadie was handling the situation far better than I could.

"You are no more married than I am!" Beth was continuing, scarcely pausing to take a breath, her poisonous wrath spurting out uncontrollably, " ..... you hoodwinked Jack Henderson, even going so far as to have a child by him, and now you're trying to snare my brother! Well, I will not allow it; do you understand, *Miss* Northcot! I am going to make sure you never see him again!" her words emerging as one long venomous hiss.

"Very dramatic and how, may I ask, do you plan to do that?"

"I'm sure you would like to how," her voice changing to a sneer, but I continued to stand where I was; I didn't want to hear any more, but at that moment was physically and mentally unable to move away, "it wouldn't be the first time, Miss Northcot. You spoiled my life once and you're not going to do it again."

"What do you mean; I spoiled your life?"

"By stealing Jack from me, that's how."

"Dear me, Beth, you're so wrong, you know; you can't *steal* people."

"You did steal him from me and then years later I thought I could have had another chance, but that was jinxed as well."

"And you're blaming me for that?"

"Indirectly, yes; if you hadn't mesmerised Jack, he and I would have eventually married and I wouldn't have wanted Bobby."

"Bobby?" Rigid with apprehension, the sweat breaking out on my forehead, I waited, desperately wishing I was anywhere else but outside Sadie's house listening to the outpourings of a mad woman.

"You sound surprised."

"Very little surprises me, Beth, but I don't want to hear any more. I think it's time you went."

"I'm going to tell you anyway, Miss Northcot. The man I'm talking about was Bobby Henderson, Jack's son, but there was something about him which I hadn't realised."

There was silence; obviously Sadie had chosen to make no response.

"Bobby," Beth Grayson spat out, "was a homosexual and he had *laughed* at my advances. He humiliated me, but then, I had the upper hand; I had no intention of allowing him to get away with that!"

I heard a chair scraping on the tiles which would have been Sadie's, followed by, presumably her footsteps, walking further along the terrace.

"I have no wish to talk to you, Beth; would you kindly let yourself out." she said in the same level tone she had used from the beginning. I was now able to see her; she had walked on to the grass and was standing with her back turned to me at the far end of the garden. It was silent now, with only the distant drone two houses away of a lawnmower; again, I heard footsteps, Beth Grayson's, then the sound of a door banging somewhere inside the house and, not wanting to be seen, I made my way back to the car and waited until I saw Beth emerging from the front door and stride across the road to where she and Charles Grayson lived. As I drove home, I made up my mind to phone Sadie later and make sure she was alright, but I tried a number of times only to find the line was engaged and the last time Sadie must have switched over to the answering phone; by then it was well after ten, considering she would very likely be in bed. I had another seminar the following day, this time in Edinburgh, and it was late, almost midnight, when I finally got home. I didn't hear about Sadie until the next evening when I continued to get the answering tone, and called round to find out if anything was wrong. One of her neighbours saw me outside Sadie's house and told me Sadie had died sometime on Tuesday night apparently, she thought from a heart attack.

Just like that. A heart attack. Did Sadie have a heart condition? She must have had. She had never mentioned she was on any medication, but then she wouldn't have done; that wasn't her way. The neighbour had said sometime on Tuesday night; it must surely have been after ten; my last attempt to call her had been around that time and up to then her line had been busy; had she made that call or had someone called her? My mind was brimming with questions, speculations; each of them scrambling for position, but once I was home and had poured myself a stiff whisky, I knew without any doubt who was responsible for causing Sadie's death and that was Beth Grayson, recalling every single word of what she'd said to Sadie earlier on the Tuesday evening. Had that been sufficient to trigger off the fatal attack later? A rapid increase of heart rate and blood pressure. Sadie had always seemed to me a calm and unexcitable person, but what did that mean? Blood pressure, I knew, was a question of balance; too low, being equally as serious as too high, with no visible signs of detection.

I woke up earlier than usual the next morning, having slept badly, with a raging headache. This was no ordinary headache and I knew from experience it would probably stay with me for most of the day, similar to those I'd been having around the time Jeff had walked out on me, and further back when Bobby had been killed. And now, having heard what Beth had said to Sadie, I couldn't even bear thinking of him without the mental pain of believing Beth had somehow been responsible for his accident. Sun, pouring through the bedroom window, acted as a mockery; another warm sunny day, but Sadie wouldn't see it, she wouldn't be taking her first cup of coffee out on her terrace, neither would she enjoy the sights and sounds around her, while meanwhile, the woman we had labelled 'the witch', was free to continue living her dark and miserable existence. The unfairness of it all was utterly depressing, but what could I do to change that; Sadie, who had been a good friend, had died, while Beth Grayson, who very likely didn't have any friends, was alive. I did manage to get some work done, thankful I had no need to leave Calder Bay, my next assignment being again in Edinburgh, and by late afternoon, my headache having gone, I decided to walk down to the bay and have a swim.

Chapter Fourteen

Howard was told by the receptionist that Dr Michael Innis was on holiday and wouldn't be back to the surgery for another week and, rather than ask to see someone else in the practice, he decided to walk along to Blanchards, the Chemists, having noticed from Sadie Northcot's prescription that they dispensed the drugs for her each month. It was early, not yet nine-thirty, but already there was a queue waiting to be served; perhaps this was normal, he thought, for a Monday morning, waiting until it was his turn, but Caroline Muir who was checking the toiletry shelves stopped what she was doing and came over to him.

'Good morning, Howard,' she smiled, 'but perhaps I should be calling you Inspector.'

'It would feel strange if you did, Caroline, after all this time.'

He had known her for years; Caroline had been a close friend of his sister and had often been in their house when they had all been growing up, therefore, as he had just said it would have been strange hearing her give him his official title.

'How can I help you, Howard; I take it you are on duty?'

'I am, that's right;' telling her one or two anomalies had turned up in relation to the recent death of Sadie Northcot and showing her the prescription, 'if you could just clarify these items, Caroline.'

'Right, as you've probably noticed, the prescription is in two sections; the first being for a six-month period, for two separate medications for regularising the blood pressure and heart beat, a thirty-day supply; the other section is for a further tablet but only to be taken when required. For example, if there were signs of any spasmodic palpitations intensifying, perhaps caused by a nervous panic attack, but these are only for a one-off prescription, only to be repeated if the doctor should consider it necessary.'

'I understand,' he said, 'and according to the commencement date of the first two tablets, there should have been at least a further two weeks' supply remaining at the time of Mrs Northcot's death.'

'Yes, that's right and weren't there?'

'None were found by her daughter; if she hadn't come across the prescription she wouldn't have known her mother had been on medication.'

'I don't suppose Mrs Northcot wanted to worry her; she was a very proud lady and it was sad to hear she'd died, but it's strange about those missing pills; no wonder you're asking questions, Howard.'

'Can you tell me how long she had been taking them, Caroline?'

'I'd have to check on the computer in the dispensary to be sure, but I think it must have been about a year and a half ago; it will only take a couple of minutes, if you would like to come in with me; better than standing out here. It's always the same on Mondays,' she added, 'it's actually our busiest day of the week, would you believe.'

'An over-indulgent weekend, perhaps.'

'You could be right.' smiling as she led the way into the dispensary.

As she had said, it didn't take long before she had Sadie Northcot's details up on the screen and scrolling back to when she started the treatment.

'Here we are,' she said, 'the thirtieth of April 2002 was the date of the first prescription, followed by the second six-monthly one on the twenty-eighth of October and this last one on the twenty-sixth of April this year, expiring on the twenty-sixth of October.'

'And was the dosage always the same?'

'Fairly constant, except for the medication for regulating the heart beat,' she said, reading from the screen, 'when the strength was increased from seven point five to ten milligrammes, this commenced with the last prescription.'

'And the one-off medication?'

'This had been the first time Dr Innis had prescribed it for Mrs Northcot.'

'And of course, we have no way of knowing whether she had taken any of those pills.'

'I would say it was doubtful, Howard, because normally in a situation like that, the patient would have had a further consultation with the doctor; these pills should only be taken in extreme cases when the patient feels they are at risk of having a heart attack.'

'They are not a cure though are they?'

'No, but they act as an immediate stop gap, or safety valve if you like, until the patient can obtain medical help.'

'Thank you, Caroline,' he said, 'you've been very helpful and it's given me a clearer idea of what could have happened. You mentioning panic attacks made me think that if something had either shocked or frightened Mrs Northcot, she could have panicked, even to forgetting where she'd put those pills, she may not have kept them in the same place as the others; it's only speculation, but you've given us something to go on, so thanks again.'

By the time he had returned to the office, the feedback from British Telecom had come through. Six calls had been made to Sadie Northcot's number during the hours of nineteen hundred and twenty-two hundred on Tuesday, the seventeenth of June. All the calls were made by the same subscriber; namely, Miss Elizabeth Grayson. Presumably Charles Grayson hadn't got round to changing the name following his sister's death, Howard thought, and taking the report with him, went along to David McIntyre's office, wanting to give him also an update on Sadie Northcot's prescription.

'Why should Beth Grayson be phoning her, I wonder,' David commented, 'especially when, according to Mrs Baird, she disliked Sadie Northcot so much and refused to even mention her name.'

'I don't like the sound of this, sir.'

'Neither do I, Howard; the woman was up to something.'

'Unless she wasn't phoning, but it had been Charles Grayson.'

'A very good point; he is still a suspect for Natasha Paton's murder, in spite of those belongings of hers being found in his sister's wardrobe. We need to have another talk with him anyway, Howard, verify how he spent the evening when Sadie Northcot died and at the same time find out where their phone is situated in the house; of course there may be more than one. Also,' he went on, 'it might be interesting to learn whether he was friendly with Sadie.'

'With the way our initial investigation is going, it will only be a matter of time before word gets out that there could have been more than one murder.' Howard remarked.

'You mean local gossiping?'

'Not only that, sir,' he answered thoughtfully, 'I was thinking more of the media.'

'Ah, yes, of course; so far they've let us off fairly lightly, no doubt because of lack of any real interest in the murder of someone almost thirty years ago, but once they get an inkling we are treating a couple of deaths which happened recently as having some connection, however tenuously, the media will immediately have their interest re-kindled.'

'There's not a great deal we can do about that, is there, sir?'

'Afraid not; the media, if we're talking primarily about the press, are in the business of selling newspapers and nobody can put any reigns on them; we just have to try and be more than one step ahead.'

'Freedom of the press.' Howard said dryly, having a pretty good idea what it will be like in the town once the reporters descend on them.

'Quite. Going back for a minute to those missing pills, all I can come up with is that they must have been stolen; if so, why should anyone steal pills prescribed for someone else? Have you any ideas?'

'I don't think they were taken to be consumed, I think it's more likely it was to prevent Sadie having access to them, not necessarily the regular ones as, presumably, if she missed one dosage, she would have been able to quickly renew her prescription, but if she needed to take one of the emergency pills and found they weren't where the left them, that could have proved fatal.'

'I think you could be right and once again we find ourselves lacking a motive. If for the present, we concentrate on the Graysons as possible suspects, we have to ask ourselves which one of them is guilty: Charles or his sister.'

'Beth Grayson does sound the more likely suspect, sir.'

'I agree she does. And it's from here the questions start piling up: was her strong dislike for Sadie Northcot sufficient to go so far as to not only want her out of the way, but to actually take steps to orchestrate her death? Had she been aware Sadie was on medication and the type of drugs she had been prescribed? And, if that had been the case, did she know where they were kept and, equally as puzzling, Howard, how did she acquire them?'

'There's only one of those questions I can make any attempt to answer,' Howard said, mentally collating the various aspects of the points they were covering, 'and that's whether she would have had sufficient impetus to dispose of her; I believe she would have had, sir; Beth Grayson was without any doubt unbalanced, perhaps mentally ill, but that's something we'll never know.'

'There's something else we don't know,' David put in quickly, 'whether she was also on medication; officially, she died as a result of a heart attack. Charles Grayson may know, but I don't expect so; presumably she would have been registered with a doctor, so that should be easy enough to find out.'

'Something else to ask him.'

'That's right; meanwhile, it's time one of us had a word with those two lads who found her on the beach. I'm not happy with that verdict; we've been told she had been a strong swimmer and cramp or no cramp how did she manage to swim back to the shore?'

'They may not have been the only people around that evening.' Howard suggested, 'I'll make arrangements to see them, shall I?'

'Right, and while you're doing that, Howard, I'll go along and have another chat with Mrs Baird, but before I do that, I'll give Charles Grayson a ring and ask him to come in later this afternoon when, hopefully, we'll have more supporting evidence to bring, at least part of this investigation, to a satisfactory conclusion.'

Calder Bay's Cottage Hospital, where Beth Grayson had been taken, had the mobile number of one of the boys who had called them and he had answered immediately when Howard rang him. He was called Ben

Park and lived in Whitehaven, a village further up from the bay, and once Howard had explained he would like to ask him a few questions about the evening when he and his friend had assisted Miss Grayson, he said that as he was planning to come into the town, he could call into the Police Station, adding that Craig McKay, who had been with him at the time, was on holiday this week and wouldn't be back until Sunday.

It might not be necessary to see both of them, Howard thought, as he waited for Ben to arrive; it all depended on whether he had spotted anyone else that evening, particularly if they were close to where Beth Grayson had been swimming. A long shot and he wasn't all that confident of learning anything further, but nevertheless, they couldn't afford to overlook what could turn out to be relevant.

The desk sergeant showed Ben into his office shortly after two o'clock; Ben Park, still in his teens; tall, lanky and sun-tanned; his light brown hair bleached by the sun which indicated he must spend most days on the beach.

'Good of you to come in, Ben,' Howard said, shaking hands and gesturing towards the chair in front of his desk, 'and we apologise for interrupting your holiday.'

'That's alright, Inspector,' he grinned, 'makes a change; I've never been inside a police station before.'

'If you're interested,' Howard suggested, 'I'll ask one of our sergeants to show you round later.'

'I would be interested, sir,' he said, 'I've been thinking of trying to join the police force for some time.'

'Good. However as I mentioned on the phone, there are a few questions, routine ones I might add, I need to ask you, Ben. Incidentally, your action in calling for an ambulance was very public-spirited; not everyone would have done that.'

'But she still died, didn't she, Inspector?'

'She did, that's true.'

'Craig and I thought she was dead already when we found her lying there, but the ambulance people told us she was still breathing.'

161

'We understand that you and Craig had been fishing on the rocks and were on your way back to the beach when you spotted her.'

'We were, yes.'

'Had you noticed her before then, perhaps when she was swimming?'

'We did; first when she walked to the edge of the water, that must have been about three-quarters of an hour before we found her, then again, once or twice when she was swimming.'

'You think it was the same woman?'

'Oh, yes, because she was wearing a bright red swimsuit and had long black hair, although she'd tied it up in a sort of a knot at the top of her head.'

'Can you remember what time it was when you and Craig arrived that afternoon?'

'I think it was about four-thirty.'

'Were there many people on the beach then?'

'Quite a lot, but by five-thirty or so, they all started to pack up and leave.'

'How long would you say Miss Grayson had been in the water?'

'It's a bit difficult to be accurate, sir,' he said slowly, obviously trying to work it out, 'but it must have been about six when she waded in because I remember hearing St. Paul's church bells ringing for the evening service.'

'That would tie in with the time she was admitted into Casualty at seven-fifteen. Was she the only person swimming during the time she would have been in the water; you had mentioned that by five-thirty everyone had left the beach.'

'There was someone; I'd forgotten about him, but not long after Miss Grayson had started to swim, he walked down from one of the sand dunes; he must have changed there because he was already wearing his swimming trunks.'

'On his own?'

'I think so, I didn't see anyone else.'

'And did you actually see him swimming?'

'For a few minutes Craig and I watched him; this was because he was really a brilliant swimmer. I had never seen anyone who could swim as fast as he did, except on television when I've watched the Olympic swimmers; he was doing the breast stroke, his head going under the water and then, seconds later, he would emerge again.'

'But you only watched him for a few minutes.' Howard prompted him, experiencing the familiar frisson when he was on the periphery of something as totally unexpected as Ben had just told him which could be the sort of lead they were looking for, perhaps an explanation of how Beth Grayson may have died.

'Because my mobile rang; it was my mother,' he explained, a rueful expression appearing on his face, 'she wanted to know when I was coming home, and by the time I'd finished talking to her, he'd gone. I was going to ask Craig, but he had his back to me by then and was busy sorting out his fishing tackle, but we did spot him again.'

'Yes?'

'This was when we had started to pack up our things and I looked over to the beach and he was walking back up the bank.'

'Would you know him again, Ben?'

'Not really, sir.'

'Perhaps you could give me a description then.'

'Well, he was about five-ten, I guess; broad shoulders, looked as though he worked out, very fair hair; I thought at first it was white, but I don't think it was and I noticed he was wearing a watch which must have been a diver's one.'

'What sort of age do you think he was?' realising it wasn't easy for anyone as young as Ben to work out a person's age.

'I would say he was a bit younger than my dad, but not all that much and he's forty-two.' he said without any hesitation.

'You've actually given us a very good description, Ben, thank you. Now, if you would like to wait a couple of minutes, I'll make arrangements for you to be taken round the station.

***

While they waited for Charles Grayson to arrive, they compared notes with what had transpired from the talk Howard had with Ben Park and his meeting with Mrs Baird.

Where Charles Grayson's reaction to being asked further questions had been decidedly frosty, Mrs Baird's friendly greeting when she opened her door to him was in complete contrast, but then she had nothing to hide, while it was all too plain to both David and Howard, that he had and whatever it was, David was determined that this meeting with him would produce some answers.

The ritual of the tea and biscuits was repeated and, as before, David waited until she had joined him at the table before he brought the subject round to what had been bugging him from the beginning of their investigation.

'I'd like you to think back again to the time we were talking about when I last saw you, Mrs Baird.'

'The summer of 1975, Detective Inspector.' she said without any hesitation.

'That's right, but not only have we learned the woman's identity, we believe she was murdered on Thursday the 10th July.'

'My goodness, that was clever of you.'

'Not particularly,' smiling, 'when we get information of that nature, invariably it's from the assistance we receive from the people we talk to, like yourself, Mrs Baird.'

'Oh, I see; you say you know who she was, Detective Inspector?'

'Yes, she was called Natasha Paton and had been in Calder Bay on holiday.'

'Natasha Paton.' she repeated frowning, 'I don't understand; if she was a holidaymaker, why was she in Green Lane?'

'She wasn't your regular tourist, not venturing any further than the beach or the centre of the town; she had been staying with relatives in Green Lane and I'm sorry to tell you, Mrs Baird, but she was Hilary Robertson's aunt.'

'Dear me, that's dreadful. Does Hilary know?'

'Yes, she knows.' deliberately not mentioning it had been Hilary who had identified the body. Mrs Baird may have a tough constitution, but he didn't think it fair to burden her with unnecessary details.

'Poor Hilary.'

'That's exactly what Janice Henderson said when I told her.'

'You've seen Janice?'

'Yes, I drove down on Friday to where she lives in the Lake District.'

'It's such a long time since I've seen her; not since Karen and John's wedding in fact; how was she, Detective Inspector?'

'I would say very well; she and her family live in a lovely part of the country.' David told her and giving her time to absorb what he'd said so far before leading her back to where he'd left off.

'She would naturally have been upset for Hilary; they were such good friends.'

'I think they must have been and it was from speaking to both of them we were able to pin-point the time of Natasha Paton's death.'

'Really?'

'Yes, Janice told me she remembered the exact day when Hilary told her that her aunt had left Calder Bay; this had been on the morning of the town's Fancy Dress Parade and how upset she had been because her aunt hadn't told her she was going.'

'That's very sad.'

'It is, yes; then Janice had gone on to tell me about the costume they were putting together for the parade –'

'– of course, I remember; they entered as 'The Loch Ness Monster'; five of them: Janice and Hilary, Bobby and his friend, Callum and young Dougie. I wasn't too happy about them using the travelling rugs, but Janice had been persistent, promising me they would look after them.'

'She said they had to make do with only four of the rugs as one had been missing.'

'Yes, that's absolutely right; I never could understand that, you know. Both Janice and I checked the linen cupboard, but there were only four.'

'Did you put them in the cupboard yourself, Mrs Baird?'

'Yes, I did; they weren't used very often, and I had taken them out the day before to give them a good airing.'

'You would have hung them outside to air?'

'Yes, on the line outside the back door.'

'And when you brought them back in, you were sure there were five of them?'

'Absolutely certain, Detective Inspector. I brought them into the kitchen and folded each of them up, placing them on one of the chairs until I took them upstairs to the linen cupboard and I've just remembered, I was on the point of doing this when Beth called in to have a chat, so I didn't take them up until after she'd gone.'

'No doubt you're curious why I should be asking all these questions about one missing travelling rug, but I do have a reason, Mrs Baird?'

'I'm sure you do;' she gave a little smile, 'it's something to do with what happened to Hilary's aunt, isn't it?'

'I'm afraid so,' David said, wondering how she was going to take the next piece, 'the cause of death,' he told her, although realising she may already know, 'was by suffocation and the pathologist's report stated there had been shreds of wool on the victim's face, similar in texture and colour to the fabric used in producing travelling rugs.'

'Dear me,' shaking her head, 'someone must have disliked her a great deal to do a terrible thing like that.'

'If I could briefly return to the missing rug.'

'Of course, Detective Inspector; as you have no doubt realised I'm not the squeamish type; I am just saddened there is so much wickedness in the world and only grateful there are people like yourselves working so hard to bring some kind of justice to it all.'

'We do our best, Mrs Baird, and mostly it is one hard slog; however, that rug. When you finally took them back to the linen cupboard, did you count them again?'

'No, I didn't see any need to; I just picked them up from the chair and took them upstairs.'

'And as this was only the day before Janice asked for them, it didn't leave much time for anyone to have taken one of them out of the cupboard?'

'No, I'd wondered about that and had a look round the rooms in case it had been, but there was no sign of it anywhere.'

'How soon after Beth Grayson left that afternoon, did you take them out of the kitchen? Was it immediately, I apologise for taxing your memory like this.'

'No, Detective Inspector, there's no need to apologise; probably good for my brain.' she added, 'But it was more or less immediately as I was carrying them at the same time as she left the house.'

'Did she leave by the front?'

'Oh, yes; hardly anyone used the kitchen door, besides it was always kept locked. I think I was probably the only person and that was when I went out to the square of grass where the washing lines were.'

'I see, and the front door; was it locked during the day?'

'No, it was always open; with such a big family there was a continual coming and going, especially during the school holidays.'

'Presumably there was a window in the kitchen, Mrs Baird?'

'Yes, overlooking the back garden.'

'And being summer, no doubt it would have been open?'

'Yes, it was; in fact, that was usually the first thing I did when I arrived each morning.'

'I'm trying to visualise the kitchen layout;' David said, 'for instance, where the table was in relation to the sink and the stove, that sort of thing.'

'I'll make a sketch for you, although it will only be a rough one.' she suggested, eagerness now in her voice, possibly because at last she was able to do something positive, rather than sit there answering a load of questions, and within minutes, she had taken a sheet of writing paper from one of the drawers and with a biro drawn what was quite a detailed plan of "Carbisdale's" kitchen.

'That's very good,' he complimented her when she'd finished and passed it to him, 'thank you very much, Mrs Baird.' looking at what she'd sketched. 'Could you tell me the chair on which you had put the travelling rugs?'

'That one there,' pointing to the one she had drawn next to the window.

'Right; and where were you and Beth Grayson sitting, Mrs Baird?'

'Beth, where she always sat, with her back to the window, and I was opposite to her, the reason being,' she explained, 'I could be close to where the kettle and tea things were.'

What she had told him was invaluable and far more than he had expected, wondering as he left, how long it would take her to draw her own conclusions as to what could have happened. She was an intelligent woman, there was no doubt about that, David thought, and at her own admission was not the squeamish type. There was also no doubt in his mind now who had been responsible for removing that rug and how it was accomplished. Beth Grayson had been visiting her as apparently she had been in the habit of doing in the afternoon; she would have been seated with her back to the window and near the chair with the travelling rugs and when the housekeeper's back was turned to her while she had been attending to the tea-making, she had taken advantage of the opportunity and had swiftly picked up the top rug and thrown it out of the window, going round to pick it up after she had left, possibly hiding it among bushes as near to the wash-house as she could. Circumstantial evidence, but undeniably feasible, but he wasn't finished yet, determined to make one last attempt to find the rug. It could very well have been destroyed, but perhaps not. Natasha Paton's belongings hadn't been, so why should the murder weapon fare any differently?

***

The desk sergeant buzzed through to David's office at five-thirty to tell him that Charles Grayson had arrived in reception.

'Alright, Sergeant;' David said, looking over to where Howard was seated, 'show him in.'

'This should be interesting, sir.'

'Quite; we'll just hear what he has to say.'

The expression on Charles Grayson's face was giving nothing away; he neither looked resigned nor even mildly annoyed at being called into the station. He nodded in Howard's direction; a cursory acknowledgment, electing to focus his attention on the senior officer.

'Would you like to take a seat, Mr Grayson?' David suggested, 'gesturing towards the chair in front of his desk which had been placed in such a way both of them would be in his line of vision.

'I don't see how I can be of any further assistance to you in your investigation, Detective Inspector; I've told you and Inspector Crawford everything I knew about Natasha.'

'We believe there are a number of omissions, Mr Grayson and these require to be clarified before we can move forward on this case.'

'What do you mean by omissions?' glaring across the desk at him, a look of indignation on his face.

'I'll explain;' David said calmly, 'Natasha Paton was murdered on Thursday night, the 10th of July, 1975. Earlier in the day, she informed her sister, Marion Robertson, and her husband that she was leaving to meet up with friends in the South of France. It would be logical to assume she would be using one of the Channel ferries for the crossing, but first of course, she would require transport to reach the ferry port and as, apart from her passport, there were no other travel documents in her handbag, we have had no alternative but to believe she was accompanying someone and we need to find out who that person could have been.'

'And you think *I* was that person?'

'Were you, Mr Grayson?'

'I object to your method of questioning, Detective Inspector; if I said I had arranged to take her with me to France, you would no doubt immediately accuse me of murdering her and if I said I hadn't, my position in your view would be no different. I just happen to fill your particular criteria by having known the woman and living next door to where her body was found.'

'If you think that way, which incidentally is wrong, what do you have to lose by giving me a yes or no answer?'

'Put like that,' he grudgingly admitted, 'nothing. Alright, I did suggest to her that as I was going to Nice for a few days, she might like to accompany me; this was because she had already told me she had friends living near there.'

'So what happened?'

'When I drove up to where I'd asked her to wait for me, she wasn't there; that's what happened, Detective Inspector.'

'And where was this meeting place?'

'In Carlogie Road, at the top of Green Lane by St. Paul's church.'

'Why the secrecy?'

'For the simple reason I didn't want my sister to know I wasn't going to France on my own.'

'She would have objected?'

'That is an understatement; she would have made my life intolerable when I came back home. You have to realise, Detective Inspector, I was only thirty at the time and still very much intimidated by her and had learned at a very young age not to antagonise her.'

'Were you surprised when Miss Paton wasn't waiting for you?'

'Not really; I thought she had probably changed her mind.'

'Can you remember what time you were to meet her?'

'I can, actually; nine o'clock.'

'And were you on time?'

'It must have been about ten minutes past when I got there; I'd gone to the petrol station first and had to wait to be served.'

'You didn't think she just got tired of waiting?'

'I didn't know what to think; I hadn't been all that late. I waited for a few minutes, but I didn't want to look as if I was loitering if anyone should come along, so I drove off.'

'Did you go to France?'

'Of course I did; I had everything arranged, not just at this end with my ferry ticket, but in Nice with the people who kept an eye on the villa for me.'

'While you were waiting, or at any time either when you arrived outside the church or when you left, did you see anyone?' David asked him, at the same time realising that what Charles Grayson had told him, although credibly and logically fitting into place, it would be virtually impossible to either prove or disprove.

'No, there was no-one about, and my car was the only vehicle on that stretch of road.'

'How long were you away, Mr Grayson?'

'Only a week; I was back in Calder Bay by the following Wednesday.'

'I see and of course Miss Paton wasn't there; didn't that strike you as odd?'

'Why should it have; I've already said I hardly knew her; if anything, I probably thought she was the type of woman who never stayed very long in one place.'

'We will require a signed statement of what you've been saying, Mr Grayson, have you any objection?'

'None at all.'

'That's fine.' he nodded, glancing towards Howard, 'There have been further developments following on from when you spoke to Inspector Crawford on Saturday, which he'll explain to you.'

'We talked mainly about your sister's death, Mr. Grayson,' Howard said, moving slightly forward in his chair, and looking directly at him, 'but we said nothing about another death which occurred only three days earlier.'

'Sadie?' he frowned, 'What has Sadie's death got to do with Beth, Inspector? I don't understand.' and he really looked as if he didn't, David thought; this time he felt his reaction was genuine; not the contrived indignant expression of a few minutes earlier.

'Before I explain,' Howard was saying, 'would you tell me how well you knew her?'

'She was a very good friend and I used to enjoy our conversations, especially after Jack Henderson died.'

'Were you aware she was on medication?'

'I didn't then, but Carla told me.'

'Carla Northcot?'

'Yes, I met her for the first time at Sadie's funeral, but then you probably knew that, and of course I introduced her to the Detective Inspector on Thursday,' including David in his glance, 'Carla and I had dinner together on Saturday evening and she told me about the talk she had with you earlier in the day.'

'Right,' Howard nodded, 'so you will know that Carla had been unable to find any of the prescribed drugs when she was sorting through her mother's possessions.'

'Yes, she told me.'

'They still haven't come to light, but the chemist has informed us of the constituents of the three drugs prescribed for Mrs Northcot; two were for regulating both the heart beat and the blood pressure and were to be taken daily, while the third drug was only to be taken when the patient fears the onset of a heart attack. The chemist also confirmed that should the patient experience a sudden panic attack, this could have been caused by intense stress or a shock of some kind. This may have indeed occurred, but at this stage can only be supposition. However,' Howard went on and David could see he had Charles Grayson's full attention, 'we have a strong indication that Mrs Northcot had been sufficiently agitated that night, which ultimately resulted in the fatal heart attack which possibly could have been prevented if she had been able to take one of those pills.'

'But they weren't there.' Charles said quietly, his expression grim.

'It would seem not.'

'You said you had a strong indication Sadie had been sufficiently agitated, Inspector.'

'Yes, I did. That evening, between seven and ten o'clock, she received six telephone calls, all from the same subscriber; namely, your sister, Beth Grayson.'

'My God!' the colour draining from his face. Immediately, David picked up the receiver and called the front desk, asking for a mug of hot sweet tea to be brought in.

'Are you alright, Mr Grayson?' Howard asked him.

'I'll be fine, thanks.' leaning back heavily in the chair, 'Beth made those calls? Why? Why would she have done that?'

'Drink this first.' Howard said, taking the mug from the desk sergeant and passing it to him. While he sipped the tea, his colour slowly returning, David and Howard exchanged brief glances. Probably Howard was thinking the same, David thought; that was no act. Charles Grayson was visibly shaken. Even finding those clothes in his sister's wardrobe hadn't affected him as strongly and perhaps because of this, had attributed to Howard and him thinking he had 'planted' them in there to draw attention away from himself. It was possible that mentally he refused to believe his sister would have been capable of murder, but now he was being forced to face facts that she had not only killed one woman, but had been instrumental for the death of another, and this time a friend of his. God knows what was going through the man's brain, he wondered, watching him as he finished off the tea and handing the mug back to Howard; also there was Carla Northcot. When he had seen them together on Thursday they had appeared comfortable in each other's company, she had been helping him to clear out his sister's clothes, not everyone would be prepared to undertake such an unpleasant task and then he had just mentioned they'd had dinner together on Saturday night. If it turned out that Beth Grayson was guilty on those two counts, he would have to carry the certain stigma of having a sister who'd been a murderess. Not easy to live with.

'At the moment,' Howard was saying to him, 'we have no motive why anyone should want to harm Mrs Northcot, but the build-up of evidence, particularly against your sister, indicates she did die in suspicious circumstances; there has to be a motive and we will do our utmost to discover what it was. However, there are only a couple more questions I need to ask you, Mr Grayson, one of them being how you spent the evening Sadie Northcot died.'

'I was working until about six-thirty and then went along to "The

Shipwreck" for a drink, followed by a meal in their restaurant and it was after ten when I got home.'

'Did you see your sister before you went out?'

'Normally, I probably would have, but she wasn't in the house.'

'Had you any idea where she might have gone?'

'No, I hadn't. She didn't have many friends and wasn't the most sociable of women, I just thought she may have gone for a walk.'

'You say she hadn't many friends, we are aware she was friendly with the Henderson's housekeeper, Mrs Baird, but who else did she know, perhaps well enough to call on them?'

'I have no idea, Inspector; Beth never told me when she was going out or where she was going.'

'Could she have been visiting Mrs Northcot, do you think?'

'Sadie? I hardly think so.'

'She *was* on the phone with her later that evening.' Howard calmly pointed out.

'But *why*? Why in this world would she have wanted to talk to Sadie, what could she have had to say to her?'

'When you returned home,' pointedly avoiding any comment, 'did you see your sister then?'

'No, she'd gone to bed I think, I noticed she had left a light on upstairs.'

'Which room would those calls have been made from, Mr Grayson?'

'Beth had the phone in her bedroom.' he answered, his voice flat and emotionless.

'You only have the one phone?'

'Only one with that number, the other phone is in my studio, but it has a different number and under my name; I had the line installed a few years ago.'

'I understand." Howard said, 'You've already said your sister hadn't many friends and that as far as you were aware, she didn't know Mrs Northcot, but if she had known her wouldn't you have thought Mrs Northcot may have mentioned this to you?'

'I'm sure she would have, Inspector, but Beth wasn't in the habit of visiting anyone socially, except Mrs Baird, but she had known her since she was a teenager.'

'She knew of your friendship with Sadie?'

'She may have done, I suppose, but I didn't tell her.'

'Why not?'

'I don't think she approved of her.'

'Did you know why this was, Mr Grayson?'

'No, I don't, but Beth was like that; she would often take a strong dislike to someone when she hadn't even met them, she never gave any reason, she would just refuse to talk about them.'

'Alright, Mr Grayson, thank you; we'll leave it there for the present.'

Charles Grayson turned to look questioningly at David, giving every impression he'd had enough for the afternoon; certainly, David thought, he looked drained.

'When you and Miss Northcot found those belongings of Natasha Paton last Thursday,' David asked him, 'did you happen to see a travelling rug in your sister's room?'

'Travelling rug?' frowning.

'Yes, a red and green tartan one.'

'Can't say that I did, Detective Inspector; why do you ask?'

'Because,' he said, choosing his words carefully; he didn't want him to pass out this time, 'one was used to suffocate Natasha Paton and regrettably it has not yet been found.'

'After twenty-eight years,' he said, appearing more in control now, 'I would say it would be extremely unlikely if you did.'

'You could be right, but it would be a crucial piece of evidence, therefore we have to continue with our search.'

'I can't see the importance.'

'Technically, the rug can be described as the murder instrument, Mr Grayson, and unless a murder weapon cannot be traced back to the assailant, invariably it is left at the scene of the crime, but that wasn't the case here; there was no sign of the rug on or near the body. We have strong evidence to support our theory that this particular travelling rug had belonged to the Henderson family and had been stolen on the afternoon of the day Natasha Paton was murdered. The theft was not discovered until the following morning by Mrs Baird and a member of the family. On the afternoon in question the rug, together with four others, had been in the kitchen waiting to be taken upstairs to the airing cupboard, but there were only four travelling rugs found in there by the housekeeper.

'I don't understand where you're coming from, Detective Inspector.'

'I think you will, Mr Grayson,' David said, 'when I tell you that during the time those rugs were in the kitchen, your sister was there having tea with Mrs Baird.'

'Beth again.'

'It would appear so.'

'You can't know for certain she took it,' he said quietly, but not with very much conviction, 'but, once again, why would she have?'

'Mr Grayson, the murders of Natasha Paton and Sadie Northcot were both pre-meditated, as yet the motives are unclear, but we believe you could provide us with the answer to your own question.'

'How?'

'By thinking back to the past; we are not psychiatrists; first and foremost, we're police officers, trained to deal with hard facts which have to be assimilated and proved beyond any doubt, but when it comes to finding and proving motives, we have to consider less tangible reasons why a person would go to such lengths as to destroy another person's life. Of course Miss Grayson is unable to defend herself or undergo any psychiatric assessment; therefore it is left for someone else, like yourself for instance, to provide us with a deeper insight into her mental state. You had shared the same house as her all your life; I would suggest therefore you had known her character extremely well.'

'I think I know what you mean,' he said, 'but surely Detective Inspector, that's half the problem, I probably knew her too well.'

David didn't pursue the conversation which wasn't going anywhere; it could be that subconsciously Charles Grayson was incapable of accepting his sister's guilt, but whether this was the case or not, their brief wasn't to sort out any hang-ups he may have concerning her.

'Incidentally, Mr Grayson,' he added, 'do you know whether your sister was on medication?'

'She wouldn't have been, Detective Inspector,' he was quick to answer, shaking his head, 'she didn't believe in traditional cures and remedies, nor did she believe in doctors and had refused to register with one.'

'Not traditional?' having a good idea what the answer might be and wouldn't have been surprised if the woman, in keeping with the reputation of being thought a witch by the youngsters in the town, hadn't brewed her own.

'Various herbs; actually, she was surprisingly knowledgeable about the properties of wildly grown berries and leaves which in most people's view should remain on the bushes and hedgerows.'

'Really,' David commented dryly, noticing a twitch of amusement on Howard's face, 'so she prepared her own, rather than purchase them from, say, a homeopathy shop?'

'Yes, that's right; Beth didn't like spending money, Detective Inspector.'

Chapter Fifteen

After Charles Grayson left the office the previous afternoon, David and Howard had discussed at some length the outcome of the various aspects of their investigation into the deaths of Natasha Paton and Sadie Northcot, and to a lesser degree that of Beth Grayson, mainly because up to now they had nothing positive to substantiate that she may have died in suspicious circumstances; all they had was what Ben Park had said about the other swimmer, together with a description of which could fit any number of men in Calder Bay. It had become apparent that Beth Grayson had not been generally liked, her only friend perhaps having been the housekeeper, but it still didn't imply any of these people would have taken the extreme action of causing her death.

'I believe there is a missing link which we need to find, Howard,' David had said, 'in order to bring us up to concluding this case. Any ideas?'

'I wish I had, sir, but I feel the same way. If there is more to Beth Grayson's death, it must have something to do with what happened to Sadie Northcot, otherwise why should she have died when she did, only a few days afterwards?'

'Those pills of hers, Howard.' David said quickly, 'Perhaps we're forgetting something here.'

'Yes?'

'It looks very much as though her death was premeditated, doesn't it?'

'I would say so.'

'The six phone calls, presumably made by Beth Grayson, had to have been made after the pills had been stolen, therefore how and when were they removed? It would have been the same day Sadie died; otherwise she would have discovered they were missing.'

'Maybe Beth Grayson had been across to Sadie's house earlier.' Howard suggested.

'Yes, and then we have to ask ourselves why she would have called to see a woman, according to Mrs Baird, she had disliked so intensely.'

'It wouldn't have been a social call.'

'No, I don't believe it would have been, but we're only guessing, Howard. The housekeeper had mentioned how she had always thought the reason for Beth's animosity towards Sadie was caused by jealousy. She was referring to years ago, shortly after Sadie arrived in Calder Bay.'

'Because of her friendship with Jack Henderson.'

'Yes,' David nodded, remembering how Mrs Baird had described Beth, 'perhaps more recently this time there had been someone else who had ignited this jealous streak of hers which may have lain dormant for the last twenty-eight years.'

'Charles Grayson.'

'I think we're getting there, Howard; he told us yesterday about his friendship with Sadie and how he had enjoyed their talks, a friendship which he kept from his sister.'

'Perhaps she found out.'

'It's possible. She could have suspected there was more to their relationship and the fact that she already disliked Sadie may have further disturbed her, to such a degree she decided to take steps to dispose of her.'

'Considering his reaction to what we were telling him, it looks as though Charles Grayson had already come to the same conclusion.'

'You're probably right. However, I think a word with the neighbour you were talking to on Saturday might be a good idea; find out whether Sadie had any visitors during the day; from how you've described Beth Grayson, she was hardly the inconspicuous type.'

The woman who came to the door was, David reckoned, in her early fifties and once she had seen his warrant card, hadn't hesitated to invite him in, leading him through to the kitchen; a long room, recently painted with gleaming stainless steel fitments along the length of one wall and opposite, glass patio doors opening out on to a tiled area and from where he could see part of the terrace of Sadie Northcot's house.

'First of all, madam,' he said, selecting his words carefully, 'I would like to reassure you there is no cause for alarm, but there are a few irregularities concerning the recent death of your neighbour, Mrs

Northcot.'

'Oh, dear.'

'When there is a sudden death,' he started to explain, 'as with Mrs Northcot's, it is always a matter of form for the authorities to examine, as far as they can, the cause and it transpires she was on medication, part of which had to be taken on a regular daily basis.'

'I understand, so she did have a heart problem; I did hear she'd died of a heart attack.'

'That was true, she did, but there was no sign of any of the prescribed drugs in the house and we are trying to find out what happened to them.'

'Do you think they were stolen?'

'We believe they could have been.'

'Who on earth would have done that? Mrs Northcot was such a nice person and I'd just got to know her; we've only been living in Calder Bay for a few months, you see.' she added, a look of sadness in her eyes as she waited for him to go on.

'Also,' David said, 'we understand she received several telephone calls on the night she died; we have investigated the source of them, but what we require to find out is why they were made as they were from the same person.'

'My Goodness!' a hand fluttering up to her mouth, 'And she was on the phone a lot that night. I was in the garden for a good part of the evening, until it got dusk as a matter of fact, and with this good weather her lounge window was open, so that's how I knew.'

'Were you able to catch anything she said, madam?'

'No, I wasn't; only that I recognised her voice, but not what she was saying.'

'Earlier in the evening,' he asked, 'or even during the day at some time, did she have any visitors?'

'I was out shopping for most of the morning, but I was at home for the remainder of the day. I didn't notice whether she had any visitors or not, but later on in the afternoon, it must have been around six because I was upstairs in the spare room doing some decorating when I saw someone park outside Mrs Northcot's house; he didn't go to the front door, but made to walk round to the back when he just stopped and stood there for several minutes before turning round and going back to his car.'

'Could you see her terrace from where you were?' he asked her, his mind working overtime; was this the missing link he had mentioned to Howard? Lucky breaks were a rarity in his profession, but when they did occur, he had learned to extract as much from them as possible.

'No, I couldn't; the room is at the front and from there I could only see the start of her side path, not as far as the terrace.'

'Had you seen him before?'

'Yes, quite a few times; he must have been a friend of hers, Detective Inspector, and he always brought her flowers when he called to see her, as indeed he had done that evening, but sadly, she would never have known, would she?'

'No,' shaking his head, 'she wouldn't have known. Could you describe him to me, do you think?'

'I'll try; he was young, still in his thirties; tall, about your height, well-built, very blond hair, almost white in fact, brushed back from his forehead, clean-shaven and each time I've seen him he is always neatly dressed, usually in a business suit as he was then.'

'As presumably he was a friend of Mrs Northcot, and as you've mentioned, a fairly frequent visitor, did you wonder why he didn't continue to walk round to the back of the house?'

'I did actually and then I decided she must have had someone with her on the terrace; she would often sit there when the weather was good, and that he hadn't wanted to intrude.'

'You could be right, madam;' he encouraged, giving her time, hoping that in hindsight she may remember something, however slight, which would give them a much-needed lead, 'and when he reached his car, did he drive off, or it could have been he waited until whoever had been with Mrs Northcot had left?'

'It's funny you should say that, Detective Inspector, but I've just remembered; he was still sitting in the car when Mrs Northcot's front door opened and –'

'– yes?'

'I was a bit surprised, that's all, expecting to see Mrs Northcot, but it was the woman who lives across the road from here; the house with all the ivy.' she explained, 'I don't know her name, but I've often seen her going in and out, so of course she must have been visiting Mrs Northcot.'

'And after she'd gone,' David asked her, 'did he change his mind?'

'No, he drove off then.'

As with the description Ben Park had given Howard, it was reasonably detailed although it could fit several males around that age, except for the hair; white-blond, short, brushed back from his forehead. Loathe as he was to start forming any preconceived ideas, David couldn't prevent himself from considering who the person could have been; Callum Ogilvie was in his late thirties and from how Howard had described him, of a similar height and build to what both Ben Park and Sadie Northcot's neighbour had said. He could very well be the same person; Callum Ogilvie had spent many of his younger years with members of the Henderson family, in particular Bobby, the one who was killed in the motor bike accident; he had known Hilary Robertson and along with Bobby and Dougie had seen her aunt, Natasha Paton, posing for Charles Grayson, their trespassing being watched by his sister, the woman they had called 'the witch'. Also, it was feasible he had known Sadie Northcot. For the first time, David found himself questioning the friendship between Callum Ogilvie and Bobby Henderson; how close had it been? It would appear that following his death, Callum had left Calder Bay, presumably losing touch with the Henderson family, to work in London and had only returned to Calder Bay a few months ago. Had it taken him all this time to reconcile himself to losing his friend? Of all the people they had spoken to so far, only he emerged as something of an enigma; where they had been able to build up fairly substantial backgrounds to the others, they had learned very little about him. If, David concluded, there was a sinister element in him being on the beach at the same time as Beth Grayson, they had to discover more about him.

He took Howard's report on his interview with Callum Ogilvie from the case file and read again what he had written. Unlike Charles Grayson when he was shown the identikit, Callum had been quick to see and acknowledge the likeness to Natasha Paton, a woman he had only seen a couple of times when she had been staying with the Robertsons. He hadn't said where he had seen her and Howard hadn't pressed him, having already heard from Dougie Henderson about the time they had broken into the garden next door to "Carbisdale". Howard had annotated the change in Callum's manner as soon as Bobby's name was mentioned; he had, according to Howard, become agitated, reluctant to talk about him, especially of the accident, except to stress Bobby had been an extremely competent motor cyclist and hadn't taken risks, all of which made it difficult for him to accept. Had Callum been justified in such a reaction, David wondered; had he believed, sub-consciously or otherwise, that the accident wasn't genuine. There would have been a police report made out, and picking up the receiver he called through to the general office. Within a matter of minutes, a print-out of the report was on his desk. At first appearance, it all seemed straightforward enough: the bike, a Honda XR100, with fifteen hundred miles on the clock, travelling north, at sixty-five miles an hour, skidded diagonally across the A92 on the outskirts of Calder Bay, crashing into a stone dyke, the force of the collision being such that the motor cyclist, Robert Henderson, was killed instantly. There were no witnesses at, or in the vicinity, of the scene. The mechanic's inspection notes were attached to the report and made interesting reading; understandably, the bike had been severely damaged, although still intact, with the exception of the area around the central crankshaft where the cotter pin had become dislodged, the mechanic concluding this could have been caused by the impact of the crash.

While that could have been the case, David thought, the fact remained that the cause of the accident remained unclear. According to the report, road conditions had been good; the surface dry and free of any debris and the only oil on the road had been from the punctured oil tank at the time of the crash. David had driven along that straight stretch of road many times, had done for years, and knew the exact position of the old stone dyke, also there were no trees nearby to throw up any unsuspecting shadows, yet from what Callum Ogilvie had said, Bobby Henderson had been an experienced cyclist, therefore it was logical to question why the accident should have happened. Either there had been something physically wrong with Bobby, but the post mortem results would clarify that, or the bike had been faulty and as the crankshaft was an integral part of the machine if the cotter pin had moved, even by a fraction, before the crash this would have ultimately affected the steering, leading to the loss of control and, no matter how skilful Bobby may have been, the crash had been inevitable.

David couldn't remember handling such a complex case, not dissimilar to opening the proverbial can of worms; first they were investigating a murder committed almost thirty years ago, followed by another one which occurred last month, then almost immediately the suspicious circumstances surrounding Beth Grayson's death and now, it looked very much as though they would have to trace back ten years to when Bobby Henderson had his accident. He remembered commenting to Howard at the start of their enquiry that there were too many deaths and it looked as if he'd been right. If it transpired Bobby's bike had been tampered with, there had to be a reason why anyone should have done this. In some convoluted way each one of the deaths appeared to be connected, which indicated there must be a common denominator. They had reached the point where they could officially close the case on Natasha Paton's murder but were being prevented from doing so because of their suspicions of Beth Grayson over what happened to Sadie Northcot and with the growing doubts surrounding Bobby Henderson's accident they would be forced to consider the possibility of Beth Grayson having been involved. Then, of course, there was the mystery behind her own demise. Had she been the common denominator they were hoping to find, recalling Janice telling him that Beth Grayson had once owned a motor bike, which could indicate she had the necessary technical knowledge to disable the bike. She appeared to have known her way around

"Carbisdale" and would certainly have known where Bobby garaged it, also when he was in the habit of using the bike, always assuming he would have owned a car, but that was something any of the family would be able to tell him, including Callum Ogilvie. With the broadening of their investigation, it would surely only be a matter of time before the developing aspects of the case would leak out and when that happened they would have the media to contend with, including, no doubt, demands to hold a press conference.

***

'It's very much like the chicken and egg situation, isn't it, sir?' Howard said later when they met to discuss the latest development, having received both the reports on the medical evidence on Bobby Henderson and Callum Ogilvie's background.

'I couldn't have described it better myself, Howard; it's tricky knowing where to start. Perhaps,' he suggested, 'we should be viewing our investigation from a different angle. Up to now, we've been concentrating on Natasha Paton's murder, allowing each subsequent incident to pile up on top of each other which has probably clouded our reasoning process.'

'I think I know what you mean;' Howard nodded, 'it's time to change our approach, maybe take a tougher line.'

'That's right,' he agreed, 'we've done enough soft-peddling; trying to keep our enquiries low-key, concerning ourselves with attracting the attention of the press, thereby disappointing those members of the general public who enjoy nothing better than a juicy scandal, or as appears to be the case here, more than one.'

'It's bound to happen anyway; sooner or later.'

'Quite. Let's start with the hard facts, Howard; what do we have?'

'The body of a woman murdered twenty-eight years ago; that Sadie Northcot's death had been instigated and, with what has transpired today, more than a suspicion that Bobby Henderson's accident had been fixed.'

'Yes, not a great deal to show for all our efforts; however,' David went on stolidly, 'we'll press on. I notice you didn't include Beth Grayson and you were quite right as we are unable to substantiate what we think may have happened to her, although now we have this report,' pointing to the background search on Callum Ogilvie, 'we do have a little bit more to go on. Incidentally, Howard,' he asked, 'did you see any possible significance in his address?'

'I did, yes. I know where the block of flats is in Bay Road; he would have had a clear uninterrupted view of the beach if he happened to be looking out of his window when Beth Grayson arrived.'

'And it may not have been the first time he'd seen her there either; according to Charles Grayson, she was anti-social and would have been in the habit of waiting until the beach had cleared at the end of each day.'

'There seems to be no doubt that it had been Callum Ogilvie and that he was the same person Sadie's neighbour had seen outside her house; the two descriptions we've been given of him match up pretty well, especially the hair colouring.'

'I believe you're right, Howard; I suggest we get him into the office and hear what he has to say. It sounds as if you may have discovered his Achilles heel the other day when you were talking to him.'

'His friendship with Bobby Henderson.'

'That's exactly what I meant. We can't afford to display any prejudices should it transpire he's gay, except to say that if there had been sexual connotations in his friendship with Bobby Henderson, it could lead to the reason behind Beth Grayson's death if in fact it was not a natural one.'

'He waited a long time, sir.'

'Yes, and we could be going down the wrong route, therefore it's best to keep an open mind. However,' he continued, 'there are a couple of anomalies in the report which require further checking.'

'Yes?'

'They are during the period he was in London;' looking at the report again, 'from September 1993 until he finished with the company he was working for in August 2002. I see that he was unemployed for almost a year from 1995 to 1996; also it would appear he didn't work again after he left the company until he arrived back in Calder Bay a few months ago.

I'm going to call the two companies he worked for in London, find out why he left them. I'll do that now and perhaps you could give Callum a ring, Howard, and arrange, if possible, for him to come in this evening at six.'

The personnel officer of Johnson Computers, Limited, the first company Callum worked for when he arrived in London, didn't take long to trace back through their records and efficiently informed him that Callum had been employed by them as a computer programmer and had left the company voluntarily on the 24th November 1995. She had nothing further to add, her tone of voice implying disinterest in an ex-employee who was only with them for a relatively short length of time. The second call he made turned out to be more productive; George Edgar was the senior partner of Edgar & Partners and had shown no reluctance in discussing one of his past employees, confirming that Callum had worked for his firm as a software designer for six years, from the beginning of February 1996 to the end of August in 2002.'

'Did he give any reason for leaving, Mr Edgar?' David asked him.

'Well –' recognising the slight hesitation in his voice, '- not exactly, only to say he had decided to return to Scotland.'

'And you thought perhaps there was another reason?'

'Nothing specific, you understand, Detective Inspector, but Callum had a number of problems; although I have to say these didn't affect his performance with us; he's an extremely clever young man and his knowledge of computers is excellent and we were sorry to lose him.'

'Were these health problems or more of a personal nature?'

'A mixture I would say.'

'I do realise you may feel uncomfortable talking about him in this way, Mr Edgar, but anything you're able to tell me will be handled with discretion. To explain briefly, we are conducting a murder enquiry here, in Calder Bay, concerning the death of a woman which occurred almost thirty years ago and in the course of our enquiry we've had to talk to as many people as possible who were living in and around where the body was discovered. It would now appear this wasn't the only murder in close proximity; one of them in 1993 and the other two less than a month ago. Callum Ogilvie is one of a number of local residents we've interviewed and where it has been easy to establish their backgrounds, where he is concerned, we know very little about him, especially during the last ten years when he was in London.'

'I understand, or at least I think I do, and I'll attempt to fill in some of those missing blanks for you.'

'Thank you, Mr Edgar;' regretting having to conduct the conversation over the phone, preferring a one-to-one approach, 'you've mentioned problems Callum Ogilvie may have had; could you be more specific?'

'Perhaps I was incorrect in saying his problems were health ones, I should have said they were more mental than physical; you see, Detective Inspector, before he joined the firm he had been receiving treatment for depression; he quite freely admitted this at the time of his interview to explain why he had been unemployed for twelve months, having, he said, found it impossible to continue working for Johnson Computers whom he'd been with since arriving in London in 1993, but he had assured me the treatment was at an end. Certainly during the time he was here he showed no signs of the recurring condition, no absenteeism and as I've said, his work was unaffected, but then, about three or four months before he resigned, we noticed a marked difference in him; he became withdrawn, obviously something must have occurred to cause what was almost a change of personality. I did ask him once if there was anything worrying him, but he said he was fine, making it clear that whatever was troubling him he was either unable or reluctant to talk about it.'

'Did you have any ideas?'

'Well, I did, actually; he had all the symptoms of someone suffering from a broken romance. I have three daughters, Detective Inspector,' he chuckled, 'and at one time or another they would subject my wife and me to their woes when some boy had ended what they had believed to be the romance to end all romances, but always, after a matter of a couple of weeks, they would have recovered and I thought Callum would also.'

'But he didn't?'

'No. He didn't get worse, but continued in the way I've described right up to when he left.'

'I appreciate your frankness,' David told him, 'and what you've told me has given me a better insight to his personality.' bringing the call to a close.

***

Callum Ogilvie arrived promptly at six o'clock. Howard introduced him to David who looked at him speculatively for a few seconds before making any inroads with the questioning, realising that the man now sitting in front of them was decidedly uneasy; unlike Charles Grayson when he had first met him, Callum Ogilvie didn't attempt to disguise this by any meaningless conversation; he merely sat there stoically, his face devoid of any animation. He was wearing a dark business suit, a light blue shirt with a buttoned-down collar. He had loosened his tie, whether as a result of the continuing warm weather or because of nervousness, he couldn't tell. He looked older than his years; also there were dark shadows beneath his eyes as though he hadn't been sleeping well. David couldn't decide whether he could be described as good-looking: even features, smooth skin, bronzed, and wondering at the same time how a woman would have viewed him. Sadie's neighbour had only mentioned his build, the way he dressed and his unusual hair colouring; she hadn't said what he actually looked like, but not wanting to be biased by what they were coming round to believing, he did seem somewhat effete; too smart, too neatly turned out, too controlled in his speech; well, David thought cynically, that could very well change within the next ten minutes or so.

'Did you know a woman called Sadie Northcot, Mr Ogilvie?' David asked him, breaking the silence in the room.

'Yes,' he answered slowly, cautiously, giving no indication of any surprise at being asked, 'I knew Sadie.'

'When did you last see her?'

'I can't remember,' his voice remaining on the same level, 'but it must have been some weeks before she died.'

'Where would this have been?'

'Sorry?' frowning.

'Where did you see her; did you bump into her in the street or did you visit her?'

'Oh, I see what you mean;' the frown disappearing, 'I always went to her house. Why do you want to know any of this, I don't understand.'

'You will, Mr Ogilvie.' deciding it was time to change tack, 'When Inspector Crawford spoke to you last Friday, we were focusing our investigation on the murder of Natasha Paton, but since then, there have been a number of developments which require looking into, developments which may have a certain bearing on Mrs Northcot's death.'

'Is that why you're asking me about Sadie?'

'Indirectly; we believe there is a strong link between the two deaths and possibly a third; namely, that of your friend, Bobby Henderson.'

'Bobby.' the name emerging as no more than a whisper, his eyes clouding over as though he was finding it difficult to focus.

'We have had reasons to look closer at the reports made out at the time of the accident, Mr Ogilvie. On the surface,' David went on steadily, 'it did in fact appear to have been a motor bike accident; a bike going out of control and crashing into a stone wall, instantly killing the cyclist, except that the evidence can be viewed differently.'

'You're saying someone arranged it.' his voice flat, emotionless, as he looked across at him.

'We believe that may have happened, we also believe, if we are correct, that you know who that someone was, Mr Ogilvie.'

'I'd like to know how you arrived at that idea, Detective Inspector.' this time showing a slight modicum of response, his eyes narrowing and remaining on David's face.

'And I intend to tell you.'

'I'm listening.'

'The person who tampered with your friend's motor bike also instigated Mrs Northcot's death; you overheard a conversation three weeks ago, on the 17th June, between Sadie Northcot and the person responsible which gave you this information, Mr Ogilvie.'

'Did I?'

'I would remind you,' David said, moving fractionally forward in his chair, 'we did not ask you in here this afternoon to play games; you either deny what I have just suggested, or you admit you were there, outside Mrs Northcot's house, that evening.'

'Well, I wasn't.'

'I see; you're prepared to sign a statement to that effect?'

'Of course.'

'We will return to the motor bike accident.' glancing over towards Howard.

'Mr Ogilvie,' Howard said, 'when I saw you last Friday, you made a point of stressing that Bobby Henderson was a competent and responsible motor cyclist. You also said you had found it hard to accept his death and that you couldn't understand how it happened.'

'That's what I said and that's what I meant.'

'If, as the Detective Inspector has put to you, you knew who had caused the accident and although you may not know how it was done, you would have discovered *why* anyone should want your friend to die.'

'I don't know who it could have been; I've already said that.'

'Very well;' Howard nodded, 'the day of the accident, Mr Ogilvie. You will no doubt remember exactly when that was.'

'Of course; Sunday the 4th July 1993.'

'How did you spend the day?'

'Nothing special; I didn't get up until late; had a swim in the afternoon, a couple of beers in "The Shipwreck" later on and watched television for the rest of the evening.'

'On your own?'

'Except when I was in the pub, yes.'

'A quiet day.' Howard remarked blandly; 'would you have described it as a normal Sunday?'

'Yes, except during the winter months; I always go to the indoor pool in Arbroath then.'

'You obviously enjoy swimming?'

'Very much.'

'Did Bobby?'

'We all did.'

'I was wondering why he hadn't been with you.'

'Well, he wasn't.' he was tightening up, David thought, no doubt becoming confused as to where Howard's questions were leading.

'Was he still living at "Carbisdale"?'

'Yes.'

'As you were familiar with the house and grounds, presumably you would have known where he kept the bike?'

'In the garage.'

'And where were you living at the time, Mr Ogilvie?'

'At home with my parents in Carlogie Road; what has that got to do with anything, Inspector?'

'Was the garage kept locked?' pointedly ignoring his question and then, as obvious as a coin dropping into a slot, he became aware of the trap which had been set for him. It was apparent to both David and Howard by the defeated expression on Callum Ogilvie's face that he realised he could be suspected of arranging Bobby's accident if he refused to admit he'd overheard Sadie and Beth's conversation; the irony being if the latter, he knew he would be accused of what happened to Beth Grayson. Like a rabbit in a snare, they could practically read his mind; whichever way he turned, the end would be the same; he would be charged with murder, whether Beth's or Bobby's in the final analysis, it wouldn't really matter.

'I don't think the door was kept locked.' he answered at last, taking so long, David was beginning to wonder if he was going to.

'So,' Howard persisted, 'anyone could go in there?'

'I suppose so.'

'Did you, Mr Ogilvie?'

'Did I what?'

'Did you ever go into the Henderson's garage?' Howard said,

enunciating each word.

'A few times over the years, with Bobby of course.'

'Never on your own?'

'No, why should I have done.'

'Thank you, Mr Ogilvie; a signed statement will be required confirming everything you've said to me at this interview.' the formal tone in his voice not being lost on Callum Ogilvie, David noticed. Howard had, systematically and skilfully, manipulated the questioning in such a manner that by this time, Callum was showing further and more pronounced signs of edginess.

'Before we finish this interview, Mr Ogilvie,' David said to him, 'I'll ask you once again whether you saw Sadie Northcot on the day she died.'

'What I said earlier, Detective Inspector, was true; I didn't see her that day, although I had intended to, but when I arrived at her house I realised she had someone with her and decided to call another day.' he said, presumably recognising the temporary lifeline he needed to extricate himself from the situation.

'How did you know she already had a visitor?'

'Because I heard voices on the terrace.'

'How far away were you when you heard them?'

'I had just started to walk along the path to her back garden.'

'This other person,' David pressed on, but not expecting anything productive to emerge, 'male or female?'

'It was a woman's voice.'

'Did you recognise it?' anticipating the answer.

'No, I didn't, Detective Inspector.' on cue, but as a matter of form he had to ask the last question.

'Were you able to hear what was being said, even a few disjointed words?'

'No.' too glibly, 'As soon as I heard them talking, I turned back and drove home.'

'I see; this additional information will be included in your statement, Mr Ogilvie and we would be obliged if you would return here tomorrow afternoon at six for the necessary signing of the two statements. Before you leave, in case we need to contact you, would you let us have your mobile number?'

'I have a business appointment in Edinburgh tomorrow, Chief Inspector,' he said, 'and don't expect to get back to Calder Bay until quite late, well after six in fact.' he added, 'but I can manage to be here on Thursday if that's alright.'

He could be stalling, David thought, but either way it wasn't a big issue and deciding to give him the benefit of the doubt, also realising it would give them the time needed to do some further checking, find out whether there had been anyone who had seen anything untoward that evening on the beach; so far they only had the two lads as witnesses, and it wasn't enough.

'Fine.'

'I'll give you one of my cards;' he said, taking a card from his wallet and handing it over to him; 'both the land and mobile numbers are on it, also my address, but I expect you have that already.' he finished just a shade too quickly and not quite disguising his relief. Relief they hadn't pressed him further, or relief they hadn't mentioned Beth Grayson's name in respect to what happened to her? It was fairly conclusive that it had been Beth Grayson talking to Sadie when he had called to see her. He may not have recognised her voice, which was unlikely, but as he was still in the car when she left the house he couldn't have failed to have seen her and had instantly known who she was; he had seen her often enough in the past when he'd been at "Carbisdale". He had been foolish to lie. Surely Callum Ogilvie had the intelligence to realise he had placed himself in a compromising position. To have changed what he had said earlier must mean he realised he had been seen outside Sadie's house that evening, but he wouldn't know they had two witnesses to say he had been swimming at the same time as Beth Grayson on the night she died, although that evidence was too thin; somehow, they had to find out more.

Chapter Sixteen

AILEEN & DOUGIE

'We need to talk, Dougie.'

'I suppose we do, Aileen; when do you suggest?'

'This lunchtime, if that's alright with you; how about "The Royal" around twelve?'

'Okay, no problem; I'll be there.'

Dougie had shown no surprise on hearing from me during the week when I knew he would be working, but what I wanted to say to him couldn't wait until either of us had a free evening. Howard Crawford's visit earlier this morning had disturbed me to such an extent I had to share with someone in the family. Talking to John would have been a waste of time and he probably would not have been interested; Janice was too far away and there would be no point in alarming her, at least not yet, therefore it would have to be Dougie.

I was seriously coming to the conclusion there must be a curse on our family; as if the discovery of Natasha's body hadn't been enough, it now seemed the police were looking into Bobby's accident. My first reaction when Howard Crawford started asking questions about what we had all been doing around the time of the accident and where he had kept his bike, including the name of the garage who carried out maintenance checks, was why the hell hadn't they been more thorough ten years ago. Also, I was still mentally reeling from meeting Sadie's daughter last Saturday; the striking likeness to Janice was incredible, so much so, I couldn't dismiss it as one would normally do by glibly saying everyone has a double. I instinctively knew when I saw her that she was my half-sister and realised my manner towards her had been unreasonable, but I was frantically trying to cope with conflicting emotions and at the same time to act normally. I had always known Sadie had a daughter and that she was called Carla, but I had never seen any photographs of her; Sadie wasn't that sort of mother. I suppose I first became friendly with her about thirteen years ago, around the time of my divorce; I'd gone back to "Carbisdale" to live for a few months, but it wasn't until much later when Godfrey and I were married, that she and I used to meet regularly for coffee, but we seldom talked about family, mostly about the time when Sadie had been an actress. She knew how much I enjoyed hearing her theatre experiences and the snippets of gossip about her fellow actors. Thinking back to last Saturday, I didn't know why I told Carla I had been waiting to meet her, because it hadn't been true. In actual fact, I had practically forgotten Sadie had a daughter. Perhaps my unfriendliness towards her was caused through jealousy; she'd had a mother all her life while I only had mine for nine years. As basic as that. It wasn't her fault any more than it was mine, and as to blame? Well, I thought, who could you blame? Sadie, who was already married, although not living with her husband? Or father, who was cheating on his wife? If I was being honest with myself, I did think he had been in the wrong. I knew how old Carla was because Sadie had once told me, which was a year younger than me; this made her the same age as John. I couldn't help wondering who else in Calder Bay had seen the likeness to Janice when Carla had been here. Charles certainly, although given his friendship with father, he may have known about her already. The most important question was, surely; did Carla know? But, I decided, in the end, did any of this really matter?

Dougie was already in the lounge bar when I arrived and waved over as soon as he saw me.

'Hi,' he said, kissing me lightly on the cheek, 'what would you like to drink?'

'A white wine, please, Dougie; shall we sit outside, it's a bit stuffy in here?'

'Sure,' he agreed, 'perhaps you can find a table and I'll follow you out once I've got the drinks.'

I chose one of the tables at the far end of the terrace and away from most of the other customers. I didn't recognise anyone I knew which was just as well because I didn't want us to be interrupted as so often happened; the downside of living in such a small town.

'Here you are.' he said, putting my wine down in front of me.

'Thanks.'

'Cheers.' he said automatically, raising his glass.

'Cheers. Have you had another visit from Inspector Crawford?' I asked him, taking an appreciative sip.

'No, I haven't.'

'Well,' I sighed, 'I have; he turned up at nine-thirty this morning.'

'What on earth for?'

'You may well ask; what I'm going to say may come as something of a shock, it certainly did to me. Apparently, the police are now, after a space of ten years, looking into the circumstances surrounding Bobby's accident.'

'Good Lord! What road are they going down now?'

'Your guess is as good as mine, Dougie. No doubt they have their reasons, but he wasn't exactly forthcoming. What he wanted to know was how I spent the day preceding the accident, also about his bike, such as where he kept it and the garage he would have used for the maintenance checks. All I could tell him was that usually he kept it in the main garage and that, no, we didn't have a padlock for the door and as you know, I wasn't living at "Carbisdale" at the time, and as far as maintenance checks, he would probably have used the same garage as we all did.'

'Didn't he give any kind of explanation? They just can't go around asking those sort of questions; it's tantamount to putting ideas into people's heads, one positive way of starting rumours.'

'I know, you're right. All he did say was that they had cause to re-examine the police report, in particular the one submitted by the mechanic who checked the bike at the time it happened and have found that the damage to the steering mechanism could have happened prior to the accident.'

'I doubt it,' indignantly, 'Bobby was meticulous and I can remember only two days before, he'd had the bike serviced; he would have known immediately if there had been something wrong.'

'He didn't use the bike every day, though.'

'No, he used his car most of the time, so he only took the bike out at weekends, but on the Saturday, the day following the service, he gave it a good spin; he and Callum went up to Aberdeen for the day. What are you getting at, Aileen?'

'I'm not getting at anything, but don't you see what the implications are, Dougie? The police are inferring that the damage had been caused maliciously and if it turns out they are right, our family name will really and truly end up in the mud, that is, as far as the locals here are concerned.'

'It probably already has in certain quarters, but we're made of much stronger stuff than that, Aileen. We'll weather this, just as we have with the business going to the wall.'

'I suppose you're right.' I agreed reluctantly, grateful for his level headedness. I had often accused him of being too matter of fact, but now wished I could be more like him, instead of continually looking on the obverse and becoming even more worried.

'It's not that what you've told me doesn't concern me, you know,' he said slowly, pausing long enough to take another sip of his lager, 'because it does, but I don't see what you and I can do about it; we'll have to wait and see if and what they come up with.'

'Do you think his bike may have been tampered with?'

'I honestly don't know what to think; look at it this way, if it had been who would have wanted to take such drastic steps. Bobby wasn't the kind of guy to fall out with anyone; if you ever got mad with him, it was always short-lived.'

'Apart from Callum, do you know whether he had any other friends?'

'Not as far as I know; he may have done -'

' – you've thought of someone?'

'No, it's just that –'

'Come on, Dougie, what are you trying to say?'

'I wasn't going to mention it, but I had a drink with Callum on Sunday, I think he's trying to pick up the threads from when he left Calder Bay, and he made an admission which in spite of these liberated times, quite frankly, took me by surprise. You see,' he added, 'he told me he was gay.'

'What, just like that?'

'Yes, he had absolutely no need to, and I wish he hadn't; it was when I asked him why he'd decided to return to Calder Bay and he explained it was mainly because he'd been let down by his boyfriend, a guy called Jeff, apparently.'

'Did you honestly never think he was, Dougie?'

'No, I didn't, but the thing is, once he'd told me I started to wonder about Bobby.'

'It's certainly taken you a long time to arrive at that conclusion.'

'You mean, you knew.'

'Oh, I didn't actually *know*, but I always suspected they both were. Always together, even right through University, and afterwards, and perhaps more importantly, neither of them showing any interest in the opposite sex; all the signs were there, Dougie.'

'Oh, I guess you're right.'

'Is it so important?' I asked him, slightly amused by his perplexed expression, 'It wasn't as if the pair of them ever openly displayed any signs of being other than good buddies, not the way many of the gays I've met carry on, making an embarrassing exhibition of themselves.'

'Permissive times, eh?'

'As you say, permissive times and we have no choice but to accept them.'

'I know,' he nodded, 'Callum had aged a lot since we last saw him.'

'Still as intense as ever, I suppose?'

'Yes, looks as if these last ten years haven't been easy ones, sounded happy enough to be back though.'

'No doubt I'll bump into him sometime.' I said, hoping it wouldn't be too soon; I had quite enough to think about without hearing any of Callum Ogilvie's woes. 'Incidentally, Dougie, I met Sadie's daughter on Sunday.'

'Really; what's she like?'

'It's not *what* she's like,' I told him, wondering how he was going to react when he heard, 'but *who* she is like.'

'Why so cryptic?'

'Are you ready for this?'

'It would seem I have no choice.' a lopsided grin appearing as he looked across at me.

'Janice.'

'What?'

'She looks like Janice.'

'Wow!'

'Is that all you can say? Wow! And please do not say everyone has a double.'

'But what you've just said is, well it's staggering. How old is she, do you know?'

'She's the same age as John; Carla, she's called and lives in London; she was up here to attend Sadie's funeral and sort out her house and personal effects, also she was with Charles Grayson when I saw her.'

'How did she meet him, I wonder.'

'I don't know, but I would say as he was a great friend of Sadie's, he would have been at the funeral and no doubt introduced himself to her.'

'You knew he was friendly with Sadie?'

'Yes, Dougie,' honestly, I thought, my younger brother must go about this town with his eyes closed, 'for the simply reason Sadie told me. Surely you realised Sadie and I were friends and she happened to mention this to me one day; I'm sure I told you Sadie and I often met for coffee and a chat.'

'You may have done, obviously I've forgotten. So,' pursing his lips and uttering a silent whistle, exactly as he used to do when he was a kid, 'you reckon we have another sister –'

'– *half*-sister.' correcting him.

'You can't be one hundred per cent certain, though.'

'No,' I admitted with reluctance, 'but if you saw her, Dougie, you would think the same. Her resemblance to Janice is remarkable; the same heart-shaped face and the way her eyes slant downwards slightly, even her hair, only the style was different. What more can I say?' shrugging.

'If you had seen the similarity, Charles would have done also.'

'He probably has, but remember, he spent quite a bit of time with father who may very well have confided in him.'

'It's possible, I suppose.'

'If you ask me, in our family anything is possible.'

***

I found it extremely difficult to concentrate for the remainder of the afternoon once I'd returned to the office and by five, an hour earlier than usual, I was more than ready to finish work for the day. The apartment had never appeared more welcoming as it did when I finally got home. Although I had made every attempt to make light of what Aileen had been telling me about the police looking more closely into the circumstances of Bobby's accident, I did share her concerns about how the final outcome of their enquiry would affect us. I couldn't begin to imagine what had prompted them; none of us had questioned the police of how the accident actually happened, having been told at the time that the bike had been out of control and crashed with some force into the stone dyke up on the main road. I think we must have been too stunned to ask why it had gone out of control, and then, within a matter of hours, we were all up at the cottage hospital where they had taken father and for the second time that day had learned of another death in the family and now, ten years later and looking back, it was hard to recall with any accuracy what we said to each other, or even where we went after we had left his bedside. Those days and weeks before and after the funeral had been bleak, featureless and although July had been, like this one, warm and sunny, I don't believe any of us really noticed. Father and I were not particularly close and I had always gained the impression, probably unjustified, that he blamed me for my mother dying when she did, but at least in the fullest sense I did have a father, while Carla Northcot, if what Aileen believed was true, although having one, she hadn't been acknowledged by him and presumably had never even seen him. All a bit too much to take in, I decided, taking a beer from the fridge and, picking up my mobile, dialled Charles Grayson's number.

'Charles, it's Dougie Henderson here,' I said as soon as he answered, 'hope I'm not disturbing you –'

'– not at all, Dougie. Good to hear from you actually; how are you these days?'

'I'm fine thanks. Have you got time to come up to the apartment for a beer; there's something I'd like to talk to you about.'

'Of course; a beer sounds exactly what I need at this time of the day, Dougie.'

'Were you working?'

'No, just finished, as a matter of fact.'

'You know where I'm living, don't you?'

'Yes, that rather splendid renovation of one of the old properties at the top of Carlogie Road.'

'That's right; I'm on the top floor. There is a lift.' I added.

'That's what I like to hear,' he chuckled, 'I'm on my way, should be with you in about ten minutes.'

In just under ten minutes I heard the whirring of the lift as it left the ground floor, stopping as it reached my landing.

'Hi,' he greeted me, 'I've been trying to remember when we last saw each other; it must have been a couple of years ago.'

'At least,' I said, leading him into the kitchen and taking a can of beer from the fridge, 'I expect you were surprised to hear from me?'

'Not really, Dougie; with what has been happening recently, I think I would have been surprised if you hadn't got in touch.'

'Don't tell me you've been questioned by the police as well?'

'Who hasn't in and around the vicinity where the body was found.'

'Actually, Charles,' I said, noticing for the first time how tired he looked, 'that wasn't what I wanted to talk to you about.'

'No? I must say that's a relief; we all seem to have talked about nothing else these last couple of weeks.'

'I'm sure the police will get to the bottom of it all; they appear to be pretty thorough in the way they're going about their enquiry. But, I suppose it's only fair to warn you, Charles,' I went on, 'you may very well be hearing from them again.'

'Really; why?'

'I met up with Aileen at lunchtime and she was telling me she'd had a further visit from Inspector Crawford, don't know whether you've met him yet, and it would appear they are now furthering their murder enquiry into re-examining the circumstances surrounding Bobby's accident.'

'I don't believe it!'

'He didn't say so in as many words, but he implied that someone may have tampered with the bike which resulted in it going out of control the way it did.'

'Good God! What on earth has made them think along those lines?'

'I've no idea.'

'What do you feel about it?'

'It's difficult to know how I feel, or how I should be feeling; Bobby died in tragic circumstances, whether contrived or not, and there's not one damn thing I, or any of the family, can do to stop police procedure.'

'You're right of course, but not pleasant all the same.'

'No;' shrugging, 'so best to let them get on with what they've been trained to do; thank God I'm not in the police force.'

'*Touché.*'

'Anyway, Charles, I'm hoping you will be able to clarify something else Aileen told me today.'

'If I can, Dougie.'

'She was saying that you introduced her to Sadie's daughter on Sunday and has absolutely convinced herself –' struggling to find the right words.

'- it's okay, Dougie,' he smiled, 'I can see you're embarrassed, although there is no need to be, you know. Presumably, Aileen saw the resemblance of Carla to Janice. Well, I can put your mind at rest I don't believe Carla will object to me telling you, but Sadie had a brief affair with your father not long after she came to live in Calder Bay, Carla being the child of that relationship.'

'Did father tell you this?'

'No, it was Sadie; this was after he died and I became friendly with her. She was a very good friend, Dougie and I miss the talks we used to have.'

'And she stayed on here; she didn't leave.'

'No, she stayed; your father provided for Carla's education, but apart from that he didn't acknowledge her.'

'Did Carla know?' I asked, appalled at such callousness; to have had a child and to totally ignore her existence was incomprehensible to me. I had always realised that father was a hard man, certainly couldn't have been described as paternal, but at least we all lived with him in the same house and knew he would be there when we needed him.

'She only learned after Sadie had died; she had left a letter for her.'

'My goodness; that must have been a shock for her.'

'I think it was, Dougie, but Carla is a most resilient woman; she's also a lovely person.'

'It feels really strange to know I have another sister, but it must be more so for Carla; all her life believing she was an only child, then discovering she had four half-siblings.'

'I think she's more curious than anything else; by the way, Aileen hasn't been the only one to see her likeness to Janice.'

'I did wonder about that.'

'Inevitable in a town as small as this; your old friend Callum Ogilvie actually thought she was Janice and then there was Hilary Robertson the other day.'

'I heard Hilary had been here; you would know that the woman's body has now been identified as her aunt?'

'Yes, I know, Dougie.'

Chapter Seventeen

The Henderson family had used Paterson's Garage for years, since the days when a young Jack Henderson had started to drive and had bought his first car from them. From those days, the business had moved progressively into the twenty-first century and were fully conversant with computerised records; Tom Paterson was eager to demonstrate this skill by rapidly scrolling down the screen until he arrived at the entries for the year 1993 and within minutes had the cursor pointing to the date, Friday the 2nd July, when the maintenance service was carried out on Bobby Henderson's motor bike, together with the name of the mechanic.

'There you are, Inspector,' Tom said, swivelling the screen round to face him, 'Harry Middleton; he's one of our senior mechanics, he'll be able to answer your questions I'm sure; he's in the workshop, so if you would like to follow me, I'll take you through.'

Howard had brought a copy of the police mechanic's report on the bike with him and once Tom had introduced Harry Middleton to him and returned to the outer office, he handed it to him to read.

'I realise Bobby Henderson's accident happened ten years ago,' Howard said, 'but perhaps you'll remember carrying out the maintenance service.'

'I do as a matter of fact, Inspector,' he answered, 'because it was the day before I went on holiday and Bobby's Honda was my last job that afternoon.' reading through the report, a frown appearing on his forehead as he reached the end.

'You look puzzled.' Howard commented, but not wanting to appear to be making too much of his reaction; the frown could be one of concentration.

'I am a bit; you see, I know that bike was in perfect working order when it left the workshop, and although this report of yours mentioned the impact of the crash could have caused the cotter pin to become dislodged, I would have thought it more probable it would have resulted in more than that, to the extent of the crankshaft being damaged, but it says here that the bike was still intact.'

'I see,' Howard nodded, 'in your professional opinion, Harry, would you say it was more likely the pin had been loosened prior to him taking the bike out on to the road on Sunday?'

'It would have to have been done manually, Inspector,' he said hesitatingly, 'and I do realise the inference of what that implies, but while I don't want to contradict the mechanic saying the pin could have become dislodged at the time of the crash, I don't believe it did. I have seen a fair number of damaged motor bikes and invariably the accidents are either as a result of speeding or when road conditions are treacherous, such as wet surface, heavy rain and of course fog and mist, and as driving conditions were good that evening, I have to say this reinforces my opinion. Hondas are excellent bikes with a good track record, sturdy and reliable and provided they are well maintained, shouldn't give any trouble. I had one myself up until a couple of years ago,' he added, 'and it never let me down.'

***

"Bay View Apartments" was a relatively new building: three storeys, stone-built, dark blue wrought-iron balconies and set back a few yards from the pavement in Bay Road. Sergeant Lilian Wood pushed open the heavy glass doors and walked into the foyer; a spacious high-ceilinged area, parquet flooring, plate glass windows facing the bay, large tubs of scarlet geraniums and a couple of cream and beige upholstered armchairs with copies of "Country Life" and that day's edition of the "Scotsman" on an oval coffee table; all of which made an effective statement of what one could expect from the apartments themselves. To Lilian, it merely served as a reminder that she would never be able to afford to live here, not that it really appealed to her, far too contrived and lacking in any real warmth, going over to read the names printed on the metal plaque by the lift. Surprised there was no concierge in evidence, noting how vulnerable the residents were, especially during the daytime; presumably the main door would locked at night, but at this time, an open invitation for anyone to enter the building, press the lift button and be taken to whichever floor they chose. Still, she decided, security wasn't her brief; hers was, as Inspector Crawford had pointed out earlier, to find out whether anyone had remembered seeing any activity on the beach the evening Beth Grayson had been out there. There were only six apartments in total, two to each floor, noting that Callum Ogilvie occupied number 2A, and hoping, as she pressed the button for the first floor, that of the remaining five residents there would be someone who just happened to be looking out of their window that evening.

She drew a blank at the first two; getting no answer from the first one and a negative response from the other; the second floor was no better; the woman who lived next door to Callum Ogilvie told him she had been away on holiday at the time, but the elderly man on the floor above who had been quick to inform her that he was a retired naval commander and spent a good part of each day out on his balcony, was eager to tell her that with the aid of an excellent pair of binoculars he had a perfect view of not only the stretch of coastline, but as far as the horizon.

'Yes, Sergeant,' he said without any hesitation when she asked him, 'I remember that evening very well; I'd seen the woman a number of times, in fact,' he had gone on garrulously, 'she used to come for her swim around the same time each evening; this was no different; the bells of St. Paul's had just stopped ringing when she appeared on the sand directly below my balcony and walked to the water's edge. She swam quite far out, but then she usually did, and about five or six minutes later she was joined by her friend, at least I took it to be her friend, because they swam side by side for a while; I must say he was a damn fine swimmer, most athletic, and she managed to keep up with him until, probably getting tired, she slowed down a bit.'

'Was she struggling, do you think, Commander?' Lilian asked him.

'Not struggling exactly, no, I wouldn't say that, and then she seemed to rally somewhat because he started diving under the water and she managed to do the same. I would say he was showing off, you know, well, that's the impression I got. Anyway,' and there was no stopping him now, not that she wanted him to, 'I could have only looked away for a fraction of a second and he was swimming back to the shore.'

'And the woman?' prompting him for the first time.

'Oh, she was still out there, although by then she was swimming much slower, but I watched for a couple of minutes before coming inside to pour myself a drink and to switch on the seven o'clock news; this was when I heard the ambulance; I hadn't realised it was coming along here, but when I went out to the balcony again, I saw it parked across the road with its lights flashing.'

'Except for the man and woman you've mentioned, Commander, had there been anyone else nearby?'

'There had been earlier in the afternoon, but after they had gone there were only the two young lads who'd been on the rocks fishing. They'd come back up the beach by this time and I assumed one of them must have telephoned for the ambulance because there was no-one else around.'

'Had you seen the man before?'

'The person she had been swimming with you mean, Sergeant?'

'Yes, that's right.'

'I have seen him quite often in recent months; I don't know his name, but he only moved into the apartment on the second floor recently. As I said, he's a good swimmer, therefore living so close to the sea must suit him very well.'

***

"The Gazette", Calder Bay's weekly newspaper came out on a Thursday and by midday, both newsagents in the town had sold out, the lead story on the front page creating renewed interest in the Henderson family. One of the first people to buy a copy was Ken Morris from "The Shipwreck".

'Good Grief!' he muttered under his breath as he read the headlines, 'What's going on in this town?'

"MYSTERY SURROUNDING DEATH OF CALDER BAY RESIDENT

The funeral of the late Sadie Northcot took place three weeks ago and only now an official police enquiry is being carried out, following evidence to support that her death had been maliciously contrived. It has transpired that her medication had been stolen from her home in Green Lane on the day of her death and it is a known medical fact that if she had been able to have access to this at the time of feeling unwell, the ensuing, and fatal, heart attack she suffered could have been avoided. It is believed that during the hours leading up to her death she had been continually subjected to a series of telephone calls, purporting to be from the same person, which contributed to the mounting stress culminating in the heart attack.

"Meanwhile, once more, the residents of Green Lane are having to endure police presence in an area of the town which was always considered to be a quiet and much sought-after oasis away from the bustling centre, but it would seem to be undergoing a certain metamorphose since the macabre discovery of the woman's body in the grounds of "Carbisdale" which, paradoxically, is close to where Mrs Northcot had lived. There are no valid reasons for surmising there is anything more than coincidental in this, but now the identity of the woman has been officially confirmed as that of Natasha Paton who had been staying in Green Lane on holiday at the time she was murdered, one cannot help but speculate on the relevance."

Ken opened the bar promptly at eleven, having had time before then to read through what the journalist had written. Bruce Struthers had been working for "The Gazette" for years and Ken could remember when he had been a cub reporter; even back then, almost forty years ago, he'd had a flair for words and had known just how much to tell the reader and, as with what he'd written today, leaving one with the distinct feeling he knew one hell of a lot more than he was letting on. Of course he had to be constantly aware of the slander laws, Ken realised that, but all the same, it didn't take the brains of Great Britain to work out the underlying meaning behind the implications of his weekly column. To Ken, who had always considered himself as being something of a sleuth, enjoying nothing better than a good who dunnit and making a stab at solving a mystery before reaching the end, spent the minutes before his first customers arrived trying to make some sort of sense out of a real who dunnit practically on his doorstep. The first question he was asking himself was what could Sadie Northcot, a lady he had often seen coming into their restaurant, and the lass, Natasha Paton, possibly have in common, apart from living so close to each other. There was almost thirty years between when they had died, a long time, so perhaps whoever was responsible, that is if it was the same person, had to have been around since then. The more he tried to unravel what Bruce Struthers had described as a mystery, the more muddled he became, but he couldn't help thinking there was a link. Somewhere.

'Morning, Ken,' Charles Grayson said, coming into the bar, 'you're looking very pensive.'

'Oh, good morning, Charles; sorry, I was miles away. Your usual?'

'Thanks, Ken.'

'I suppose you've seen "The Gazette" this morning' he asked, pouring out his beer.

'Yes, I have, and I would say most of Calder Bay has as well; Morrisons only had a couple of copies left by the time I got there.'

'I thought it had been too quiet these last few days; most folk seemed to have given up talking about the murder of that young woman, but this news about Sadie Northcot will stir them all up again. I know we like to learn what's been going on, but when it's so close to home, well it all becomes a bit much.'

'You're right.'

'The police don't seem to be having much success in solving the first murder.'

'Oh, they'll get there, Ken, don't you worry.'

'I hope so, but now with what's happened to Mrs Northcot, somehow it seems a lot worse.'

***

As he had done on Tuesday, Callum arrived as the clock above the town hall was chiming six, the difference this time that instead of being directed to the Detective Inspector's office, he was taken along the corridor to one of their interview rooms where David McIntyre was waiting for him, seated at the end of the table with a tape recorder at his right-hand side.

'Good afternoon, Mr Ogilvie,' he said, pointing to the chair opposite, waiting until Callum sat down, before continuing, 'the two statements covering what was discussed on Tuesday have been prepared and are ready to be signed by you, but before I read them through to you and to give you the opportunity of making any changes to what you said previously, I will be conducting this interview along official lines which will be recorded and may, in the event of any court appearance by yourself, be used as evidence. Is this understood?'

'Perfectly.' and as previously, limiting his response.

'Also, at this point in the proceedings, Mr Ogilvie, it is your prerogative to have your lawyer present.'

'That won't be necessary.'

'Very well, but if at any time you should change your mind, I will bring the interview to a temporary close.'

Only a slight nod indicated his acknowledgment and David leaned over towards the recorder and pressed the switch.

'Thursday, the 17th July 2003, 6.10 p.m., I will first refer to the death of Mrs Sadie Northcot, which we are now treating as murder, the evidence we have supporting this being irrefutable; the degree of harassment she experienced on the day she died had been sufficient to exacerbate her heart condition which had up to that time been successfully regulated by medication. She had been instructed by her doctor that in the event of any sudden change in her health, she was to take one other tablet which would immediately forestall any heart attack and allow time for further medical assistance to be obtained, but that night she was unable to find the prescribed drug because it had been stolen during the same day by, we believe, the person you saw leaving her house when you had called to see

Mrs Northcot. When you were questioned this Tuesday, Mr Ogilvie, you stated you were unable to hear what was being said between Mrs Northcot and her visitor, Miss Beth Grayson. Do you still maintain that this was the case?'

'Of course; I was too far away from where they were.'

'You had commenced to walk along the path at the side of the house when you heard their voices.'

'That's what I said.'

'And yet you heard them?'

'Yes.'

'And recognised Mrs Northcot's, but not the other woman's voice?'

'That's right.'

'Why did you stay on the path for as long as you did?'

'I told you before; I turned back as soon as I heard them.'

'You told us that, yes, but it wasn't true, was it?'

'Why shouldn't it be true?'

'Because we have a reliable witness who says you stood there for up to ten minutes before returning to your car.'

'Whoever told you that was wrong.'

'Also, Mr Ogilvie, you didn't drive off straight away; you remained in your car until Mrs Northcot's visitor had left the house.'

'That's nonsense.'

'I can think of only one reason why you waited several minutes before leaving; you were listening to what they were saying.'

'How many times do I have to tell you I couldn't hear what they were talking about?'

'Mr Ogilvie, if you persist in refuting what my witness has told us, I will have no option but to consider the reasons behind your reluctance to contradict what are in essence, should my witness, under oath, be questioned in court, hard indisputable facts.'

'What do you mean?'

'What I mean is,' David pressed on relentlessly, 'why you are not admitting you overheard their conversation.'

'No comment.'

'Your attitude is not acceptable; either you re-phrase what you've just said, or I will have to charge you with deliberately withholding information which is crucial to our enquiry.'

'What I meant,' he said, taking his time to answer, 'was that there is no more I can add to what I've said to you already.'

'Right. Let me explain further; while all the evidence in respect to what happened to Mrs Northcot does go a long way in concluding that Beth Grayson was the person who instigated her death, what we don't know is why she would have gone to such extreme lengths; in other words, what was her motive? We strongly believe that the content of their conversation that afternoon is the clue we need and there is the possibility that in the absence of not finding sufficient evidence against Beth Grayson, we will be forced to consider someone else as being responsible. Therefore,' he went on, watching Callum Ogilvie's expression, gratified to see it gradually changing from one of stubborn denial to what appeared to be a resigned acceptance; he was intelligent enough to realise he really had no choice but to be amenable, 'I am going to ask you again, Mr Ogilvie; did you hear what the two women were saying?'

'It wasn't a pleasant conversation,' he said, taking so long to answer, David was beginning to think he was going to revert to his monosyllabic replies, 'not on Sadie's part, but Beth Grayson's. She was extremely unpleasant, but although I wanted to intervene, to support Sadie I mean, I hesitated because I could tell by the way she was handling her, I would have been more of a hindrance -'

'- yes,' he prompted, 'did Mrs Northcot sound distressed?'

'No, she didn't, quite the contrary; she didn't seem all that ruffled by Beth's rudeness, treated her quite calmly in fact.'

'Did you gather why she had called to see Mrs Northcot?' having to ask a direct question, rather than allow him to ramble on, recognising it would be a ploy to allow him more time to select exactly what he was going to extract from what he'd overheard.

'Yes, Beth wanted her to have nothing more to do with her brother; it was quite obvious Beth didn't like her, she was jealous I think, and then accused Sadie of taking Jack Henderson away from her; apparently, this was years ago which didn't make much sense because she would only have been in her teens and I doubt very much whether Jack would have been interested in someone like her.'

'Did you know Beth Grayson?'

'No, although we all knew who she was; this was when we were kids, we used to call her the witch.' he added.

'I see,' David nodded, 'going back to their conversation; would you have described Beth Grayson as being threatening towards her?'

'I don't know about threatening, just mad talk really. Anyway, Sadie told her to leave which she did a few minutes later.'

'You say Beth Grayson mentioned Charles' name, also that of Jack Henderson, did she mention anyone else?'

As soon as he asked him, David knew he'd hit on a nerve. The expression on Callum's face was identical to how he had looked when Bobby Henderson's name came up on Tuesday. Could they be coming close to finding out why his bike had been tampered with, especially as now, after Howard's talk with the mechanic, it seemed it had been?

'She was talking wildly and not making any sense,' Callum said at last, 'this was when I decided I'd heard enough.' sidestepping the question.

'Her words may well have appeared meaningless to you, Mr Ogilvie, but could you give me the gist of what they were; they could have some bearing on his enquiry?'

'Oh, she was going on about how Sadie had spoiled her life by stealing Jack Henderson away from her and then –' hesitating, but this time David didn't interrupt.

'- then she went on to say if Jack hadn't been mesmerised by her, they would eventually have married and she wouldn't have wanted – she wouldn't have wanted Bobby –'

'- wanted?'

'I told you it was mad talk,' he said quickly, 'everything she said was crazy; Bobby would never have given her any encouragement; like the rest of us, he didn't like her, so it was probably understandable for him to laugh at her advances.'

'What do you think she meant by advances?'

'Presumably sexual; the woman was obviously deluding herself, but in any case it sounded as though Bobby had enraged her because she said that this time she'd had the upper hand and wasn't going to let him get away with it.'

'And, that's what she told Sadie?'

'Yes, that's what she told Sadie.' his voice flat and expressionless.

'And that was all?'

'Isn't that enough, Detective Inspector?'

'That remains to be seen, Mr Ogilvie; however, what you have told us today could take us a little further in establishing whether your friend's bike had been tampered with. At this stage, having spoken to the mechanic who carried out a maintenance check on the bike only days before the accident, there are very strong reasons to suspect that a crucial part had been damaged prior to the crash; in other words, we have nothing to support that it was simply an accident.'

'I see.'

'I will now bring this interview to a close,' David said, 'the time being 6.50 p.m. on Thursday, the 17th July 2003.'

When Callum finally left the room, having signed the statements, David played through the tape, mentally picking up the salient points of the interview, returning again to what Callum had told him about when Beth Grayson had brought Bobby Henderson's name into the conversation. He was only too well aware that they only had Callum's word for what he'd said; for reasons best known to himself he could have been lying, or perhaps omitting the full content of the two women's conversation. Whether it constituted a motive remained questionable; Beth Grayson had been a deeply disturbed woman; to have verbally accused Sadie of spoiling her life for something, imagined or not, which occurred over forty years ago, was without doubt unreasonable, verging on the paranoia, and continuing to harbour this belief for so long. Surely, David reasoned, any normal person, while feeling bitter when she believed she had been usurped, would in the course of time have ceased to dwell on the experience, but then, from what they had learned from those whom they'd spoken to, Beth had not emerged as normal, far from it. Even that business with Bobby Henderson laughing at her happened years ago; therefore it was reasonable to believe it was someone else more recently which once again brought him back to Charles Grayson. Had she visited Sadie for the sole purpose of telling her to stop seeing her brother? Outrageous as that sounded, it could have been that her intense hatred of Sadie had intensified when she knew about her friendship with him to such a degree she planned her murder. David could only think of one other way to strengthen their case against her and this was to speak to Charles once more in the hope he could give them a fuller analysis of what his sister had been like from as far back as he could remember and in the absence of her no longer being alive, could contribute, as satisfactorily as possible, to them reaching a conclusion and to ultimately charging Beth Grayson posthumously with the three murders.

David had chosen for the time being not to question Callum about the day Beth Grayson had died, deciding on a different approach. He was working on the premise that up to now, it wasn't public knowledge that they suspected anything irregular about her death, although aware it was possible that from today the situation may change with Sergeant Wood's visit to the property in Bay Road. While the retired naval commander had supplied them with further evidence that it had been Callum Ogilvie swimming in the bay the same time as Beth Grayson, and that his description of what he'd seen had been sufficiently succinct, it wasn't enough. They needed to know more before calling Callum in again. So far, they were at an advantage in being ahead of him that he shouldn't have any idea why they wanted to see him, and David was determined they would remain like that up to the moment when they would put their surprise attack into action.

***

Richard Bryant-Pennington was out on his balcony on Friday evening enjoying a glass of 'Famous Grouse' whisky, while watching, as he often did during the summer months, the holidaymakers on the beach below as they collected their belongings together to make their way back to the town, when he saw his neighbour, whom he now knew to be Callum Ogilvie, having been curious enough following Sergeant Wood's visit the previous day, to check on the residents' name board downstairs in the hall. This evening, he had the beach to himself, not even the usual lads on the rocks were there and, as before, once he reached the water, he continued walking until he was in far enough to swim, not the breast stroke, but the crawl, his arms powerfully propelling him through the water at what seemed to Richard Bryant-Pennington, an incredible speed. At the point where he expected him to turn back, he carried on, steadily in a straight line towards the open sea and to where focusing on him became difficult, but with the aid of a pair of binoculars he'd had for years, he managed. They helped, but after five minutes or so, Richard had lost him. Where the hell was he heading, he muttered; there was no land for miles, and surely, no matter how strong a swimmer he might be, the man would eventually weaken. He would never have sufficient strength to make the length of the return. It just wasn't possible.

Richard spent the next few minutes deliberating; should he forget seeing him and assume he would be able to get back to the shore or, should he contact the police? As a good citizen, he knew what he must do and going back inside the apartment, picked up the receiver and phoned Calder Bay police station, asking to speak to Sergeant Lilian Woods.

Lilian wasn't on duty that evening, but the desk sergeant put him through to Inspector Howard Crawford who didn't waste any time after reassuring Richard he had done the right thing by reporting the incident, before striding along the corridor to David McIntyre's office.

'Yes, Howard?' he said as soon as Howard appeared in the open doorway.

'It could be a false alarm, sir,' he said quickly, 'but there's been a call from one of the residents from the Bay View Apartments who saw

Callum Ogilvie swimming out to sea; this was at least twenty minutes ago and so far he hasn't returned.'

'Twenty minutes,' David repeated, 'a long time, Howard. Was he one of the residents Sergeant Wood spoke to yesterday?'

'Yes, the retired naval commander, Richard Bryant-Pennington he's called, and his apartment is on the third floor.'

'Right,' David said, standing up from his desk, 'we'll go along there and if he has returned, we can use the opportunity to ask him some more questions, although,' he added grimly, 'it doesn't sound promising, it's possible he's got the wind up.'

'If that's happened,' Howard put in, 'he has beaten us to it.'

'It's possible; remembering his past mental health record, perhaps we shouldn't be surprised.'

It took them less than ten minutes to drive along to Bay Road, pulling up outside the apartment block. Richard Bryant-Pennington was still on his balcony, standing against the rail; a tall, erect man with a shock of white hair and looking every inch what he had once been. As soon as he spotted them, he shook his head, which they interpreted as meaning Callum Ogilvie hadn't come back. To make sure, they took the lift up to the third floor and had a quick word with him before going back down again and walking down the bank and on to the sand.

'Before we go any further and put a call out, Howard, let's have a look along these dunes; he must have changed on the beach, I can't see him walking from the apartment block wearing only swimming trunks.'

'He would have needed a towel, and his keys to get back into his apartment.'

'True.'

Callum Ogilvie's clothes: shorts, tee-shirt and trainers, in a neat pile on top of a folded beach towel, were all in the second dune they went to; in the pocket of the shorts, a bunch of keys and a mobile phone.

David called the Station for them to put an alert out to the coastguards, and once again they were in the lift, but this time taking it to the second floor and with one of the keys on the ring, opened the door to Callum

Ogilvie's apartment. The white envelope propped up against the carriage clock on the mantelpiece caught their attention immediately. In small neat hand-writing it was addressed to Detective Inspector David McIntyre, Calder Bay Police Station.

Callum Ogilvie's suicide note was brief, but succinct in that he didn't over-elaborate, neither did he display any signs of remorse for causing Beth Grayson's death, giving as his reason that she was responsible for destroying his life by murdering his dearest friend, Bobby Henderson.

Events moved swiftly, Callum Ogilvie's body was recovered from the sea within a matter of hours, Richard Bryant-Pennington having given them precise and accurate directions as memorized by him from the moment he first saw Callum wade into the sea and start to swim in a straight line until he was no long visible. The activity on the beach on this occasion attracted a crowd of onlookers, including the local television camera crew and an interviewer, paradoxically the same woman who had announced the discovery of Natasha Paton's body two weeks earlier. It wasn't clear who had contacted them so quickly, but judging by the eagerness of Richard Bryant-Pennington to answer her questions, it could have been him. Even after the body had been taken away and there was no evidence of the short-lived drama enacted in their midst, a few stragglers remained, reluctant it would seem to leave.

'It's amazing, isn't it, sir,' Howard commented as they walked back to the car, 'how a tragedy can excite some people?'

'Human nature, I suppose, Howard.'

Chapter Eighteen

CHARLES & CARLA

Carla was among the first passengers on the British Airways flight from Heathrow to come through from Customs. It had been one hell of a week, and one I thought would never end, but now following yet another meeting with David McIntyre, it was almost at an end. Carla had phoned me a couple of nights ago to say she was coming up to Edinburgh for the weekend and wanting to know whether we could see each other; just to hear her voice had acted as an immediate fillip to my flagging spirits as each successive development had unfolded. So much had happened in Calder Bay since she left on Sunday, most of which I wanted to forget, although I realised we would be spending some of the weekend going over the various elements, most of which affected us both. Carla would have to accept and eventually come to terms with the fact that her mother had not died a natural death, but as a direct result of what Beth had done, while I had to try and put the knowledge that my sister had been a murderess, but more importantly how Carla would react to this unpalatable fact. It made little difference to the way I was feeling about the whole business with Detective Inspector McIntyre suggesting it was likely Beth would be certified, while not insane, certainly mentally unbalanced; whichever way you looked at it, to me it made no difference; Beth, in cold blood, had been responsible for murdering three people and not one of them, I am positive, had done anything to harm her in any way. A bitter pill.

And there she was. Carla, the woman I was falling in love with, walking up to the end of the barrier towards me, that teasing little smile which I found irresistible on her lips.

'Charles, dear Charles.' she said, putting her one free arm round my shoulders and kissing me on the cheek.

The warmth of her, the faint muskiness of her perfume, was intoxicating.

'I can't tell you how happy I was when you said you were able to get away;' I said, taking her travel bag from her, 'you must have had a hectic week.'

'No more than usual, but I've decided to rearrange my priorities, but I'll tell you about that later. So, where are we staying; you said on the phone you were going to surprise me.'

Hoping she wasn't going to be disappointed, I told her of the serviced apartment on the ground floor of a Georgian townhouse where I stayed when I had to be in Edinburgh for any length of time; it was perfectly positioned in Great King Street in the New Town and within easy walking distance to dozens of restaurants and bars, and of course if Carla was interested, close to the shops in George Street and Princes Street. I'd had time to call in there before driving out to the airport, leaving my holdall in one of the bedrooms and checking that basic food supplies were there for preparing breakfast.

'It's a lovely idea, Charles, it really is and far more comfortable I'm sure than staying in a hotel; also,' she added, 'it will give you an idea of what it would actually be like to live here.'

The journey from the airport to the centre of Edinburgh didn't take long in spite of the various traffic holdups once we had left the motorway and joined the A720, caused mainly by the mass exodus of commuters leaving the city at the end of the working day. Gilmour House was halfway along Great King Street and, parking the car at the rear of the property, we went inside. I could tell by her delighted expression that Carla liked what she saw and she walked from room to room admiring the sheer elegance of the apartment.

'Very, very attractive, and so tastefully done; no expense has been spared, has it?'

'I'm glad you like it.'

'I love it, but how did you first find it, Charles?'

'Through an old friend of mine, I'd like you to meet him sometime, Carla, I think you would like him; Gareth used to own the house and about ten years ago, his company transferred him up to Aberdeen and rather than sell the place, instead he had it converted into flats, only three, but this one,' I added, 'he doesn't rent out, but keeps solely for himself and his family when they are in Edinburgh, and close friends.'

By now it was almost seven and I suggested we went to "The Standard Bar" in Howe Street, only a five-minute walk away, for a drink and something to eat. During the many times I'd stayed in Edinburgh, "The Standard" had become my local, even to the extent of getting to know a couple of their regular customers. It was a cosy place and, either seated at the bar or on one of the leather banquettes in the grill area, it was hard to believe you were actually in the heart of a bustling city.

'Surprised?' I asked Carla as I followed her inside.

'Very,' she smiled over her shoulder at me, 'and so different from the London pubs, although,' she admitted, 'just as busy.'

'For many,' I grinned, 'Friday night is party night!' pulling out one of the chairs for her at the far end of the bar where it was less crowded. 'What would you like to drink?'

'I'm really thirsty, so I'd like half a lager, please.'

'And I'll have the same.'

'I haven't asked you yet,' she said, 'but what has your week been like; pretty grim?'

'Let's say, I've had better.' raising my glass to her, 'I had yet another meeting with the Detective Inspector this morning and it would seem to be fairly conclusive that Beth was responsible for all three deaths.'

'Three?'

'Of course, I should have realised, you won't know about the questions being asked about Bobby Henderson's accident.'

'They're saying it wasn't an accident?'

'It would seem so.'

'How awful.'

'Carla,' I said tentatively, but I had to ask, 'what do you feel about what happened to Sadie; Beth's involvement, I mean?'

'Don't look so worried,' she smiled her gentle smile, placing a hand on mine, 'Beth's guilt has nothing to do with you, Charles.'

'She was my sister.'

'Look,' she said, 'don't think I don't realise what you must be going through, but Beth obviously had major mental problems; how they started, we'll probably never know, but they were *her* problems, Charles, not yours. Perhaps they were psychological, I don't know, I'm no psychiatrist, but I am a lawyer, and I've been trained to be objective, to view situations and attempt to make some sort of sense out of them, but, well,' she shrugged, 'when it comes to mental illness, that's something else. Leave it to the experts, Charles.'

'You're right, of course,' I agreed, grateful for her rationalism, 'Beth was a strange person, but that's something I've always known. I've been trying to remember when I first realised this, but it's difficult; perhaps it was round about the time our mother died; Beth was seventeen then, but mother had been ill for a number of years and for my part, being a schoolboy of thirteen, I'd got used to not having her around, but maybe it had been different for her.'

'It's possible, especially if she had never been a very outgoing sort of person, finding it difficult to make friends, living inside herself, that kind of thing.'

'Depressing.'

'Please don't let it be, Charles.' she smiled again, 'Anyway, how are the renovations going?'

'Very well, actually, the builders would have finished all the external work this afternoon, which means I'm well ahead of the schedule I'd set for myself and, then, next week most of the furniture will be removed and the redecorating can be done.'

'That's great. It will do you good to finally get away from Calder Bay.'

'Don't I know it! I've already begun making inroads into renting; I thought that would be better than buying straightaway, give myself some breathing space.'

'That's a good idea. Now,' the return of the teasing smile, 'do you want to know what I meant when I said I had decided to rearrange my priorities?'

'Go on, then; surprise me.'

'Oh, I think I'm going to;' she laughed, 'I've been considering for some months about making a few changes to my life; you see,' she went on, more seriously now, 'I have always put my career first, and slotting in everything else if and when I had the time. My own fault of course, but you know what they say; all work and no play and all that?'

'A form of escapism?'

'Could be, although I enjoy my job and couldn't imagine not working, but I've allowed myself to become blinkered; cut off from what most people would describe as a more balanced way of living. For instance, I haven't had a holiday for three years and that in itself is unhealthy. I've been too committed to my company which, in turn, has made them complacent in respect to me; they have come to expect that I'm always there and when, as recently, I had to be away for a couple of weeks, they didn't like it.'

'But it's your entitlement surely; to take compassionate leave, sick leave and holidays.'

'I know it is, Charles and as I've said, I'm entirely to blame.'

'How do you plan to alter this situation?'

'I've already made a start actually.'

'You're intriguing me.'

'I told you I worked for Gallaghers Pharmaceuticals, didn't I?'

'Yes.'

'Well, about twelve months ago they opened a branch in Scotland, with offices in Aberdeen and Edinburgh and yesterday I met with my board of directors and requested a transfer to their Edinburgh office.'

'My goodness! How did they take that?'

'At first, not well at all, but since going back on Monday I had made a number of enquiries and knew they were looking for a corporate lawyer, therefore I felt I was in a stronger position to persuade them and after an hour of wrangling among themselves, they agreed and on Monday morning I have a meeting with the Managing Director here in Edinburgh.'

'You really are serious, aren't you?'

'Of course.'

'I hope you won't regret such a radical change, Carla; it's a big step, but then you don't need me to tell you that.'

'I won't regret it, Charles.' she said quietly, her eyes sparkling as she looked at me and I longed at that moment to put my arms around her and hold her close, to show her how deliriously happy I was. 'What do you think?' her head tilted to one side as she waited for me to answer.

'I'm overwhelmed; in less than a week you've accomplished so much and I'm delighted we will be living in the same city, but what about your friends; won't you miss them?'

'Not all that much,' she said ruefully, 'most of them are more colleagues than friends, besides,' shrugging her shoulders, 'I'll make new ones, and perhaps this time they won't be working for Gallagher's.'

We walked through to "The Standard's" Grill after we had finished our drinks and while we waited for the food to arrive, I ordered a bottle of Bordeaux.

Carla had asked me what I recommended from the menu and I had no hesitation in suggesting the beef olive stuffed with crumbly pork sausage meat, and sauté potatoes and baby carrots. We both had the goat's cheese and caramelised onion tartlet which lived up to its reputation of being a perfect mix of sweet and salty flavours. We weren't able to manage their desert speciality of chocolate profiteroles, stuffed with Chantilly cream, but instead decided on a coffee while we finished off the wine.

It was almost eleven when we returned to the apartment and while I poured us a nightcap, Carla switched on the television to catch the eleven o'clock news. I came back into the lounge with the drinks at the same time as the Calder Bay coastline flashed up on the screen and in the foreground facing the cameras, the presenter with her microphone almost touching the mouth of the elderly man standing next to her.

' ..... Commander Bryant-Pennington,' she was saying, moving even closer to him, 'did you recognise the man you saw swimming earlier this evening?'

'Can't say I did; he was too far away.'

'You saw that he was in difficulty through?'

'Not at all; the reason why I contacted the police was because he didn't return to the shore.'

'And yet you were able to give them accurate details of the direction where he was heading.'

'Yes, that's right.'

'Thank you, Commander.' and by her closed-in sulky expression obviously disappointed in his curt and uninformative replies, 'it would appear,' she went on, stepping away from him, 'there is some mystery surrounding the actions of the man whose body a short time ago was recovered from the sea by divers. Once again, Calder Bay is the focus of public attention following the macabre discovery of a woman's body in the grounds of one of the town's oldest properties .... ' the picture fading, to be replaced with the studio, the newscaster covering another topic.

'What now, I wonder.' I said, handing Carla her drink.

'Sounds like a suicide.'

'It does; well, this will set all their tongues wagging once again.'

'They've certainly had plenty to talk about recently.'

'Anyway, Carla, no doubt we'll hear in due course who the man was, perhaps even why he should have made such a dramatic exit.'

'And why that particular stretch of sea; there's a wide expanse to choose from out there.'

'Which I suppose could indicate he may have lived nearby.'

'Yet another task for the Calder Bay Police Force; they're having a busy summer.'

***

I lay awake for a long time before drifting off to sleep; an uneasy sleep, interrupted by disturbing dreams which, as most dreams, made no sense whatsoever and soon forgotten, except for the last one; I was back in Calder Bay and walking along the road in the direction of the bay. The tide was out, leaving the sand a darker shade where the water had reached. I was on my own; the beach was deserted and no passing motorist to break the stillness. I had no idea of the time, except it must have been around midday as the sun, a shimmering golden ball, was directly overhead. I had reached the deep curve of the bay before stopping at the edge of the grassy bank to gaze out as far as the horizon and, as I did, becoming aware of a change, not only in the weather which had grown chilly, but in the silence; not nearby, but further away. Someone was singing; a woman's voice, but I wasn't able to make out the words and although the tune was familiar I couldn't remember what it was and then it faded away to be replaced by laughter, closer this time; a child's laughter, loud and shrill, not a joyous sound as it should have been, but too excited, too uncontrolled and echoing as though he or she was being joined by other children. I shivered, not so much from the fall in temperature, but a feeling of menace in the atmosphere, of being watched; I looked down at the sand below where I was standing, but it remained deserted and then, I noticed someone swimming slowly to the water's edge. I wanted to step back, get away from there, but I wasn't able to; my limbs felt heavy and useless, my whole body rigid with a dreadful fear as the woman emerged from the water and walked up the sand towards me. I wanted to scream, to shout out, but I couldn't. She had almost reached the bank when I felt a pressure on my shoulders; hands, the fingers digging into my flesh, turning me round and dragging me towards her ......

...... I must have woken at that point because I don't remember any more.

'Carla. Carla.' Charles called out softly, 'You're alright,' he said, coming into the room and sitting down on the side of the bed, 'you've had a nightmare, but,' he insisted, 'you're alright, you're safe now.'

'Oh, Charles, I'm sorry, did I wake you; it was such an awful dream.'

'Ssh, you can tell me about it if you like; help it to go away. Anyway, I was in the kitchen when I heard you call out.'

'What time is it?'

'Eight o'clock; I've made us some coffee.'

We sat in the kitchen and drank our coffee while I tried to describe what must have been the worse dream I'd ever had. He listened without interrupting, now and again nodding his head, until I reached the end.

'Some dream.'

'It doesn't seem so bad now; thank you for rescuing me.' I smiled across the table at him.

'No doubt a dream therapist would be able to explain it to you, but when you consider what has been happening these last few weeks, I suppose it's hardly surprising your brain has been working overtime while you were asleep.'

'You're probably right,' I agreed, 'while I can understand perhaps why I should dream about Calder Bay and that particular spot, I can't give any explanation of why I should have heard the woman singing and more especially, those children.'

'They could be a conglomerate of things you're read, films you've seen, or even from when you were a child; in other words, take your pick.'

'Quite frankly, I'd much prefer to forget about it.'

'Best way; breakfast, Carla; what would you like?'

Charles cooked some scrambled eggs and made another pot of coffee while I showered and unpacked the few clothes I'd brought with me. I hadn't liked to mention to him that although I had never met his sister and hadn't known what she looked like, I had been positive that the woman in my dream had been her and that she wanted to tell me something. It was only an impression, but there was no doubt in my mind, only thankful I had woken up in time. Beth Grayson had obviously been an extremely disturbed woman and perhaps hearing that the police were considering she had been responsible for a third person's death had triggered off a train of thought in my brain which surfaced as a dream of such nightmare proportions. Although I had been shocked when Charles had told me that Bobby's death hadn't been an accident, it was impossible for me to feel more than that for a half-brother and one I had never known, remembering the conversation I'd had with his friend, Callum

Ogilvie, particularly when he had talked about his friendship with Bobby and for the first time wondering just how close the pair of them had been. Callum had struck me as being a highly emotional sort of person, when after ten years he appeared still to be grieving over the loss of his friend, and recalling how upset he had sounded when Sadie's name had been mentioned. All this introspection is not good, I decided, and giving my hair a final brush, I went back into the kitchen to join Charles.

We spent the morning in and around George Street, mostly window-shopping, although I was tempted to buy a turquoise linen two-piece and an ankle-length silk dress in a creamy lemon, from one of the boutiques in Thistle Street and Charles treated himself to a pair of leather moccasins from Harvey Nichols in the city's Multrees Walk, home, apparently, to the big names in fashion. Before stopping for a lunchtime drink we took a stroll through Princes Gardens, which at this time of the year, the height of summer, looked splendid; immaculate lawns, winding footpaths bordered by flowers in full bloom and, as ever, towered over by the impressive Edinburgh castle.

Charles suggested Brown's Bar & Brasserie in George Street for lunch, telling me as he had already reserved a table for our evening meal at the Pompadour Restaurant in the Caledonian Hilton, perhaps we should have something light to eat. I couldn't remember having spent such a pleasant morning, the city of Edinburgh, living up to all my expectations, but I was enjoying being with him so much. He was a good listener and unlike so many men I had known, he wasn't continually talking about himself, scarcely mentioning his work. If anyone was to ask me to describe him, I would say he was a modest man, unaccustomed to the harsher and highly competitiveness in the business world and I could well understand why he had continued to live under the same roof as his jealous and possessive sister, although as he had explained to me, he had long ago mentally moved away from her dominance.

In the afternoon, we did the 'touristy things': starting with a visit to Edinburgh Castle and walking round the war memorial, queuing up to look at the Scottish Crown Jewels and the famous Stone of Destiny; from there, we walked down the Royal Mile to the Palace of Holyroodhouse, once the home of Mary Queen of Scots where works of art from the Royal Collection is now exhibited, aware of becoming immersed in centuries of Scottish history, my life in London seeming a thousand miles away and the recent troubled events in Calder Bay even further and noticing how, in a matter of a few hours, Charles had become more relaxed, knew he must be feeling the same way. Of course he would have to return there, but hopefully this short break away would have helped him to accept what had been happening. As for myself, although it saddened me still that Sadie had gone, I no longer viewed how she must have died with such intensity as when I learned who had been responsible. Apart from her own violent death, I'm sure Beth had continued to live her life the way she had done and that in itself surely must have been a form of mental suffering for her which only death could bring to an end.

'This has been a truly wonderful day, Charles.' I said to him later.

'I wanted it to be special for you.' he said simply, placing his hand gently on my cheek, 'These haven't been easy weeks for you, losing Sadie and everything else that's been going on.'

'Nor for you.'

'Well,' he shrugged, 'I've been doing a lot of thinking and you were right what you said yesterday; while it never pardons what she did, I realise now that Beth must have had serious mental problems, which only a psychiatrist would have been able to fathom out. There's nothing I can do and I'm stuck with that whether I like it or not.'

We were in the Magnum Restaurant, having placed our order from an impressively varied menu and were sipping our *kir royale* aperitifs. The restaurant, stylishly elegant; twinkling fairy lights surrounding the outside of the tall arched windows creating an enticingly warm glow and inside, glittering crystal chandeliers, flickering candles and sumptuous furnishings provided a marvellously serene atmosphere.

It wasn't until the following morning when we learned anything further about the drowning; no doubt it would have been on the news earlier, but neither of us had wanted anything to spoil our weekend. I suppose we should have known better than to buy the Sunday newspapers, but as I was taking my turn to cook breakfast, Charles had offered to walk along to the newsagents at the end of the road. I could tell by his expression that what he was going to tell me wasn't going to be pleasant, and without saying anything, I took "The Times" from him and read the main front page article:

"ANOTHER MURDER IN CALDER BAY!

Following the recovery of a man's body from the sea on Friday night, it can now be revealed he has been formally identified as Callum Ogilvie, a resident of Calder Bay; the seaside town on the East Coast of Scotland which has in recent weeks attracted considerable media attention in the wake of a succession of mysterious deaths. Callum Ogilvie, a suicide victim had left a hand-written confession of being responsible for causing the death of Miss Beth Grayson who had also lived in Calder Bay.

"At a press conference yesterday, Detective Inspector David McIntyre, who has been leading the investigation, announced that irrefutable evidence has emerged to substantiate their case against Beth Grayson being guilty on three counts; namely, the murder of Natasha Paton on the 10th July, 1975, the instigation of the deaths of Bobby Henderson on the 4th July 1993 and Sadie Northcot on the 17th June of this year, and will accordingly be charged posthumously. With the conclusion of this triple murder case, it is to be hoped that the lives of the people of Calder Bay will be permitted to return to normality without the shadow of conjecture and suspicion which they have had to endure recently."

I handed the paper back to him, reluctant to read any more, realising there would be some follow-up piece on the inside pages.

'I told you I'd met Callum, didn't I, but only because he made the mistake of believing I was Janice.'

'You did, yes; what did you make of him?'

'Heavy-going,' I admitted slowly, 'an intense kind of person which became more pronounced when he talked about Bobby; it was obvious he hadn't got over his death.'

'That could explain why he decided to deal with Beth, but I don't suppose we'll ever know.'

'You mean he may have found out that she tampered with Bobby's bike?'

'It's possible, Carla; Beth was a prowler, by that I mean, she had a habit of moving around, always silently, watching people, listening to what they were saying. I knew she used to stand outside my studio door when I was working and sometimes she'd be in the garden, just pottering about, but I knew she was there and now and again she would stop what she was doing and look over towards my window.'

'Didn't it get on your nerves?' I asked, appalled, imagining what it must have been like for him.

'I didn't like it of course, but I'd learned to ignore her.'

'No wonder you'll be glad to leave Calder Bay.'

'A new beginning, Carla,' he said, pulling me towards him and kissing me, not as previously on the cheek, but on my lips and we stood there, in the centre of the kitchen on a warm sunny Sunday morning, and for the first time in my life I recognised what it was like to feel totally committed to someone; this time I wasn't making any mistake.

Chapter Nineteen

News of Callum Ogilvie's suicide note confessing to the murder of Beth Grayson, and that she would be charged posthumously for the three other deaths received different reactions among those who had known the victims and, to a lesser degree, to many who a couple of weeks ago had never even heard of Calder Bay, far less anyone who lived there.

Commander Richard Bryant-Pennington was enjoying a certain notoriety around the town, but continued to remain tight-lipped about providing the inquisitive with any additional snippets of information, knowing from experience there were many who, with nothing better to do, would circulate exaggerated versions which would bear no resemblance to what he had said in the first place, but when the young man from "The Times" rang the bell of his apartment on Sunday morning, he couldn't resist the temptation to waver from this decision. In his opinion to be personally quoted in a prestigious national newspaper such as "The Times" was indeed an accolade and he had no hesitation in discussing at some length why he had come to the realisation that his neighbour, Callum Ogilvie, could have been in some difficulty and how he had been able to give the police accurate directions, enabling the drivers to locate the man's body in a relatively short time.

'Were you on the shore when this was taking place, sir?' the journalist, who had introduced himself as Ken Radcliffe, had asked him.

'Indeed I was; not a pleasant sight I might add. Do you know,' he added, 'there was actually a smile on his face, but then that does happen I understand; a graduation of hypothermia when the person loses all sense of feeling when they are in water of extremely low temperatures, as it would have been out there at that depth, followed by experiencing an increasing warmth and glow of a non-existent euphoria, a phenomenon which nobody can understand, before finally drifting off into unconsciousness and descending to the sea bed.'

'Did you think at the time he had committed suicide?' Ken Radcliffe asked him, waiting patiently until he had the chance to curb the flow, the gist of which he was already familiar.

'There was no doubt in my mind; he swam too far out, you understand, and had reached the point where I knew he wouldn't have the strength to make it back to the shore.'

'Was he in the habit of swimming in the bay, Commander?'

'When the weather was as fine as it has been for a number of weeks now, I would often see him out there.'

'You will have read today's papers, I presume?'

'Yes, I have and grim reading they make too.'

'Indeed,' Ken agreed, 'you will have learned about Callum Ogilvie's confession in that case.'

'I certainly have.'

'Did you know Beth Grayson?'

'Only by name, but I'd never met her.'

'Apparently, she was swimming in the bay on the evening she died; did you see her then?'

'I most certainly did, Mr Radcliffe, and I also noticed that she swam with Callum Ogilvie for a while, so naturally I presumed they knew each other.'

As he left the Bay View Apartments, Ken Radcliffe was not in possession of very little else to justify providing his editor with any further article on the recent events in Calder Bay, concluding that the whole business, including further public interest had already reached saturation point and would soon fall into the annuls of newspaper history.

By Friday, exactly a week after his death, Callum Ogilvie was cremated; a short ceremony held in the chapel adjoining the crematorium, attended only by a few mourners: an aunt and uncle from Aberdeen and a cousin and his wife who lived in Yorkshire, Mrs Baird, Dougie Henderson and his sister, Aileen Hope.

***

'I didn't expect you to be there, Aileen.' Dougie said after the service and they were in "The Royal" having a drink.

'It was the least I could do,' she said, 'poor Callum; he didn't have many friends, did he?'

'No; he was to be pitied more than anything else, even although he'll always be remembered as a murderer.'

'Theoretically, you're right, of course, but Beth Grayson was evil.'

'Even although she may have been mentally unstable?'

'That doesn't make any difference to me, Dougie; mad or not, she *was* a murderess; she took it upon herself to destroy three people's lives! All three of them would still have been alive today if it hadn't been for her, and that in my book is evil!'

'Okay, Aileen; anyway,' he added calmly, 'it's all over now, thank goodness.'

'I heard the other day that Charles was leaving Calder Bay; can't take the aftermath, I suppose.'

'You can hardly blame him; you know as well as I do what the people are like here; they forget absolutely nothing and metaphorically, they will always be pointing a finger at him, reminding each other that his sister was a murderess.'

'Did you know he was planning to leave?'

'Yes, I had a drink with him the other night in "The Shipwreck" and he told me then.'

'Where's he going?'

'Edinburgh.'

'He always said he'd like to live there, but I never thought he would ever get round to it, but then I don't suppose he would have if his sister had still been alive.'

'I'm not so sure, you know. Oh, I admit when he was younger she did have a strong emotional hold over him, but he's quite different now.'

'Probably his new lady friend has something to do with that.'

'What do you mean?'

'So, Dougie, you don't know everything that goes on around the town after all,' she was laughing at him, 'but I would say that Carla Northcot is with him quite a lot these days.'

'Carla Northcot?'

'You look surprised.'

'I suppose I am' I hadn't realised they knew each other that well.'

'I would say they know each other extremely well.'

'Where do you get your information from, Aileen?'

'Most of it from applying my well-developed instincts and, well, I've seen them together.'

'And that's all?'

'It's enough, Dougie; believe me.'

***

At first, when Janice heard the news on Saturday that their friend, Callum, had committed suicide she couldn't believe what she was hearing, but Dougie, who had phoned her immediately he'd listened to the midday news, assured her it was true alright as, apparently, he had left a suicide note, although no information had been given of the contents, only that it had been addressed personally to Detective Inspector David McIntyre. She didn't know what to make of it all; she had known Callum for years, ever since Bobby had brought him back home from primary school one afternoon for their ritual tea of tomato sandwiches and sponge cake. They had all realised how distraught he'd been when Bobby was killed and they fully understood why he had felt the need to get away from Calder Bay. She hadn't realised he had returned until Dougie told her, which again hadn't surprised her all that much, reckoning that one day he would come back. But the most puzzling thing of all was leaving that note for the Detective Inspector. What did it mean? And then, the following morning when the Sunday papers were delivered and she read the headline, she knew. The shock of learning he had been responsible for Beth Grayson's death became inconsequential when she read about Bobby, so much so, she had sat rigidly with the newspaper clutched in both hands as she tried to absorb the truth behind what really happened to him. Sam had found her there ten minutes later, in the same position, her face ashen beneath the suntan and her eyes staring sightlessly in the direction of the open patio doors. Gently, he had unclasped her fingers from the paper and pushing it further along the table, he took her in his arms.

'Janice, love.'

She had leaned heavily against him and he could feel the tension gradually leave her body and tilting her face up to him, he kissed her, stroking her hair back from her damp forehead. Only then, did she cry, not loudly, but sobbing; the tears streaming down her cheeks. He hadn't said anything, keeping his arms around her, giving her the time she needed.

'Oh, Sam,' she said at last, allowing him to wipe the tears away, exactly as he used to do with the children when they were young, 'it's about Bobby —they're saying it wasn't an accident – they're saying – they're saying,' she repeated, 'that Beth Grayson was responsible.'

'I'll read it, shall I, love?'

'Please.' and watched him, her eyes never leaving his face, until he had reached the end of the piece and for the second time he pushed the newspaper to one side.

'All I can say is that it's a great pity you had to learn about it the way you did; no wonder you were so stunned.'

The telephone in the hall started to ring before he had finished speaking and, giving her shoulders a comforting squeeze, went through to answer it. He wasn't away for long and when he came back he sat down beside her again, taking both her hands in his.

'That was Detective Inspector McIntyre; he wanted to speak to you, but I told him you weren't up to it, love.'

'Why was he phoning?'

'Somewhat belatedly, but he wanted to warn you about that article in the paper; he apologised for not doing so before, which of course he should have done.'

'I'm not blaming him; he's enough to do I'm sure without having to phone everyone who would react in a similar way.'

'You never liked that woman, did you?' he asked her.

'None of us did, Sam. She must have been mad.'

'More than likely, but I don't suppose that makes any difference to how people thought of her, is it?'

'Callum must have found out somehow that she was responsible for Bobby's accident and perhaps the knowledge was too much for him if you realise the strength of his friendship with him.'

'It's Charles Grayson we should now feel sorry for; must be dreadful for him continuing to live in the same place where people will immediately think of his sister every time they see him.'

'You liked Charles, didn't you?'

'I did, yes; he's alright. As you know, I only met him two or three times when he was visiting your father.'

'Perhaps he'll move away from Calder Bay now; it always surprised me he stayed on there for so long.'

'Best thing he could do, I would say, love.'

***

The burial of Natasha Paton took place in the village where she had been born, her grave alongside those of her parents and sister in the small cemetery of the ancient village church, followed by a simple service conducted by the same minister. Hilary had been surprised to find that nearly all the pews had been taken, mostly by old friends of the Davies family, all attending out of respect, many of them remembering Natasha as a child. This was the fourth time she had been in the church, each of them sad occasions; none of them weddings or christenings, but for the funerals of both her grandparents, her mother's and now Natasha's. So much sadness, she thought, taking Pete's hand as they had walked out of the church and into the brilliant sunshine, thankful he was with her this morning.

Neither of them said much on the way back to Oxford, but it was a companionable silence, Hilary needing this limbo-like time to run through in her mind the sequel of events leading up to the final conclusions so starkly conveyed to them the previous Sunday. She was thinking it ironic that, for her at least, it all started with the discovery of Natasha's body and ending today with her funeral, whereas for the Hendersons and for Charles Grayson as well, any inner turmoil they may be experiencing could well continue for some time, knowing, although she hadn't said as much to Pete, she would never return to Calder Bay. She had been shocked to hear about Callum, remembering when she had last seen him and how tense he had appeared, actually saying little about what he had been doing, appearing more interested in their lives as though intentionally avoiding anything too personal. When they had all been young, he had been quite different; outgoing, fun-loving, everything a young boy should be, but he had changed a lot and it didn't take too much imagination to work out why that could have been. He had never recovered from losing Bobby, his closest friend and possibly, his idol; why else had he left Calder Bay so soon after Bobby was killed? But, then he returned? Why? It's unlikely anyone would ever know, including why he had been sufficiently motivated to murder Beth Grayson.

They arrived back home around seven and before doing anything else she changed out of the sombre black dress into one of her colourful cotton shifts, while Pete opened a bottle of chilled *Chablis*, handing her a glass when she came back downstairs.

'Cheers, darling.'

'Cheers,' she replied, at the same time noticing the two British Airways' flight tickets on the table in front of her, 'flight tickets, Pete; where are we going?'

'To Hong Kong.' he said, his grey/blue eyes sparkling with amusement as he watched her amazed expression.

'We're going to Hong Kong?'

'Yes, that is if you want to.' teasing her now.

'Oh, Pete, what an absolutely marvellous surprise. I can't wait to tell Kirstie.'

'Darling,' smiling broadly by this time, 'she already knows; I phoned her a couple of days ago, told her it was going to be a surprise for you, but not until this afternoon was over.'

'I don't know what to say, honestly I don't.'

'You don't need to say anything.' he said, leaning over to kiss her.

***

As was often the case with John Henderson, whenever he learned of anything unpleasant, whether this concerned him personally or not, made little difference. While the piece in "The Times" didn't fall into the category of affecting him, or even now, as presumably the murder enquiry was closed, causing him any further inconvenience, he chose to ignore the whole business. He just wasn't interested, not that he ever had been.

Mrs Baird seldom phoned her daughter, but after she'd been to Bobby's funeral she felt compelled to talk to someone and that person could only be Karen.

'It's not like your mother to call, Karen.' he'd commented when she came off the phone.

'I know; she wanted to tell me she'd been to Callum's funeral this morning.'

'Why in the world did she do that?'

'Why shouldn't she have, John; she'd known Callum a long time and treated him as one of the family.'

'But the guy was a self-confessed bloody murderer! So,' he spluttered, 'you condone what he did?'

'No, of course I don't, but if you think about it, John, reading between the lines in Sunday's papers, it sounded as if it could be in retribution to that Beth woman fixing Bobby's accident.'

'You're not usually so philosophical, Karen; what's got into you?'

'It's what has got into you, John; it's your brother we were talking about here, not some stranger.'

'I don't need reminding.'

'I'm sure you don't, but ever since you read about it all you've never so much as mentioned the subject; it's as if you don't want to know.'

'Spot on, my dear wife; I very much wish I hadn't read that damn article; Bobby, even in death, continues to emanate as a disturbing presence.'

'I'm sorry; I don't know where you're coming from.'

'Bobby was gay, Karen; my brother was an out and out poofter!'

'I knew that, John.'

'What! And you never said?' he gasped, looking at her disbelievingly.

'I didn't see there was any need to, dear.'

'I suppose you knew that Callum was as well?'

'Naturally.'

'Naturally! There's nothing natural about being a poofter; just as well father never found out. If he had, he wouldn't have thought as much of him as he did.'

'Don't you think your father may have guessed?'

'I've had quite enough of this pointless conversation.'

'Just as you wish, John.'

***

'Well, Howard,' David McIntyre said at the end of the week, 'I think we've wrapped up everything now. An unusual case, without the satisfaction of making any formal arrests; in other words, both culprits, Beth Grayson and Callum Ogilvie, escape the justice of the law.'

'And presumably,' Howard put in, 'if Beth Grayson hadn't been killed, she would have ended her days in a mental institution.'

'Quite.' David agreed, shaking his head, 'And the same could perhaps be said for Callum Ogilvie if he hadn't pre-empted his arrest. Incidentally, Howard, I had a call from Edgar & Partners on Monday; George Edgar had read the news about Callum, in particular that he had committed suicide; he was quite apologetic as a matter of fact, telling me that Callum had already made a suicide attempt, but he hadn't liked to say anything about it to me when I spoke to him before.'

'How did he find out, sir?'

'This was when Callum started working for them and had explained the reason why he had been unemployed for twelve months was because he was receiving treatment for depression which was true, although Callum had neglected to tell him about the suicide attempt and George

Edgar, being a fairly thorough sort of person, made some enquiries around the area where Callum lived and in the process, discovered that he had mixed with a local gay community and had, after a broken relationship, taken a drug overdose.'

'What went wrong; with the attempt, I mean?'

'Well, we've no proof, not that it is relevant now, but I would suggest he tried to overdose on the medication he was being prescribed for depression and had perhaps misjudged the strength of the dosages. Or,' he smiled wryly, 'it could have not been a serious attempt.'

'A cry for help maybe.'

'Possibly, Howard; he was pretty mixed up after all. Although if we had known, we would have been pre-warned of him having suicidal tendencies, I suppose.'

'All in all, he was in a sorry state.'

'Not dissimilar to Beth Grayson.'

'You're right, although you have to admit, Howard, she went too far. In fact, an extremely dangerous woman and probably would have continued disposing of people who threatened her in any way.'

'You could say she was also indirectly responsible for Jack Henderson's death.'

'A frightening thought, eh; I don't believe there would have been any end to her activities. No doubt when she heard about his death, she considered in her sick mind that she had truly achieved her goal by punishing him for the rejection she had been nurturing for all these years.'

'By killing two birds with one stone, you could say.'

'Most profound, Howard.'

Other titles by Margaret Alty:

Tangled Web – ISBN: 978 1 84549 422 3

Search for the Lion – ISBN: 978 1 84549 627 2
Sequel to *Tangled Web*

Jenny – ISBN: 978 1 84549 442 1

Camouflage – ISBN: 978 1 84549 478 0

The Last Orange – ISBN: 978 1 84549 560 2

A Reflective Image – ISBN: 978 1 84549 681 4

A Meadowbank Mystery

Murder in Meadowbank –ISBN: 978 1 84549 494 7

Double Act –ISBN: 978 1 84549 537 4

Murder After Hours –ISBN: 978 1 84549 579 4

A Gathering of Crows –ISBN: 978 1 84549 594 7

All published by arima Publishing.

www.ingramcontent.com/pod-product-compliance
Lightning Source LLC
Chambersburg PA
CBHW071146260626
47162CB00003B/935